FALLING FOR GRACIE

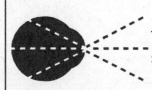

This Large Print Book carries the
Seal of Approval of N.A.V.H.

FALLING FOR GRACIE

SUSAN MALLERY

THORNDIKE PRESS
A part of Gale, Cengage Learning

GALE
CENGAGE Learning·

Farmington Hills, Mich • San Francisco • New York • Waterville, Maine
Meriden, Conn • Mason, Ohio • Chicago

Thorndike Press® Large Print Romance.
The text of this Large Print edition is unabridged.
Other aspects of the book may vary from the original edition.
Set in 16 pt. Plantin.

LIBRARY OF CONGRESS CATALOGING-IN-PUBLICATION DATA

Names: Mallery, Susan, author.
Title: Falling for Gracie / by Susan Mallery.
Description: Large print edition. | Waterville, Maine : Thorndike Press, 2017. | Series: Thorndike Press large print romance
Identifiers: LCCN 2017008920| ISBN 9781410496522 (hardcover) | ISBN 141049652X (hardcover)
Subjects: LCSH: Large type books. | GSAFD: Love stories.
Classification: LCC PS3613.A453 F35 2017 | DDC 813/.6—dc23
LC record available at https://lccn.loc.gov/2017008920

Published in 2017 by arrangement with Harlequin Books S. A.

Printed in Mexico
1 2 3 4 5 6 7 21 20 19 18 17

To Hazel, with love and thanks.

CHAPTER ONE

"Gracie? Gracie Landon, is that you?"

Trapped, standing in the middle of her mother's front lawn, a newspaper in one hand and a mug of coffee in the other, Gracie Landon glanced longingly toward the escape that was the front door.

In theory, she could bolt for freedom, but that would mean being rude to Eunice Baxter, neighbor and octogenarian. And Gracie had been raised better than that.

She pushed her sleep-smashed hair out of her face and shuffled in her younger sister's Tweetie Bird slippers over to the low wood fence that separated the Landon property from Eunice Baxter's.

"Morning, Mrs. Baxter," she said, hoping she sounded cheerful instead of trapped. "Yes, it's me. Gracie."

"My stars, so it is. I haven't seen you in forever, but I swear, I would have recognized you anywhere. How long has it been?"

7

"Fourteen years." Half her life. She'd been so hopeful that people would forget her.

"Well, I'll be. You sure look pretty. When you left, and I mean this in the kindest way possible, you were a dreadfully ugly child. Even your poor mother used to worry that you wouldn't grow into your looks, but you did. You're as bright and shiny as a magazine cover model."

Gracie didn't exactly want to reminisce about her homely period — the one that had lasted for nearly six years. "Thank you," she said, inching toward the porch.

Eunice poofed her shellacked helmet of curls, then tapped her chin. "You know, I was just talking about you to my friend Wilma. We were saying that young folks today don't know how to fall in love. Not like they used to in the movies, or like you did with Riley Whitefield."

Oh, God, oh, God, oh, God. Not Riley. Anything but that. After all this time, couldn't her reputation as a young, crazed teenaged stalker be put to rest?

"I didn't exactly love him," Gracie said, wondering why she'd agreed to come home after all this time. Oh, yeah, right. Her baby sister's wedding.

"You were a testament to true love," Eunice told her. "You should be proud. You loved that boy with all your heart and you weren't afraid to show it. That takes a special kind of courage."

Or insanity, she thought as she smiled weakly. Poor Riley. She'd made his life a living hell.

"And that reporter fellow wrote about you in the town newspaper so everyone knew your story," Eunice added. "You were famous."

"More like infamous," Gracie muttered, remembering the humiliation of reading about her crush on Riley over breakfast.

"Wilma's favorite is the time you nailed his girlfriend's doors and windows shut so she couldn't get out for their date. That's a good one, but my favorite is the time you laid down right in front of his car right there." Eunice pointed to the bit of road in front of her house.

"I saw the whole thing. You told him you loved him too much to let him marry Pam and if he was going to go ahead with the engagement, he should just run you over and put you out of your misery."

Gracie held in a groan. "Yeah, that *was* a good one."

Why was the rest of the world allowed to live down their childhood humiliations but everyone wanted to talk about hers?

9

"I guess I sort of owe Riley an apology."

"He's back in town," Eunice said brightly. "Did you know?"

As pretty much everyone she'd run into in the past couple of days had made it a point to tell her, yes. "Really?"

The old woman winked. "He's single again. What about you, Gracie? Anyone special in your life?"

"No, but I'm very busy with my work right now and . . ."

Eunice nodded knowingly. "It's fate. That's what it is. You two have been brought together to be given a second chance."

Gracie knew she would rather be staked out naked on a fire ant hill than ever have anything to do with Riley Whitefield again. She didn't need any more humiliation where he was concerned. And who knew what tortures he would be willing to endure to avoid the likes of her?

"That's really nice, but I don't think I —"

"Could be he's still sweet on you," Eunice said.

Gracie laughed. "Mrs. Baxter, he was terrified of me. If he saw me now, he'd run screaming in the opposite direction." Honestly, who could blame him?

"Sometimes a man needs a little push."

"Sometimes a man needs to be left alone."

Which was exactly what she intended to do. No more running after Riley. In fact, she planned to avoid any functions where he might be. And if they did happen to bump into each other, she would be cool, polite and distant. Maybe she wouldn't even recognize him. Whatever feelings she'd once had for Riley were gone. Dead and buried. She was way over him.

Besides, she was a different woman now. Gracious. Mature. No more stalker girl for her.

"Who was that?" Vivian asked when Gracie walked into the Landon family kitchen. "Did Mrs. Baxter trap you into talking to her?"

"Oh, yeah." Gracie put the paper on the counter and took a long drink of coffee. "I swear, it's as if I just left town last week instead of fourteen years ago."

"Time is different for old people," Vivian said as she shook back her cascade of strawberry-blond curls and yawned. "For one thing, they get up too early. Mom was out of here before seven this morning."

"She said something about a special Saturday sale at the store." Gracie slid onto a stool in front of the counter and set down her mug. "Which you're supposed to be

11

helping with."

"I know." Vivian stretched. "It's my own fault for picking out a three-thousand-dollar wedding dress. My choices were to either blow the budget on that and have nothing for the guests to eat, or chip in." She grinned. "At least I'm getting a fabulous wedding cake for free."

"Lucky you."

As a sister of the bride, Gracie had volunteered one of her masterpieces for the reception. She eyed the calendar tacked up on the wall. The wedding was exactly five weeks from today. A smarter woman would have hidden out until the last minute, then shown up with the cake, enjoyed the celebration and left. But frantic phone calls from their mother, Vivian and Alexis, their other sister, had churned up enough guilt in Gracie's acid-prone stomach that she'd agreed to come home to help with the planning.

Her reward was baking all the cakes she had on order in a strange oven she wasn't sure she trusted and being tortured by old ladies who insisted on talking about Gracie's questionable past love life.

"Not my idea of a good time," she mumbled into her coffee.

Vivian grinned. "Did Mrs. Baxter mention that Riley Whitefield is back in town?"

Gracie glared at her. "Don't you have to be somewhere?"

Vivian laughed as she raced toward the stairs.

Gracie watched her go, then opened the newspaper and prepared for a quiet morning. That afternoon she would be moving into the house she'd rented for the six weeks she would be in town, but until then, there was nothing to occupy her time except —

The back door burst open.

"Oh, good. You're up." Alexis, Gracie's older sister by three years, glanced around. "Where's Vivian?"

"Getting ready to go to the hardware store."

Alexis frowned. "I thought she'd be gone already. Doesn't the sidewalk sale start at eight?"

"I haven't a clue," Gracie admitted.

She'd been home all of two days and was still finding her bearings. While Alexis and Vivian had grown up in this house, Gracie had left the summer she turned fourteen and had never been back.

Alexis poured herself a cup of coffee and took the stool next to Gracie's.

"We have to talk," her older sister said in a low voice that shook slightly. "But you

13

can't tell Vivian. Or Mom. I don't want them to worry. Not when they already have the wedding to deal with."

"Okay," Gracie said slowly, knowing there was no point in asking if everything was all right. If things were all right, Alexis wouldn't be here demanding promises of confidentiality or looking panicked.

"It's Zeke," Alexis said, then pressed her lips together. "Dammit, I told myself I wouldn't cry."

Gracie tensed. Zeke and Alexis had been married for five years — happily from all accounts.

Alexis sucked in a breath, then let it out. "I think he's having an affair."

"What? That's not possible. He's crazy about you."

"I thought so, too." Alexis brushed her free hand across her eyes. "It's just. . . ." She paused as they heard thumping noises from overhead. "He disappears every night and doesn't get back until three or four in the morning. When I ask him to tell me what's going on, he says he's working late on the campaign. But I don't believe him."

Gracie carefully closed the newspaper. "What campaign? Doesn't Zeke sell insurance?"

"Yes, but he's running Riley Whitefield's

14

campaign for mayor. I thought you knew."

Gracie was more out of the loop than she'd realized. "When did that happen?"

"A few months ago. He hired Zeke because —"

Footsteps thundered on the stairs. Seconds later Vivian burst into the kitchen.

"Hey, Alexis," she said as she fastened her long hair into a braid. "Want to take my place at the store today?"

"Not really."

Vivian grinned. "It doesn't hurt to ask. I'm off to do slave labor to pay for my wedding dress. Don't have too much fun while I'm gone."

The back door slammed shut behind her. A minute later, a car engine started, sputtered, then caught.

Alexis walked to the window over the sink and stared out toward the street. "Okay, she's gone. Where were we?"

"You were telling me that your husband now works for Riley Whitefield. How did that happen?"

"Zeke spent two years after college working for a senator from Arizona." Her worry faded a little as she faced Gracie and smiled. "I was at Arizona State and he . . ." Alexis shook her head. "God, that was a lifetime ago. I can't believe he'd do this to

15

me. I love him so much and I th-thought. . . ." Her voice cracked. "What am I going to do?"

Gracie had the uneasy sensation of being trapped in the middle of a fun house. Nothing was as it seemed and she didn't know her way out.

Sure, Alexis and Vivian were her sisters. Her family. They looked enough alike that no one could mistake the genetic connection. Long blond hair — pale for Alexis, strawberry for Vivian and gold for herself — big blue eyes and the same average body build. But she'd been doing this sister thing long distance for half her life. She didn't know how to slide back into confidences and advice mode without a little warm-up.

"You don't know for sure Zeke is doing anything," Gracie said. "Maybe it *is* the campaign."

"I don't know, but I intend to find out." She took a step forward.

Gracie got a bad feeling in her already queasy stomach. "I'm going to hate myself for asking, but how?"

"By spying on him. He's supposed to have a meeting with Riley tonight and I'm going to be there."

"Not the best idea in the world," Gracie said as she reached for her coffee. "Trust

16

me. I speak from experience. Riley experience."

"I'm going to do it," Alexis said, her eyes filling with tears, "and I need your help."

Gracie set down her coffee cup. "No. No. Alexis, I can't. You can't. It's crazy."

Tears trickled down her sister's cheeks. Pain darkened her blue eyes. Alexis personified agony and Gracie didn't know how to fight that. But she tried.

"It will only lead to disaster," she said firmly. "I won't be a part of that."

"I u-understand," Alexis said as her mouth quivered.

"Good. Because I'm not going with you."

Late that night, Gracie found herself following her sister along a trimmed hedge just east of a massive old house. Not just any house, either. The Whitefield family mansion, home to umpteen generations of wealthy Whitefields and now Riley's main residence.

"This is insane," Gracie whispered to her sister as they paused to crouch a few feet from a back window. "I stopped spying on Riley when I was fourteen. I can't believe I'm doing this again."

"You're not spying on Riley, you're spying on Zeke. There's a big difference."

"I doubt Riley will see that, if we're caught."

"Then we won't be caught. Did you bring your camera?"

Gracie grabbed her trusty Polaroid from under her arm and held it out. Light from the streetlamp glinted off the narrow lens.

"Get ready," Alexis said. "The library window is around the corner. You should be able to get a really good picture from there."

"Why aren't you getting the picture?" Gracie asked as dread made her legs feel as heavy as bronze.

"Because I'm going to stay here and see if any floozy bitch runs out the back way."

"If Zeke were having an affair, wouldn't he just go to a motel?" Gracie asked.

"He can't. I pay the bills. Besides, when we were dating, he let some guy use his apartment for a lunchtime rendezvous. I'm telling you, Riley's doing the same for Zeke. Who holds campaign meetings until two in the morning?"

It sounded logical in a twisted psychotic way, Gracie thought as she inched toward the side of the house. Especially if one ignored the reality of sneaking onto private property to snap pictures through an open window.

"We don't even know if they're in the

18

library," Gracie said in a low voice.

"Zeke says they always meet there. If he's really at a campaign meeting, that's where it should take place."

"Can't I just look through the window and tell you what I see?" Gracie asked.

"I want proof."

What Gracie wanted was to be far, far from here. But she recognized Alexis's stubborn expression and her own guilt. Even if she *wanted* to turn her back on her sister, she couldn't. Better to simply take the pictures and get out than stay crouched and arguing.

"Get ready," Gracie said as she once again moved toward the house.

The bushes under the building were thicker than they first appeared. They scratched her bare arms and tugged at her khakis. Worse, the library window was higher than her, which meant she had to hold the camera above her head, point down into the room and take a picture without being sure what, or *who*, was in there.

It would just be her luck to focus the camera just as someone looked out the window.

"Here goes nothing," she muttered as she stretched up on tiptoes and pushed the red button.

Hot, bright light exploded in the night. Gracie instantly dropped to her knees as she swore under her breath. The flash! How could she have forgotten about the flash?

"Because I use the camera to take pictures of wedding cakes, not to spy on people," she muttered as she scrambled back to her feet and started running toward the car.

There was no sign of Alexis, nor did Gracie know if she'd actually gotten a picture of anything. Not that it mattered. She just wanted to get out of here before —

"Freeze!"

As the forceful command was accompanied by something hard and very gunlike being jabbed between her shoulder blades, Gracie did as instructed. She froze.

"What the hell are you up to? If you're a thief, you're a piss-poor one. Or do you always announce yourself with a flashbulb?"

"Not if I can help it," Gracie said as she sucked in a breath. "I'm sorry if I startled you. I can explain."

As she spoke, she turned, and as she turned she saw the man holding the shotgun and he saw her.

Both of them jumped back. While Gracie wished the ground would open up and swallow her, he looked as if he'd seen a ghost.

"Sweet Jesus," Riley Whitefield breathed. "Gracie Landon, is that you?"

CHAPTER TWO

As the ground-swallowing was taking too long, Gracie began to wish for a large, people-eating dinosaur to rise from the grave and devour her whole. Or aliens. She would accept aliens swooping her up into their visiting craft if she didn't have to stand here and stare at Riley's gorgeous face. She would even endure the medical experiments without complaining.

She hadn't seen him since the summer she'd turned fourteen. He'd been all of eighteen, caught in that half-boy, half-man stage that was both appealing and awkward. He'd grown up, filled out and gotten sexier and more dangerous looking. But the disbelief in his eyes made her want to die right there on the spot.

"I can explain," she said, then wondered if she really could. Were there any words that would convince him she wasn't still crazed stalker girl recently released from a mental institution?

"Gracie Landon?" he repeated.

She noticed he'd lowered the shotgun so it wasn't pointing directly at her. That was something.

"This isn't what you think," she said and took a step back. Maybe it would be better for both of them if she just disappeared into the night. And where was her sister? How just like Alexis to fade away when the going got tough. She'd always let Gracie take the fall for things.

"You weren't lurking outside my house, taking pictures?" Riley asked.

"Okay, yes, I was doing that, but it wasn't about you. Not technically."

His eyes were the color of stormy midnight. At least that's how she'd described them when she was a teenager. She'd written really bad haiku about his eyes and his mouth. She'd imagined how he would kiss her when he finally came to his senses and realized they belonged together. She'd even written poems to his various girlfriends — after he'd dumped them — commiserating with their pain.

Yes, my dear Jenny, I alone can understand, the magic of the moment, when he takes your hand.

Gracie placed her palm on her stomach

23

where she could feel the acid churning. Most days she couldn't remember where she'd left her car keys, but she could recall lines of horrible poetry written a lifetime ago?

"There's something seriously wrong with me," she muttered.

"I'll second that," Riley said.

She narrowed her gaze. "You're not helping the situation. You know that? I know this looks bad, but here's a news flash. I'm not here for you. My brother-in-law, Zeke, is supposed to be helping you with your campaign for mayor tonight. That's what this is all about." She waved the camera in his face.

He frowned. "You have a thing for your brother-in-law?"

"What?" she yelped. "No. Yuck. Of course not. My sister, Alexis, asked me to —" She pressed her lips together and turned away and started for the car — assuming Alexis hadn't driven off in it after slinking away. "Just forget it."

"Not so fast," Riley said as he grabbed her arm. "You can't show up like this, take pictures, then walk away. How do I know you haven't put a bomb in my car?"

Gracie jerked free of his grip, then squared her shoulders before turning around to face him. "I never tried to hurt you," she said as calmly as she could when what she wanted to do was run screaming into the night. This was so not fair. "When I had a crush on you, I tried to keep you from seeing your girlfriend, but I never actually hurt anyone."

"You threw yourself in front of my car and begged me to run over you."

Heat exploded in her cheeks. Why couldn't everyone just leave the past where it belonged? Why did every humiliating detail of her life have to be dissected in public?

"That was about *my* pain, not doing injury to you." She drew in a deep breath. Peaceful thoughts, she reminded herself. And a couple of antacids. That's all she needed. "I'm sorry to have bothered you. I'm sorry I let my sister talk me into coming here. I knew it was a bad idea. It won't happen again. Whatever her problems with Zeke, I'm not getting involved. Ever."

His gaze narrowed. "What problems with Zeke?"

"That's personal."

"Look, lady, the second you started taking pictures in my windows, it became my business."

He had a point. Not a very big one, but still . . . "Zeke has been acting funny — staying out late, not talking about things.

He says he's busy with your campaign all the time but Alexis thinks he's having an affair."

Riley swore and grabbed her arm again. "All right. Come on."

"Let go of me."

He didn't and he started walking, dragging her along with him.

"Where are we going?" she asked.

"Inside. We have to talk. If my campaign manager is cheating on his wife, I want to know about it."

"I don't think he is. He just doesn't seem the type. What time did your meeting with him end tonight?"

Riley stopped on the front porch. Light from the big fixture by the front door illuminated his perfect features — dark eyes, high cheekbones and the kind of mouth that made normally reasonable women want to run out and do something really, really sinful. He still wore an earring, but a diamond stud had replaced the gold hoop she remembered so well.

"We didn't have a meeting," he said flatly. "I haven't seen Zeke in three days."

The churning got worse. Gracie pulled free of Riley's grip and rubbed her stomach. "That can't be good."

"My thoughts exactly. So come inside. I

want you to start from the beginning and tell me everything you know about Zeke and his affair."

"For one thing, I don't know if he's even having one. Alexis could be overreacting."

"Does she usually?" he asked as he held open the front door and motioned for her to step inside.

"I don't think so. Maybe. I live in L.A. I don't actually spend all that much time with her."

She walked into the house and came to a complete stop in the foyer. The place was huge. Old, but beautiful with high ceilings, carved moldings and enough furniture, knickknacks and artwork to monopolize an entire month of *Antiques Roadshow.*

"Wow. This is pretty cool," she said as she turned in a slow circle. "I think my entire house would fit in the foyer."

"Yeah, it's big. The library's in here."

Once again he grabbed her arm and dragged her along. She caught a glimpse of a formal dining room and a parlor or living room before he pulled her into the library. He released her and walked to a liquor tray set up by the window. After setting the gun on the desk, he poured what looked like Scotch into two glasses. She set down her Polaroid.

"Let me say for the record — ouch," she said as she rubbed her arm again. "I don't remember you manhandling women before."

He glared at her, then handed her a drink. "I don't trust you."

"It was fourteen years ago, Riley. You really need to let go of the past."

"I was happy to until you showed up again. You tortured me for two years. They wrote about it in the newspaper. The 'Gracie Chronicles.' "

Embarrassment made her want to squirm. "Yes, well, that part wasn't *my* fault. Can we talk about something more relevant? Like Zeke."

"Why does Alexis think he's having an affair?"

Gracie shrugged. "He's coming home late and not saying where he's been."

"How long has this been going on?"

"About six weeks. At first she figured he really was working on the campaign, but the nights got later and later and when he wouldn't talk about what was going on. . . ." She stopped and glanced at him. "Why *are* you running for mayor? You don't strike me as the political type."

Riley ignored the question and pointed to her drink. "Do you want something

28

different?"

Gracie sniffed the glass, then put it on the desk. "No, it's great. It's just stress makes my stomach unhappy." She pulled a roll of what looked like antacids from her pocket and popped a couple in her mouth. "Terrific room."

Riley followed her gaze as she glanced at the twelve-foot-high bookcases filled to overflowing. He didn't bother telling her that the library was one of the few places he felt comfortable in the oversized house.

"Tell me about Zeke," he said.

"You tell me." She walked to the leather sofa across from the ornate fireplace and flopped down. "He's your campaign manager. Is he having an affair?"

"Hell if I know." Riley paced to the desk and leaned against it. "He talks about Alexis all the time. I would say he adores her."

"But your meetings don't run until three in the morning."

He smiled. "I'm running for mayor, not president."

"Yeah, that's what I thought, too. Well, I guess I have to tell Alexis that he wasn't here. She's not going to like that."

Riley didn't much like it, either. The election was only five weeks away and he couldn't afford a scandal. Not when he was finally making progress with the good citizens of Los Lobos.

He set down his drink and tugged at the picture still hanging from the camera. After peeling off the protective layer, he stared at the Polaroid photo.

It showed the ceiling of the library and a few shelves, but nothing else.

"You're not very good at this," he told Gracie.

She rolled her eyes. "I'm not trying to be. Despite what you think of me, I didn't grow up to be a spy or a professional stalker. I bake wedding cakes for a living."

She was annoyed and indignant, but also embarrassed. Color stained her cheeks and her bottom lip trembled slightly. She'd grown up, filled out, but the basics were still the same. Big blue eyes, long gold-blond hair and an air of determination that had scared the bejesus out of him back then.

"I'm sorry," she said. "For this and for all that. You know. Before."

"Are we talking about the itching powder in my boxer shorts?"

"Yeah. I guess. I just. . . ." She leaned forward and traced a pattern on the coffee table in front of the sofa. "Looking back, I can't believe what I did to you. It was horrible."

"Folks around here are still talking about it."

She sat up and looked at him. "Tell me about it. Everyone else gets to leave their past behind, but not me. Noooo. I become a legend. I have to say, it seriously sucks."

He thought about the laxative she'd managed to sneak into his soup the afternoon before the homecoming dance. "You were creative."

"I was a menace. I just wanted . . ." Color flared again. "Well, we both know what I wanted."

"Date much now?"

She tossed her head. "Some. I'm careful not to bring them here."

"You don't want them hearing about the time you lured a skunk into my car, then locked it inside for a couple of hours?"

She winced. "I paid for the cleaning."

"My car was never the same. I had to sell it. At auction." He raised his glass to her. "You were hell-bent on breaking up me and Pam." Based on what had happened, maybe he should have listened.

Gracie's knowing expression had him thinking she would agree with his assessment. But instead of commenting on that she said, "So what happens next?"

"I find out what Zeke's up to. I don't need

31

any trouble right now. Can you get your sister to back off until I have some concrete information?"

When Gracie hesitated, he stared at her. "You owe me," he reminded her.

She shivered. "I know. Okay — I'll do what I can with Alexis. But I can't promise more than a couple of days. She's a woman on a mission."

"And we all know what happens when you Landon women set your mind to something."

"Exactly." She stood and looked at him. "I'm really sorry, Riley. I know the apology is about fourteen years too late, but I mean it from the bottom of my heart. I never meant to make your life hell."

"I appreciate that."

"Do you want me to leave my cell number so you can get in touch with me about Zeke or do you want to call Alexis directly?"

Riley decided on the devil he knew. "Your number is fine."

He handed her a pad of paper. She quickly wrote on it and passed it back.

"My camera," she said.

He gave it to her.

"How long are you in town for?" he asked.

"A few weeks. My younger sister, Vivian, is getting married. I'm here to help out with all the details and to make the wedding cake. I rented a house at the edge of town. I need a kitchen to complete my other orders."

"I'll be in touch."

She nodded, then turned the camera over in her hands as if she wanted to say something else. He waited, but she only shrugged, then walked toward the hallway.

He followed her to the front door. She stepped out into the night, then glanced back at him.

"I wasn't wrong about Pam," she said.

"I should have listened."

Her lips curved up in a smile. "Really?"

"Sure. Even a blind squirrel finds an acorn sometimes, Gracie. Good night."

He closed the door, but didn't step away. Sure enough he heard a thud, as if she'd just kicked the door.

"That was a low blow, Riley," she yelled. "A real low blow."

Despite everything that had happened and everything he had yet to do, he found himself grinning as he returned to the library.

Gracie fumed as she stalked away from Riley's house. "A blind squirrel," she muttered. "My opinion on Pam wasn't based on dumb luck. Talk about ungrateful. If he'd listened to me, he wouldn't have married her in the first place. But no."

She stomped her foot once for good measure, then stopped on the sidewalk. No sign of Alexis *or* the car. While Los Lobos wasn't huge, the distance from the Whitefield manor side of town to her mother's more middle-class neighborhood would definitely qualify as a serious workout.

She turned left and started walking. The night was pleasantly cool with a hint of brine in the air. Even though she'd been gone forever, the town felt familiar. She liked the closeness of the ocean and the quiet residential streets. She might live in a suburb back in Los Angeles, but it was a whole lot louder than this.

At the corner, she glanced back at Riley's house. He might have grown up poor, but he fit in there now. As she walked across the street, she smiled. Man oh man, had he looked good. She supposed she could take comfort in the fact that even at thirteen she'd had fabulous taste in men. Riley had only gotten better with age. He had the brooding, dark, good looks of a fallen angel. An angel with a diamond stud earring.

Despite her shock and embarrassment at seeing him again, she'd felt something.

34

Sparks. Attraction. No doubt as completely one-sided as it had ever been, which meant she had to make sure she didn't even pretend to act on it. No way was she willing to be stalker girl again.

A car pulled up beside her. Gracie glanced over and saw Alexis's Camry. Her sister rolled down the window.

"You got away," she said quietly. "I'm glad. Get in."

"What do you mean I got away?" Gracie asked as she opened the door and slid onto the passenger seat. "Were you seriously concerned Riley would take me prisoner and torture me for information?"

"I didn't know what would happen. I can't believe your flash is that bright and loud."

Gracie glanced at her aging camera. "Me, either. Guess it's really not what I should use for my undercover work." She returned her attention to her sister. "You *left* me back there. What's up with that?"

Alexis hunched over the steering wheel. "I'm sorry. I couldn't risk being caught."

"Oh, and I could? Do you have any idea what Riley thought when he found me lurking outside his windows?"

"Nothing he hasn't thought a million times before."

That hurt, Gracie thought. "I would like

everyone to remember I've grown up since then." She sighed. "It doesn't matter. I have the information you wanted."

Her sister looked at her. "What do you mean?"

"I asked Riley about Zeke."

"What? No!"

Alexis slammed on the brakes, making Gracie grateful she'd fastened her seat belt securely.

Gracie braced her hands against the dashboard. "I talked to him about the problem. He has answers. Why is this a big deal?"

"Because it's private," Alexis shrieked. "I didn't want anyone to know. It's family stuff and supposed to be a secret. Not that I would expect you to understand that."

Gracie flinched. She didn't know if her sister meant the family part or the secret part, and she wasn't sure it mattered.

"You dragged me into this," she reminded her sister. "I went along to help you."

"I know. I'm sorry. It's just . . ." Alexis sighed. "What did he say?"

"That to the best of his knowledge, Zeke loves and adores you. But he wasn't working on the campaign tonight." She thought about mentioning that Riley was going to talk to Zeke about his extracurricular activi-

36

ties but wasn't sure she wanted to hear the screeching again.

"Anything else?"

Gracie hesitated.

Alexis pulled up in front of the Landon family home and turned off the engine. "What?" she demanded.

"Riley is going to talk to Zeke about where he goes."

Alexis dropped her head to the steering wheel and moaned. "Tell me you're kidding."

"I'm not, but it's not such a bad idea. You're not willing to talk to your husband about it and someone has to get the truth. Once you know he's not running around, you'll feel better." Gracie touched her sister's arm. "If you'd just talk to him yourself," she began.

Alexis opened the driver's door. "You don't understand. It's not that simple. I'm not sure I want to know what he's doing. If he *is* fooling around . . ." She swallowed. "I don't want to have to leave him, but I will."

Gracie didn't want to be having this conversation or any other, at the moment. She had only been home a couple of days and already a week of root canals seemed so much more pleasant.

"Why don't you wait and find out the

truth?" she asked softly.

"Good point. I will. Are you coming in?" Alexis jerked her head toward the house.

At this point Gracie was more than ready to escape to her rental, but she nodded and stepped out of the car. She would duck inside, yell out a greeting and leave. She could rationalize the decision by saying she had to unpack, but the truth was she wanted to be gone because she needed some distance. Too much family stuff too quickly, she thought.

They walked toward the house. As Alexis pulled open the front door, Gracie realized she could hear shouting inside.

"That can't be good," she said.

"Sounds like Vivian." Alexis shook her head. "I hope the wedding isn't off again."

"What? Off?" But before Gracie could press for details, her sister had stepped into the house. Gracie trailed after her.

Vivian stood in the center of the room, her face streaked with tears and bleeding mascara, her hands on her hips, her mouth petulant. Their mother sat on the sofa, several brides magazines open on the coffee table.

When she saw Gracie and Alexis, their baby sister sniffed. "I hate Tom," she said defiantly. "He's selfish and mean and I'm

38

not going to marry him."

"Of course you are," Alexis said soothingly. "You just had a fight. Now tell me what you were arguing about."

"The bachelor p-party," Vivian said over a sob. "He said I couldn't come. But if I'm not there, how will I know what he's doing? I don't care about movies and drinking and stuff, but I don't want him to have s-strippers."

"Does he want to?" Alexis asked.

Vivian hiccupped. "He s-said it wasn't up to me. He s-said until we were married, he didn't have to do what I said."

Gracie wanted to be anywhere but here. She didn't know if she should simply excuse herself and make a quick dash for her car or pretend an urgent need to use the bathroom. Then she stunned herself by opening her mouth and talking.

"Did you explain that your being at the bachelor party isn't so much about you telling him what to do as it is about making sure you can begin your marriage in a state of love and trust? I've never understood the need for men, or women for that matter, to have a big party where plenty could go wrong that could potentially destroy the relationship they're trying to celebrate with a wedding."

Everyone turned to stare at her. Alexis shook her head, as if trying to discourage a not-very-bright child, her mother rose and walked over to Vivian, who had started a fresh storm of sobbing.

"I'll take that as a no," Gracie murmured, feeling more out of place by the second.

"It will be fine," her mother said as she pulled Vivian close. "You and Tom will talk in the morning and things will be better."

"I g-guess," Vivian mumbled against her mother's shoulder. "I j-just want him to love me."

"Of course you do. It's all right. Everything will be all right."

Gracie waved toward the door. "I should leave you to deal with this. I'll just be going."

"Good idea," her mother mouthed.

Gracie did her best *not* to feel as if she'd made a difficult situation worse and headed back out into the night. She drove across town to her rental house and gratefully walked into the dark quiet.

A few clicks of light switches took care of the gloom and a glance around the kitchen restored her spirits.

She'd already put away her special cooking pans, slipping the ones that wouldn't fit anywhere else into some open shelves meant

40

for cookbooks. Her cooking schedule was magneted to the refrigerator and she'd used poster tape to tack up her two-page spread from *People* magazine. The one with the headline What's Gracie's Secret?

She crossed to it now and traced the picture of the popular sitcom star from *Olive's Attic* as she fed a piece of luscious Gracie-made wedding cake to her husband at the wedding. The second page showed several of Gracie's cakes, along with a picture of her carefully decorating one of them.

That was her world, she reminded herself. Her house in Torrance, her orders, her perfect kitchen with three full-sized ovens, built-in cooling racks and southern exposure. It was a world she understood — where she was just Gracie. Not anyone's sister or daughter. She didn't mess up there. She didn't feel as if she didn't belong.

Had it been a mistake to try to come home? The decision had been made and there was no unmaking it.

"Just a few weeks," she reminded herself. Then she could walk away from all of this and never look back.

CHAPTER THREE

Gracie walked into Bill's Mexican Grill promptly at noon only to find her friend Jill already seated and waving her in.

"You're always early," Gracie said as she approached.

Jill stood and hugged her. "I know. It's a disease. I'm thinking I need a twelve-step program."

Gracie stepped back from her friend and looked her over. "Very fabulous," she said. "Would I recognize the designer?"

Jill wiggled her hips as she turned in a slow circle, modeling her tailored shirt and trim pinstripe slacks before she took her seat.

"Armani. I'm still working through my big-city lawyer clothes. Tina, my assistant, keeps ragging on me about dressing too fancy for Los Lobos, but if I don't wear them to work, where will I?"

Gracie sat next to Jill and fingered the

sleeve of her silk blouse. "I'm guessing not for cleaning the bathroom."

"Exactly." Jill leaned forward and grinned. "I'm *so* happy to see you. It's been ages. What? Five months?"

"Just about. We were last together at your wedding up in Carmel, where I have to say you were far more interested in the groom than in me. This despite the fact that I made you a pretty fabulous cake. What is up with that? I'm your oldest and dearest friend. He's just some guy."

Jill laughed. "You're right. He's some guy. Some great, amazing, hunky —"

She broke off when the waitress approached to take their drink orders. Gracie asked for diet soda while Jill chose iced tea.

Her friend had changed, Gracie thought. In the past few years Jill had been on the legal fast track at a huge law firm in San Francisco. She'd worn stiff suits, worked impossible hours and had tamed her fabulous curly hair into a sleek, painful bun at the nape of her neck. Now she looked . . . Gracie smiled. Soft. All feminine and comfortable in her skin. Long cascades of curls tumbled down Jill's back. The shadows were gone from under her eyes and she seemed to glow.

"You like married life," Gracie said.

43

"I love it. Mac is amazing. I was a little nervous about being a stepmother, but Emily is wonderful and very patient with my mistakes. My only regret is that we have to share her with her real mom. I wouldn't mind having her around all the time."

"Wow. That's so cool."

"It's just how I feel. I adore them both."

Gracie grabbed Jill's left hand and studied the diamond ring guards surrounding an impressive solitaire.

"I like a man who isn't intimidated by a good-sized rock," Gracie said with a grin.

"Mac knows how to do it right," Jill admitted. "In many ways."

Gracie held up both hands. "If you're going to talk about sex, I'm not listening. I can be blissfully happy for your newly married self, your great husband and perfect stepchild. I won't even begrudge you a dog, but I draw the line at sex."

Jill patted her hand. "Because you're not getting any?"

"Exactly. David and I broke up three months ago and I haven't been inspired to start the whole dating nightmare again."

The waitress returned with their drinks and chips and salsa, then asked if they were ready to order.

"What's good?" Gracie asked.

"They make a delicious taco salad," Jill said.

"Works for me." She had her antacids in her purse for the inevitable attack later.

"Make it two," Jill told the waitress. "Thanks." She turned back to her friend. "I thought you really liked David. What happened?"

"I don't know. Nothing. Everything. He was great, but . . ." She sighed. "I want sparks. Is that so horrible? Not an actual fire event but a few singes would be nice. I want to be excited when I know I'm going to see the guy I'm with. I want to use words like amazing and heart-stopping, not nice or very pleasant. David was very pleasant. We got along. We never fought. We never . . . anything. How can I get serious about a guy when I barely notice if he's there or not?"

"Despite your earlier attachment to a man we will not name, you're not a drama queen," Jill said.

"Maybe that's the problem. Maybe I'm so concerned about reverting to stalker girl that I'm not letting myself care about anyone." She picked up her drink. "I could be a drama queen if I wanted."

Jill smiled. "Sure you could."

The idea had appeal, except Gracie knew that she actually preferred order in her world. Surprises were all good for presents, but in the rest of her life, she liked predictability. Which might explain a long series of really dull guys.

Besides . . . "I think Vivian got all the drama queen genes in our family. She and Tom had a huge fight yesterday over the bachelor party and she was threatening to call off the wedding."

Jill's eyes widened. "Do you think she will?"

"I haven't a clue. But if she does, I'm going to be very cranky about coming up here and renting a house for six weeks. I have orders lining up like crazy."

"I thought you would have stayed with your mom," Jill said. "Couldn't you use her oven?"

"It's not just the oven. It's the refrigerator and freezer, not to mention an entire dining room table for decorating and most of the cupboards for my supplies. Plus I like to stay up late and work. The cake part is easy — it's the individual decorations that take forever."

What she didn't mention was how uncomfortable she felt in her mother's house. She hadn't lived there in so long, it had ceased to be home. She was trying to fit in and not doing a very good job of it so far.

46

"Is it weird to be back?" Jill asked.

"Yes and no. I feel different, but no one sees me that way. I'm still Gracie Landon — in love with Riley Whitefield."

Jill picked up her iced tea. "You know he's in town."

Gracie narrowed her gaze. "Don't you start in on me. I've already heard that from my mother's neighbor, my landlord, the clerk at the grocery store and some woman on the street whom I don't remember at all. It's more than scary — it's a *Twilight Zone* moment."

"It's the articles in the newspaper," Jill said. "Even people who'd never met you felt they were a part of the romance."

"Tell me about it."

"Have you seen him?"

Gracie hesitated. She didn't know how to say she had without spilling Alexis's private business.

"You have!" Jill leaned forward. "I want to know everything. Start at the beginning and talk slowly."

Gracie sighed and picked up a chip. She turned it over then bit into it. "You can't say anything," she told her friend when she'd chewed and swallowed. "I was checking out something for Alexis and no, I can't tell you what."

"So you ran into him at the store or something?"

"Not exactly. I was sort of lurking around his house."

Jill's brown eyes widened. "You have to be kidding. You were *spying* on him?"

"No. I was spying on someone else. But he caught me and it was horrible and awkward and I think he's going to be getting a restraining order against me."

Jill grabbed a chip. "What did you think? Isn't he still amazing looking?"

"Oh, yeah. Dark, brooding, dangerous."

"Sexy," Jill added. "I love the earring. I tried to talk Mac into getting one, but he's pretty much ignoring me on that."

"I'll admit the earring is appealing."

"And his butt. The man has a fabulous butt."

"I didn't get a chance to check it out, but I'll put it on my to-do list."

Jill threw the chip across the table. "Oh, please. Don't get all superior with me. We're talking about Riley. I refuse to believe you can stand in the same room as him and not feel something."

"I felt humiliation and a burning desire to be somewhere else."

"That's not what I mean. Come on, Gracie. There had to be some attraction

48

between you."

No way she would admit to that, Gracie thought. Too dangerous with the potential to make her look far too foolish. Plus it would be all one-sided. "He's firmly in my past where he will stay. Do you think I'm proud of what I did to him? I hate that everyone remembers it and talks about it. The last thing I'm willing to do is fuel the fire. What's he doing here, anyway? And running for mayor? What's up with that?"

Jill straightened. "I can only discuss things that are public knowledge."

Gracie stared at her friend. She was careful to keep her lips pressed together so her mouth didn't hang open, but she was pretty sure her eyes had bugged out.

"You're his *lawyer?*"

"I'm handling some things for him."

Gracie didn't know what to say. "How long will he be in town?"

"That depends."

"You're not being the least bit helpful." Gracie took a sip of her drink. "Do you know why he's running for mayor?"

"Yes."

"Are you going to tell me?"

"No."

"You're not very much fun, you know that?"

49

Jill grabbed a chip. "I know. I just can't." Her expression turned wicked. "But if you see him the next time you're spying at his house, you could ask him yourself."

"Not even for money. I don't want to have anything to do with Riley ever again. The humiliation would be too great."

"Fair enough. As long as you're sure he's not the one."

Gracie looked at her and laughed. "If he's the one, I'm converting to Catholicism and taking my vows."

Franklin Yardley liked watches. He had an impressive collection he stored in a custom-made drawer in his dresser. Every morning after picking out a suit and tie, he carefully chose the watch he would wear for the day. Omegas were his favorite, but he had three Rolexes because everyone expected a man in his position to wear one.

"It's all about perception," he reminded himself as he glanced down at the Omega partially concealed by the cuff of his mono-grammed cotton shirt.

Still, he wasn't interested in a watch for himself today. He turned the page of the jewelry store catalogue and paused when he saw the display of ladies' watches. No, he was shopping for a very special someone.

A simple but elegant Movado caught his eye.

"Perfect."

It was fancy enough to impress the lady in question, but not so flashy as to call attention to itself.

He made a note of the jewelry store and then checked his calendar. He would need a day or so to get the twelve hundred dollars he would need to buy the watch. It wasn't as if he could put it on his credit card. Sandra, his wife, might never have worked a day in her life, but she kept track of every single penny. Somehow he'd assumed the daughter of a self-made millionaire wouldn't care about things like budgets and spending, but Sandra did. She believed that since the wealth in their marriage came from her, she had the only say on how it was spent.

Still, after twenty-eight years of marriage, Frank had made his peace with her tight purse strings and had figured out more than one way around them.

She often commented on his nice things, the ones she hadn't bought for him, but he never explained, not even when she told him to his face she didn't trust him. He didn't particularly care what she thought — she would never leave and she looked good at parties. It was more than enough.

Frank slipped the catalogue into his leather Tumi briefcase, then unlocked the desk's bottom drawer. Under the city seal and several other important documents was the checkbook for the account especially set aside for the mayor's discretionary funds. Frank liked to think of it as his private play money. He tucked the checkbook next to the catalogue and pushed the buzzer that would summon his assistant.

The door to his private office opened and Holly walked in. Tall, blond, raised in San Diego and all of twenty-four, she had the perfect pretty looks of a third-generation surfing family. But behind those big blue eyes and high cheekbones was a brain of extraordinary sharpness.

"I have the figures you requested," she said as she put a folder on his desk.

Hers was the figure that interested him the most. He imagined how pleased she would be when he gave her the watch later this week.

"It's not good," she added. "Riley White-field is gaining in the polls. People are starting to listen to his message." She frowned slightly, drawing her perfect eyebrows together. "They're saying we should discuss the issues more. I think you should give a few more speeches."

He adored everything about her. The way she talked, the way she worried, the way she said "we" as if they were a team.

"What issues do you consider most relevant?" he asked.

Delight widened her eyes. "You really want my opinion?"

"Of course. You're my connection with the good citizens of Los Lobos. They'll tell you things they would never tell me."

"I hadn't thought of that. I guess being the mayor sort of separates you from everyone."

"Why don't you close the door and we'll brainstorm some topics," he suggested.

She did as he requested, then took the seat across from his. "Taxes are always an issue," she said. "But there aren't any bond measures on the ballot."

"What's Whitefield discussing?" he asked.

"Zoning, more money for schools, ways to bring tourists to town in the winter."

"I'm not sure I want more tourists around," Frank said.

Holly nodded. "They're a pain, but they dump lots of money into the economy."

"Sounds like we have our work cut out for us." Frank paused as if considering something, even though he'd long since made up his mind. "I don't suppose . . ." he began.

Holly leaned forward, her expression eager, her firm, young breasts swaying gently under her blouse.

"I was thinking you'd like to draft a couple of speeches for me."

She sprang to her feet and stared at him. "Are you serious? You'd let me do that?"

"I think you'd do a terrific job. You're bright, talented, ambitious. Are you interested?"

She laughed. "Absolutely. I could have two drafts to you by the end of the week. Is that soon enough?"

"Of course." Even better, he had a feeling her "drafts" would be word perfect. He rose. "Thank you, Holly. This means a lot to me."

"I'm really excited by the opportunity."

"I'm the one who's excited. I'm taking advantage of you. You're the kind of woman who makes a man go far."

Her smile turned knowing as she walked toward him. When she was only a few inches away, she reached for the waistband of her skirt.

"You're the kind of man who makes a woman want to do almost anything."

Her skirt dropped to the floor. Unable to tear his gaze away, he gave silent thanks.

She wasn't wearing any panties.

■ ■ ■ ■

Gracie turned the cake onto the cooling rack and expertly tapped the bottom with just enough force to let everyone know who was in charge. A challenge, considering the moody, temperamental oven she had to work with. One of the joys of renting. She counted to five, tapped again, then lifted in one clean motion that left no room for second chances.

The pan slid off perfectly, leaving the golden cake resting on the rack.

"I love it when a plan comes together," she said with a grin as she studied the multiple cooling layers that would make up a simple but elegant bridal shower cake.

Her exposure in *People* magazine, not to mention a couple of raves in the wedding issue of *InStyle* had turned her small cake business into a growing concern. For reasons not clear to her, celebrities now considered her a "must have" for their weddings and sometimes their showers. Sort of like wearing a Vera Wang original.

"I'm not about to complain," she said happily as she crossed to the refrigerator where she'd carefully stacked all the fleurs-de-lis she'd made in advance of decorating the cake. All three hundred and fifty. She would actually need about three hundred and thirty — the rest were for breakage.

The design — an elegant creation in white and gold — was a replica of a cake featured in a Renaissance painting. The bride-to-be, a popular actress with a career of movies on *Masterpiece Theater,* loved all things old. Gracie loved the challenge of something other than flowers, doves and hearts.

She walked to the counter, prepared to make yet more decorations in advance of assembling the cake, when her cell phone rang. For a second her heart fluttered, as if anticipating some wondrous event. The problem was, no one that exciting would be calling.

Oh. Yeah. Riley.

A quick glance at the display of her cell phone told her the caller was her mother, or at least someone at the hardware store.

Heartbeat quickly slowing to normal, she pushed the talk button.

"This is Gracie," she said.

"Hi. It's your mother. I'm confirming the meeting about the wedding. You'll be there, right? There's so much work to do to get things ready for Vivian's special day. I'm hoping you'll have some great ideas, what with all your wedding experience."

Gracie *still* felt the aftereffects of the previous evening when she'd been reprimanded by Alexis and left feeling more like an outsider than ever.

"Is the wedding still on?" she asked. "Vivian seemed pretty upset."

Her mother sighed. "Oh, this happens about once a week. She's flighty and impulsive, which isn't a good combination. But marriage will settle her down."

Gracie was of the opinion one should be settled before getting married, but that was just her.

"Sure. I'll be there. Should I bring anything?"

"Just your patience. You're going to need it." Her mother named the time and place, then excused herself to get back to customers at the store.

Gracie hung up and set the phone back on the counter. She'd been worried about coming home for a lot of reasons she hadn't been able to articulate. Now that she was here, she could easily list them, explain them, even file them by category.

There was Riley — not just that the town hadn't forgotten, which it hadn't, but also her reaction to him. One would think that half a lifetime away from him would reduce his appeal, but one would be wrong. Second, her relationship with her family. She remembered a lot of screaming and fighting with her sisters, but also a lot of good times. Now Alexis and Vivian were strangers to her, but close to each other. She felt like the odd man out and she didn't like it. Finally, there was her mother. She felt an awkwardness, a strain just under the surface, but she couldn't explain why it had happened. Was it because she'd been gone for so long? Or was there something else she didn't see?

She turned back to her cooling cake and wrinkled her nose. This was one of the few times she wished she did something else for a living. Something that didn't give her too much time to think. What she needed was a distraction . . . a really big one.

Riley sat in a leather chair that had been custom-made for his uncle. Donovan Whitefield had taken over the family bank on his thirty-fifth birthday and hadn't missed a day until he'd died forty-two years later. He'd been stern and difficult, a man who didn't take vacations, forgive mistakes or appreciate the foibles of others.

Or so he'd been told. Riley had never met his uncle. For nearly five years they'd lived in the same small town, but their paths had never crossed.

Riley turned in the chair and looked at the large portrait on the tall wall opposite the door. The office was stately and elegant, befitting a bank president, and the painting reflected all of that. Donovan Whitefield had been immortalized standing behind this very desk, staring out into the distance, as if the future beckoned.

Riley thought it was all a pile of shit. If he had his way, he would take the portrait down and burn it. But he couldn't — not until he won the damn election and all this was his. Until then, he played the game, and that meant sharing office space with an old and crabby ghost.

There was a quick knock on his door, then the heavy carved wood swung open.

"Good morning, Mr. Whitefield," his assistant said.

Riley shook his head. "I've told you it's not necessary to knock. You are never going to find me doing anything secret or suspicious."

Diane Evans, a sixty-something woman who had worked all her life, barely blinked.

"Of course, sir," she said in a voice that told him she would continue to knock until the last minute of the last day of her employment.

Riley knew he wasn't in a position to

complain.

Diane was efficient, quiet and knew everything about running the bank. If it hadn't been for her counsel, he would have floundered more than once. He might be able to sniff out oil in the middle of a typhoon in the South China Sea, but the world of financial institutions was new to him.

Diane had guided him through the past seven months without mussing a single strand of her short, graying hair.

"There was a call about the children's wing of the hospital again," she said evenly. Not by a flicker of a lash did she let on they'd had this conversation at least three times before and each time he'd not only refused to donate, but he'd instructed her not to mention it to him again.

He motioned for her to come in and take a seat on the far side of the desk. She moved quietly on her sensible shoes, then perched on the edge of the leather and wood chair, her back perfectly straight, her shoulders squared, her tweed suit covering her like an ugly coat of armor.

"You did promise to think about it, sir," she said.

"Funny. My recollection is that I told you hell would freeze over before I gave them a penny to build the Donovan Whitefield

60

memorial children's wing."

A pad of paper materialized in her hand, along with a pen. "Perhaps if I explained the needs of community again," she began.

"Perhaps if you got off me about this," he said.

She looked at him. Nothing about her serene expression changed. No eyebrow raised, no corner of her mouth turned down. Still he felt her disapproval all the way to his bones.

"It's for children, Mr. Whitefield," she said. "Local children who shouldn't have to go into Los Angeles to get the care they need."

He figured he owed her. She'd stayed late every time he'd asked, she'd saved his ass over and over and she'd never once thrown the memory of his grandfather in his face.

"I'll think about it," he said slowly. "On the condition you stop knocking and stop calling me Mr. Whitefield."

Diane rose to her feet. "Very well . . ." She hesitated, then pressed her lips together before saying, "Riley. I'll let the committee know you're considering a donation. In the meantime I have those reports your requested and Mr. Bridges is here to see you."

Despite the fact that the donation would cost him about fifteen million dollars if he did it, Riley still felt a measure of victory. Who knew he had it in him to negotiate with his secretary and win?

Zeke Bridges strolled in three minutes later. Tall, personable, with an air of trustworthiness about him that made you *want* to buy insurance from him, he'd been Riley's first choice to run his campaign for mayor. Zeke wasn't just well liked by most folks in the town, he had experience.

"The numbers are up," Zeke said as he slumped into the chair Diane had vacated. "Way up. We're gaining on Yardley every day. Those newspaper ads really made a difference. The old guy has to be running scared, which means we're going to have to watch for some kind of counterplay, but I'll keep on the polls so we'll know if he starts to creep back up in the numbers."

Riley grinned. "You're polling people? Zeke, it's Los Lobos and I'm running for mayor, not president."

"Sure. Make fun of me. But the truth is campaigning is all about the right information. We have to get it and use it to our advantage."

"If you say so. You're the expert and that's why I pay you the big bucks."

"Just remember that. We're only a few weeks away from the election. Every event is crucial. Sure we're ahead, but it wouldn't take much to derail the whole campaign. Yardley's a popular incumbent and people usually don't like change."

"I promise to remain cooperative," Riley said. He had to win this election, and for ninety-seven million reasons Zeke knew nothing about.

Zeke took him over the schedule for the next couple of weeks. There would be a few public appearances and some ads on local cable. When Riley had approved everything, he leaned back in his chair.

"There's just one more thing."

"Sure. What?"

"What you do on your own time is your own business, right up until it impacts my campaign."

Zeke frowned. "What are you talking about?"

"Your secret life. You're disappearing at all hours and not telling your wife where you are, which is your business, but she came looking at my place because that's where you told her you were going to be, which makes it my business."

Zeke swallowed hard. "Look, Riley, I'm sorry but I —"

Riley cut him off with a quick shake of his head. "There's no sorry. There's only the campaign. I'm only going to ask you this once. Are you doing anything that could have a negative impact on my bid for mayor? Before you answer, let me remind you that Los Lobos is a small town and people finding out that the head of my campaign is screwing around on his wife would be a big negative."

Zeke pushed to his feet. "I'm not cheating on Alexis. I would never do that. I love her." He turned away. "It's not that. It's not anything that matters to you or the campaign."

"Then what is it?"

Zeke turned back to him. "I don't have to tell you that."

"What if the information is a requirement of your continued employment with me?"

The other man looked him square in the eye. "Then you're going to have to fire me because I'm not going to tell you what I'm doing. It's not about you and it's not about Alexis. That's as much as I can say. Is it enough?"

Riley didn't want to be dealing with this right now, not with the election only a few weeks away. While he could replace Zeke, he didn't want to.

"If you're not going to tell me, you should at least tell your wife," Riley said. "She's worried. Making her think you're running around isn't the best way to prove you love her."

"Agreed. I'll explain things to her."

"By telling her what you're doing?"

Zeke shook his head. "I can't do that. Not yet. But it's not bad. You have to believe me."

Riley had learned a long time ago not to trust anyone. As much as he liked Zeke, he wasn't going to change his rule for him.

"If whatever it is you're doing spills over into the campaign, I won't just fire you, I'll do what I can to ruin you," Riley said. "Do we understand each other?"

"Sure." Zeke jerked his head toward the portrait on the far wall. "I know you never met your uncle, but I did. You probably don't want to hear this, but you're a lot like him."

No, Riley didn't want to know. "Thanks for sharing," he said dryly. "I'll talk to you soon."

When Zeke had collected his papers and left, Riley stared at the door for a long time. He wanted to believe the problem was solved, but the tension in his gut told him otherwise. Zeke was up to something and Riley wanted to know what.

He picked up the phone and pulled a

piece of paper from his shirt pocket.

"Hi, this is Gracie," a female voice said after two rings.

Riley grinned. Whoever would have thought he would one day be calling Gracie Landon on purpose?

"It's Riley. I talked to Zeke."

"And?"

He outlined their conversation.

"Alexis isn't going to be satisfied with that," Gracie said.

"I'm not either. I'm going to follow him tonight. See where he goes."

"I want to come with you."

His first instinct was to say no, but then he remembered who he was dealing with. The Gracie he knew would simply follow him, which meant they would be a very conspicuous parade.

"Fine. I'll pick you up at six-thirty. Are you back at the old house?"

"No. I'm renting a place." She gave him the address. "This is pretty cool," she said when he'd written it down. "I've never been on a stakeout before."

"Great. This is the perfect opportunity to round out your stalker past."

CHAPTER FOUR

Gracie wasn't sure of the correct fashion choice for a stakeout. In the movies everyone wore dark colors and drank cold coffee. She couldn't possibly drink coffee this late — not if she wanted to sleep or even keep her belly from going up in flames. She was nervous enough. Caffeine would simply cause an overflow of acid and the resulting pain would lay her low for hours.

"Clothes first, refreshments later," she told herself as she stood in front of the closet.

She hadn't brought all that much up with her for her stay in Los Lobos. Most of the space in her Subaru had been crammed with baking supplies and decorating tools, not to mention her nifty cooling racks. She'd limited her clothing choices to two small suitcases. Of course when she'd made that decision she hadn't planned on playing Bond girl sidekick to Riley's yummy 007.

"Black," she murmured as she sorted

through jeans and other slacks. A pair of black Dockers caught her attention. Somewhere she had a black T-shirt. That should do.

She found the T-shirt in a drawer. Unfortunately it was decorated with a white silhouette of a bride and groom and proclaimed itself to be from the 2004 Bride on the Beach show she'd attended the previous summer.

Gracie ignored the unfortunate pattern and pulled it on. She studied herself in the mirror and realized her blond hair would act as a beacon. Another quick search unearthed a battered Dodgers baseball cap. The blue didn't match the black but hey, this was a stakeout, not a fashion show. Besides, Riley was unlikely to notice what she was wearing.

Riley. Just his name made her body tense and her heart rate quadruple. She was going to have to figure out a way to counter her reaction to him. They were only together to figure out what Zeke was up to. She had a feeling that given the choice, Riley would rather spend the evening with a known mass murderer than her. Any attraction on her part was a really bad idea.

She stuffed her feet into sandals and headed for the front of the house. The light patter on the roof told her the rain promised by the local news had arrived. She picked up a windbreaker and then searched out her purse and keys.

Seconds later lights swept across the front window. He was here.

She didn't know if she should run for cover or boldly step into the night. She settled on waiting for him to knock on her front door.

"Hi," she said as she pulled it open, then was grateful she'd done the speaking thing before seeing him.

God, he looked good. Like her, he'd dressed all in black, but his T-shirt didn't advertise anything beyond the chiseled muscles of his chest and the narrowness of his waist. Raindrops winked from his slicked back hair as if bragging about their close proximity to the man himself.

"Ready?" he asked as he brushed off his bare arms. "You have a coat. Good. It's really raining."

She found herself more than tongue-tied. She felt frozen in place, as if her feet had somehow become completely stuck to the foyer tile. She might never move again. Centuries from now archeologists would unearth her and put her still upright body in some natural history museum with a little notice beside her on the wall saying they couldn't explain what she was doing, either.

She forced herself to breathe and then to speak. "Are we, um, taking your car?"

"I'd rather."

It was fine with her. She didn't feel up to driving. She doubted she was capable of much more than involuntary bodily functions at this moment. She wasn't just overwhelmed by her attraction to Riley, but also by the unfairness of the situation. She'd been gone for so long and had gotten on with her life. Was it too much to ask that she be able to come home for a few weeks and *not* make a complete fool out of herself?

No answer crashed through the heavens, so she grabbed her purse and her keys, turned out the living room light and stepped into the cool, damp, night air.

Riley led his way to his car — a sleek, silver Mercedes that still smelled of new car and high-end leather. She slid onto the passenger seat and tried not to think about the fact they were going to spend the next who-knew-how-long together. Confined.

In some circles this could be considered a date. Of course in some circles she would be considered a menace to society and in desperate need of counseling.

"Why aren't you staying at your mom's

house?" he asked.

"I thought about it, but I need the space for my work. I tend to be a night owl and a lot of people don't appreciate noise from the kitchen at 3:00 a.m."

He backed out of the driveway, then glanced at her. "Do I remember something about cakes?"

"Wedding cakes. They're very fancy. I also do cakes for showers sometimes, but most people aren't willing to pay that kind of money except for the actual wedding."

"How much are we talking about?"

She shrugged. "I'm working on a shower cake right now. It's fairly ornate and will serve fifty. I'm charging a thousand."

The car swerved slightly. "Dollars?"

"I've found it really helpful to keep my prices in U.S. currency. It saves confusion."

"For a cake?"

"A really good cake."

"But still."

She smiled. A lot of people reacted the way he did. Those who wanted something incredibly special and totally handmade were willing to pay the price.

"How many cakes do you make a year?" he asked.

"Less than a hundred. Of course wedding cakes are more expensive, but they take

71

longer. I do okay, but I'm not getting rich. I won't until I decide to expand, which I'm not sure I want to do. I like having total control."

As she talked he drove through Los Lobos. "You know where Zeke lives?" she asked.

"I've been there a couple of times."

"I have his license plate," she said, digging in her purse for the information Alexis had given her.

Riley nodded at the windshield. "If this rain gets worse, we won't be able to read it from any kind of distance."

He pulled onto a side street and slowed. Gracie had only been by her sister's house once since returning to town, so she had to check out numbers to figure out which one it was.

Riley turned off his lights and cruised to a stop across the street. He pointed. "That's Zeke's SUV."

She peered through the windshield. "Is it black?"

"Dark blue, but in this weather, anything dark is going to look black."

"Okay." She leaned back in her seat. "Now what?"

Riley glanced at her. "We wait."

She'd known that, of course. That's what

stakeouts were all about. Waiting. But thinking about it and actually doing it were two different things. Not only did Riley make her nervous, she found it really difficult to sit still. He sat there, immobilized, watching the house, while she shifted in her seat, stretched out her legs, fussed with her jacket, then tugged on her Dodger cap.

"You going to settle down anytime soon?" he asked, never taking his attention from the house.

"I'm settled. I just can't get comfortable." She sat up straighter in the seat. "I've been accused of fidgeting, but I don't understand how people can sit there like lumps. It's not natural. It's —"

"There," Riley said, cutting her off and pointing.

Sure enough Zeke hurried out of the house toward his SUV. Gracie instinctively sank down in her seat and shielded her face.

"I doubt he can see you through the rain," Riley said dryly.

"I want to be sure," she said. "Keep your voice down."

Riley grinned. "You're taking this too seriously." He started his engine and waited until Zeke pulled out before shifting into gear and following him.

Riley might think they were safe, but

Gracie stayed slumped in her seat until it became obvious Zeke was heading directly to the freeway and not trying to lose anyone.

"Where do you think he's going?" she asked as she shifted into a more comfortable position. "And what's he up to? If he's not seeing another woman, the possibilities are endless."

"Please don't list them," Riley said.

She glanced at him. "I wasn't going to."

"One never knows with you."

She bristled. "Excuse me," she said, turning toward him as much as her seat belt would allow. "You don't *know* me at all. Your impressions and assumptions come from my actions when I was barely fourteen years old and whatever you picked up reading that stupid series of articles. Until yesterday you'd never had a conversation with me or spent any time in my presence."

"We talked when you threw yourself in front of my car and begged me to kill you if I was going to marry Pam."

She felt heat flare on her cheeks and was grateful for the darkness. "That wasn't a conversation. I talked, you got in your car and drove in the other direction."

"Good point. So you're saying I should give you a chance."

"I'm saying you shouldn't judge me or as-

74

sume anything until you've gotten to know me better." Then, suddenly aware he may not *want* to get to know her better, she pointed. "He's getting on the freeway."

"I can see that."

Riley accelerated smoothly, keeping up with Zeke's car. When they were on the freeway, he backed off a little. Unfortunately another SUV moved right in front of them, blocking Zeke's vehicle from view.

"There's so many of them," she said as she looked out the side window.

Sure enough, they were surrounded by SUVs. Sort of like a weaker force being taken by a bigger enemy.

"Keep his license plate number handy," Riley said. "We'll need it if we get separated for very long."

She waved the piece of paper she held. "I have it right here." Another SUV cut them off. "Maybe *we* should have bought one of those homing devices. We could mount the little display thingie and then just follow the red dot to wherever he's going."

She felt Riley's gaze on her.

"What?" she demanded. "I've seen it in the movies. It's not as if I own one and use it on unsuspecting prey."

"I can't be sure with you."

She leaned back and deliberately turned

75

away from him. "That's what I meant about not judging me. I made a reasonable suggestion and you jumped on it."

"You thinking putting an illegal tracking device on someone's car is reasonable?"

"You really think it's illegal?"

"If it wasn't raining so hard and I didn't have to watch the road, I swear I'd be banging my head against the steering wheel."

Genuinely baffled, she blinked at him. "Why? What did I do?"

He made a whimpering sound she wasn't sure she'd ever heard before.

"Are you married?" he asked. "Do I have to worry about some burly guy showing up and trying to beat the crap out of me?"

"I'm not married, although I'd like to point out that anyone I did marry would completely understand my need to help my sister." She liked the faint touch of indignation in her voice, then nearly passed out as a thought occurred to her. "Are you?"

"Nope. Pam cured me of wanting anything long-term. Since her, I've kept my relationships strictly superficial."

Gracie wanted to ask more questions, but she spotted something. "Is that his car? Look. That dark SUV is exiting the freeway."

She glanced around for a sign and saw they were coming into Santa Barbara.

76

"What could he be doing here?" she wondered aloud.

"We don't know that it's him. I can't read the license plate, can you?"

She squinted. "No. You'll have to get closer."

Riley tried, but they missed the signal at the bottom of the off-ramp and had to hurry to catch up with the other vehicle. They shot through the intersection only to see it turn left up ahead.

"Go, go, go!" she yelled.

"I'm going."

They followed the other car through a residential neighborhood and watched it pull up in front of a two-story house.

She couldn't believe it. What was Zeke doing here?

The front door opened and a young child dashed out into the rain. "Oh, my God. He's not just having an affair. He has a whole other family. It's just like those Lifetime movies."

"Not exactly," Riley said as he pointed.

The driver had stepped out of the SUV and walked around front. Gracie relaxed as she saw a small, curvy woman reach down and pull the child into her arms.

"Oh. I guess we lost him," she said, feeling both foolish and relieved.

"You think?" Riley turned around in the narrow street and headed back the way they'd come. "I should have let you drive. You're the professional."

She raised her eyebrows and looked at him.

He had the nerve to grin. "It's true," he told her. "Okay, I'll back off. It's nearly seven-thirty and I haven't had dinner. Want to grab something before we head back?"

She couldn't have been more surprised if he'd morphed into a leopard man. Okay, that would have surprised her more, but not by much.

"You mean dinner?" she asked, trying not to sound too stunned by the invitation.

"It's the generally accepted meal for this time of day, but if you'd prefer something else, I'll see what I can do."

Her stomach clenched and for once it had nothing to do with acid. Her big eating plan had been her usual tuna salad that she generally had five nights out of seven.

"I, um, yeah. That would be great," she said calmly.

She wanted to open the window and scream out into the night, but instead she contented herself with a little inside shimmy and a very big smile. Dinner with Riley. Talk about a great ending to a good day.

■ ■ ■ ■

Riley chose a restaurant on the water and, despite the rain, Gracie found it far too romantic. If only she'd worn something different. Something sexy and flirty and . . . Oops. As they were shown to a booth by the window she had to keep reminding herself that this *wasn't* a date and that Riley wasn't interested in her in that way.

They were, um, friends, maybe. Former acquaintances brought together by a common goal — to find out what Zeke was doing when he stole away at all hours.

"You'd think she'd just ask him," she said as she was seated.

Riley settled in his chair and raised his eyebrows. "What?"

"What? Oh, sorry. Thinking out loud. Just my sister and the problem she's having with Zeke. Why doesn't she just ask him? She says it's because she doesn't want to know, but isn't knowing better than not knowing? I'd want to know. At least then you have something you can handle. But this nothingness is just too much like being left in the dark. Don't you agree?"

He shook his head. "I lost the thread somewhere."

"It doesn't matter." She picked up her menu but instead of looking at it, she stared out into the storm.

Rain pounded against the windows. Below she could see the angry surf smacking into the shore. Lights from the restaurant offered a feeble glow that quickly bled into the darkness.

"What a fabulous night," she said.

He raised both eyebrows. "You're kidding, right?"

"No. I love storms. Hey, I live in Los Angeles where we get all of nine inches of rain a year. So when there's some exciting weather going on, I like to enjoy it."

He glanced out the window. "This is nothing. I've been on an oil rig in a typhoon. That's weather."

His statement made her instantly want to ask a thousand questions. Was that where he'd been? How on earth had he gotten there when he'd started out in Los Lobos? But she settled on, "I thought they evacuated rigs during bad storms."

"Oh, we're supposed to go, but who's going to enforce the rules? I worked for a small private company. Everyone on board was a little crazy."

"Including you?"

He grinned. "Especially me."

The waiter appeared and told them about the specials.

"How about some wine?" Riley asked.

"Sure. You order."

"What are you going to have?"

She scanned the menu and picked a grilled salmon dish with a house salad. Riley chose a surf and turf, then surprised her by ordering an Australian Shiraz.

"I thought you would have gone fancy and French with the wine," she said.

"I like Australian wines. Spanish as well."

"There are some great local vineyards around here. The whole Santa Ynez valley is covered with grapes." She started to say they could go on a tasting trip sometime, but stopped herself before the words formed.

This was Riley, she reminded herself. This wasn't a casual dinner with a guy she liked. This was . . . dangerous.

"So," he said, leaning back in his chair. "How did you get into wedding cakes?"

She smiled. "The basic need for transportation. I was sixteen and I wanted a car. My aunt and uncle insisted that I contribute to the gas and insurance part of the equation, so I had to get a job. There was a local bakery a couple of streets over and I applied there. When they hired me, it was late May and wedding cake season was in full swing. I received a baptism by fire. But it turns out I had a real talent for making and designing cakes. Instead of college, I apprenticed with a master baker, then went out on my own."

She shrugged. "I tried to be a little well-rounded. I've taken some night courses on running a small business. I've been playing with the numbers as far as expanding. I'm at that awkward place where I'm having trouble getting everything done, so I'm turning away business, but I'm not sure I would have enough to support a whole other person."

"Maybe you could get by with just half of one."

"There's a thought."

They were practically alone in the restaurant. The only other couples were seated on the other side of the dining area. With the storm still raging outside, there was a sense of isolation. Between the lashing rain and the flickering candles, it *was* pretty darned romantic.

Gracie found herself wanting to rest her chin on her hands and stare dreamily at Riley while he talked, just like in those really old silly teen movies she'd loved as a kid. The dim light suited him, bringing out the shadows in his face and emphasizing the strength of his jaw and lines of his cheekbones. But it was more than that.

All those years ago she'd loved him from afar, but she'd never really known him. They hadn't had a single conversation. Her affections had been based on her own rather twisted feelings and fantasies, not the man he was. After all this time, it felt good to know that so far, she liked the person inside.

The waiter brought the wine and a basket of bread.

"Why do they do that?" she asked when he opened the bottle and poured them each a glass.

"Open the wine?" Riley asked. "Someone has to pull the cork out. I've tried simply breaking off the top of the bottle, but then there's the whole shards of glass issue. Not very inviting."

Gracie rolled her eyes. In the soft lighting the color changed from medium blue to the color of a warm, shallow bay in summer.

While the image was accurate, it made Riley want to give himself a good beating, then go watch sports. A shallow bay in summer? Where the hell had that come from? This was Gracie, the terrorizing stalker. Not a woman he found attractive. And even if he did think she looked pretty hot in her tight T-shirt, she wasn't for him. The list of reasons was endless, but the three *F's* were the most important. Gracie didn't qualify.

"Not the wine," she said, ignoring her glass and staring longingly at the basket of bread. "That. Death."

He frowned. "Bread is death?"

"Not technically, but do you know what a couple of slices can do to a woman's hips and thighs? That's where the bread goes. There's a route directly from the stomach to the fat pockets where hungry little cells scarf up bread and grow round and full."

"Okay, now you're scaring me."

She licked her lips. "You're a guy. You wouldn't understand about deep burning hunger for something so incredibly bad for you. Your metabolism allows you to eat the contents of an entire grocery store without gaining an ounce."

He might be a guy, but he knew all about hunger. If she licked her lips like that again, he was going to have to forget his rules in favor of simply taking advantage of the situation. The three *F's* be damned.

"Oh, forget it," she said and reached for a piece of bread.

He watched her smooth on the tiniest wedge of butter, then bite into the slice. Her eyes fluttered closed, her body relaxed and he would swear she actually moaned. Was it just him or had it gotten hot in here?

When she swallowed, she opened her eyes and smiled. "Excellent."

"What else don't you eat?" he asked.

"Bread's my thing. Okay, and chocolate. I can take or leave most junk food. Jill and I had lunch today at a Mexican place and while I ate a few chips, I could go months without them. But bread. . . ."

She started to take another bite. He had to look away because watching her eat it was too erotic. Bread. What was it with women and food?

"What about your cakes?" he asked, careful to keep his attention on the windows.

"Never touch 'em," she said. "I used to sample all the time. There was an ugly ten pounds. But once I perfected my secret recipe, I didn't bother anymore. Sometimes the fillings give me a little trouble, but I do my best to be strong. What about you?"

He returned his attention to her and was pleased to see she'd finished her slice of bread. "I don't bake."

"Aren't you the comedian? I meant what about your life? How did you get from your oil rig to here? And why are you running for mayor?"

"Jill didn't tell you?"

"You mean my closest and oldest friend

for years? Spill a client secret? You have to be kidding."

He reached for his wine. "Did you ask?"

She smiled. "I know you dated a lot in high school. I was there. Gee, Riley, didn't you learn anything about women back then? Of course I asked."

Her complete honesty and good humor intrigued him. All those years ago, he'd never given much thought to Gracie, except to wish her far, far away from him. It wouldn't have occurred to him he could like her.

"I'm running for mayor to meet the terms of my uncle's will."

She tossed her long blond hair over her shoulder and reached for her wine. "That doesn't make any sense. His dying request was for you to be mayor?"

"Something like that. He's left everything to me, the bank, the house, his estate, on the condition I prove that I've become respectable by running for mayor and winning."

"And I thought my family was twisted. But it's a lot of money, right? I mean that's why you're doing it."

"Excluding the bank, the estate is worth about ninety-seven million dollars."

She'd nearly finished swallowing her wine

when he spoke. Even so, she gasped, then started to choke and cough.

"You okay?" he asked, half rising from his seat.

She waved him back. "I'm fine," she said in a low croak. She coughed again, then reached for her water and took a sip.

"Did you say ninety-seven million *dollars*?"

He chuckled. "Yes. U.S. dollars. I use them, too."

"That's an incredible amount of money. I love my uncle more than I could say but all he left me was a small three-bedroom house in Torrance."

"With no strings."

"True, but for that amount of money, I'd jump rope with the strings if necessary. So, wow. You'll be the richest mayor in Los Lobos history. I guess you'll only want to serve the one term. Then what?"

"I haven't decided."

In truth, he wasn't planning to stay past the election. The will had stated he had to win, but had said nothing about serving out his term.

The waiter came with their salads. When he'd left, Gracie said, "You're running the bank, too, right? Is that weird?"

"It's my first desk job. While I was gone, I

did a lot of studying in my spare time. I earned a bachelor's in finance, which helps. Still, I'm constantly on the verge of screwing up. My secretary, Diane, is a big help."

Gracie's expression turned knowing. "Diane, huh?"

"She's a treasure. In her sixties, still wears tweed suits. Bosses me around like crazy."

"I would never have thought you were the kind of man who enjoyed being dominated by women."

"Diane is very special."

The light turned Gracie's hair to the color of gold. He liked how easily she laughed and how she seemed to take very little seriously. Her body moved in such a way that he could easily imagine her naked and wet. Just thinking about it . . .

But he couldn't think about it or do anything about it, he reminded himself. Under other circumstances, with him clearly explaining the rules, maybe. But not here. Not in Los Lobos where everyone knew everyone else's business and he had an election to win. She might be sexy and pretty and completely charming but there were ninety-seven million dollars on the line. For that price, he could keep his horny thoughts to himself.

"What are you thinking?" she asked.

"You've gone all serious."

"That we could never do this in Los Lobos."

She glanced around the restaurant. "Agreed. People would talk about nothing else for weeks. My life, our lives, would be a living hell."

"I'm getting the better deal, though."

"What do you mean?"

He smiled. "I'm the one dining with a legend. The infamous Gracie Landon who knows how to love with her whole heart."

Her gaze narrowed as her hand shot forward. She grabbed a roll and threw it at him. Riley laughed as it bounced off his chest and tumbled to the floor.

"If they could see you now," he teased.

She picked up her fork and stabbed a piece of lettuce. "You'd better watch yourself. You have a very nice car and I still know where that skunk lives."

As they pulled into Gracie's driveway, she leaned toward the window and stared out at the dark night.

"I'm glad it's still raining," she said. "It's a perfect night to bake."

Riley stopped the car and turned off the engine. "You'll do that now?"

"Yeah. I like the quiet. I can concentrate.

Plus there are some really cool infomercials on TV. You'd be amazed at the stuff you can buy. Not that I ever phone in, but I like to see them."

"Uh-huh. Sure. I'll bet you have a whole secret stash of Veg-O-Matics in that house."

She chuckled. The soft sound brushed against his skin in a way that reminded him he was a man who hadn't been with a woman in too damn long.

"No Veg-O-Matics, but if you're very, very good, I might bake you something. To thank you for helping me with all this."

"Zeke is my campaign manager. Now that you know how much I have on the line you can see why I want to make sure whatever he's up to isn't going to screw with my plans."

"Good point. I'll call Alexis in the morning and tell her we don't know anymore than we did before. I'll also try to get her to talk to him. It's the most sensible plan."

He would bet money she didn't wear perfume, but her sweet scent seemed to fill the car. Tension crackled between them. Who would have thought after all this time, he would find Gracie appealing?

He reminded himself of his mission, his rules and how much could be lost by a single night of pleasure. Then he leaned toward her and watched as her eyes widened and her pupils dilated.

"Have a good rest of the night," he said as he carefully undid the lock and pushed the door open. A blast of cold air swept into the car.

She blinked. "What? Oh. Sure. Thanks again." She gave him a quick smile and hurried up the walk toward the house.

He waited until she was inside before starting the car. But it was a long time before he drove away and that night, thoughts of her kept him hard and awake well past midnight.

The sharp sound made Gracie want to yell at somebody. She hadn't gotten to bed until almost four and it was far too early for her to be getting up. She knew she hadn't set the alarm, so what. . . .

Sleep receded. She gazed around blurrily until she realized it wasn't the clock radio making the noise but the phone. She grabbed the cell.

"Yeah. Hello?"

A deep sob filled her ear.

"Hello? Who is this?"

"It's me. Alexis." Another sob. "Oh, Gracie, I just went over to his office and I saw him. With *her*!"

"What? Who? What her?"

"P-Pam. Zeke is having an affair with Pam Whitefield."

CHAPTER FIVE

Becca Johnson's hand shook as she signed the final loan documents. "I'm scared," she admitted with a smile.

"This is the point of no return," Riley told her. "You want the chance to change your mind?"

Becca looked at him in surprise. "Are you kidding? Thanks to you, I'm getting the chance to open a business in my home. It's what I've always wanted to do. Since the divorce, I've barely been hanging on, financially." Her smile faded. "Was I supposed to tell you that?"

He did his best to look reassuring. "My loan committee did a thorough check on your credit and income. I doubt you have any financial secrets from us."

"Okay. I mean I'm good for the money." She signed the last paper and passed it over to him. "I really appreciate this."

Becca Johnson was a thirty-something

divorced mother of two interested in opening a day-care facility in her home. She'd come to the bank for a loan to cover some remodeling expenses and start-up costs. The committee had been on the fence, so the final decision had been Riley's. He'd given the woman the loan.

"I figured with so little equity in the house and all. . . ." She stopped talking and shook her head. "I should probably keep my mouth shut. I don't want you to change your mind at this late date."

"Too late for that." He tapped the signed papers on his desk. "We have a binding contract. Good luck with your new business."

"Thank you."

She rose and walked to the door of his office. "You've been wonderful, Mr. Whitefield. All the other banks in town told me no. I couldn't have done this without you."

The praise made Riley uncomfortable. He shrugged off the compliment. "You're the kind of person who pays her bills on time and that's what we want."

She nodded, then stepped out into the hallway. Riley turned his attention to his computer. The door closed, but he knew he wasn't alone. Even the air stood at attention when Diane entered a room. He glanced at his assistant.

She wore yet another of her infamous tweed suits. A green one this time, with a fussy yellow blouse underneath. Her shoes were dark and sensible — the kind that frightened small children.

"Here are Becca Johnson's loan documents," he said, handing her the file. "Please see that they're processed today and that the money is deposited in her account first thing in the morning."

His assistant took the papers, but didn't leave.

"You have something else on your mind?" he asked.

She stood there glaring at him. "I do. Your quarterly projections aren't very detailed."

"Is that a criticism?"

"It's a statement of fact." She glanced down at the file in her hand. "Funny how Ms. Johnson thinks she's just been offered the chance to make her heart's desire come true. If only she knew she'd made a deal with the devil."

Riley leaned back in his chair. "And here I thought we'd agreed you would call me by my first name."

Diane's disapproving expression didn't change. "How long does she have until her world comes crashing in on her? A month?

Are you closing the bank the day after the election or will you wait until the results are certified?"

So, she'd figured it out. Riley wondered if the woman would find any satisfaction in knowing she was right.

"All the loans will be called," she said. "Every single one. Do you know how many houses that is? How many businesses? You could destroy the town."

Riley didn't respond. Her gaze sharpened.

"Don't you care?"

"Not one damn bit."

"That's what I thought."

She turned on her heel and left.

Riley stared at the closed door. He refused to feel guilty about what he was going to do. If he won, the bank was history. If he didn't, life would go on as before. Someone else would be brought in to run things.

Diane could destroy his chances, but she wouldn't. She was from the old school — what happened within the sanctity of the workplace stayed there.

He closed the current program on his computer and accessed the databank. After typing in Diane's name, he checked for any outstanding loans. There was one on a house. Per the balance, she only owed a few thousand dollars. Even if the bank closed, she would be fine. So what did she have to get so upset about?

Fifteen minutes later, he was halfway through the weekly loan reports when someone banged on his door. Riley looked up and frowned. Diane would never bang, even if she was furious with him, which she probably was.

"Come in," he called.

The door opened and Gracie peeked around it, into the room. "Hey, it's me."

"I can see that."

"I have good news and bad news. Which do you want first?"

"Why don't you come into the office and tell me both?"

"I could do that."

She stepped into the room and closed the door behind her. After making her way to his desk, she placed a small pink box in the center and smiled.

"I made you a cake."

She spoke with a combination of pride and embarrassment that made her cheeks flush. Or maybe they were flushed for another reason — he couldn't be sure.

Her long blond hair hung down loose and sexy. She wore a short, summery kind of dress that emphasized curves. He was as human as the next man and certainly didn't

97

mind when an attractive woman wanted to spend a bit of her day with him. Even if that woman was an ex-crazed stalker. But that wasn't what held him motionless in his seat.

Instead, it was the cake.

"I couldn't sleep last night and after I'd worked on my decorations for what felt like forty-seven days I decided to do some baking. It's white cake with a chocolate cream filling. The frosting's —"

She kept on talking about the frosting and how she'd been unsure of the design, but he wasn't paying attention. Not really.

His mother had made him cakes for his birthday, of course, but that had been the extent of her baking. She hadn't been into it and he hadn't cared. Since then, well, he wasn't the kind of man women made cakes for.

"Aren't you going to open it and look?" she asked impatiently.

"Sure."

He flipped up the top and stared down at the white round cake decorated with a grinning skunk.

He laughed. "I'm impressed."

"Good. Guys don't do the flower thing and I don't know what your hobbies are or anything. I thought the skunk would be funny. Want a taste?"

As she asked, she sank into the leather chair on the visitor side of his desk and dug into her oversized straw bag. She pulled out a wicked looking knife and paper plates in a big Baggie.

"You're kidding," he said. "You travel with a knife?"

"Sure." She withdrew it from the protective cardboard covering. "You never know when you have to cut into a cake and take a taste. At least I don't." She handed him the knife, then dug around some more. "I seem to be out of forks."

"I'll make do. Want some?"

She shook her head. "I'll take a taste if you're worried about me poisoning you or something, but otherwise, no. There was that whole bread thing last night."

"You only had one piece."

"You haven't seen my thighs."

He had the sudden thought that he would like to. Very much. And maybe the rest of her.

Dangerous, dangerous territory. Better to cut into the cake.

He cut himself a piece and slid it onto a paper plate. She watched anxiously as he took a big bite.

The cake was soft and moist, with just the right texture and a delicate flavor he couldn't place. The chocolate cream filling tasted like a mousse, but not completely.

"Excellent," he said sincerely. "The best cake I've ever tasted."

She visibly relaxed. "Good. I worked hard on perfecting my secret recipe, but every now and then, I like to test it out on an unbiased person."

"You think I'd tell you the truth if I didn't like your cake?"

"Why would you care about hurting my feelings? I mean with our past?"

"Good point." He ate another bite of cake, then set the plate on his desk. "If the cake was the good news, what's the bad?"

Gracie slumped in the seat and hung her head back. "Alexis. She called me in what felt like the predawn hours but was really only about ten to tell me that Zeke had forgotten his briefcase at home so she'd gone by his office to drop it off. In the process of performing her good deed, she walked in on Zeke having what looked like a very personal relationship with . . ." She paused, straightened and looked right at him. "Brace yourself."

"I'm braced."

"Pam."

It took him a second. "Pam, my ex-wife?"

"One and the same." Gracie leaned forward and put her hands on his desk. "So, have you seen her since you've been back in town?"

"Seen her as in caught a glimpse of her in town? Yes. Seen her as in spent time with her? No." He held in a smile. "Worried?"

"Not at all. I'm fourteen years over my crush. You can see anyone you'd like. Doesn't bother me at all." She made an *X* on her chest. "Scout's honor."

He doubted she had any active interest in his personal life, but last night in the car, they'd both been interested in him kissing her.

"Zeke sleeping with Pam won't be good for anyone," Riley said. "Especially not Zeke."

"So we're on stakeout detail again?" she asked cheerfully.

"Yes, but this time we'll follow Pam."

"At least it won't be raining."

"Easier for us to follow her and easier for her to spot us."

"Life is a trade-off. Six-thirty again?" she asked.

"As we have no idea of her plans, it's as good a time as any."

"I'll be ready." She stood. "I'll even bring my camera."

He winced. "Not a good idea."

"We need proof."

"Can't you get something small and digital?"

"I'm not into technology."

She picked up the knife and cleaned it with a napkin she'd dug out of her purse. After putting the knife away and dropping the napkin in the trash, she headed for the door.

"See you then."

With a wave of her fingers, she was gone, leaving Riley with the sense of having been visited by a larger-than-life force.

There was another knock, this one soft and respectful. He guessed it would have been full of rage if she'd known how to transmit that emotion as well.

"Yes, Diane?"

His secretary stepped into his office. "Your one o'clock meeting is ready, sir."

He pushed the cake box toward her. "This is delicious. You should try some."

She raised her chin slightly. "No, thank you."

"Gracie made it for me. Gracie likes me."

Diane's expression flashed with the anger that had been missing from her knock. "That's because she doesn't know you, sir."

"There are too many details," Gracie's

mother said as she spread out the stack of folders onto the coffee table. "Vivian, honey, we're going to have to decide about a few things. We have to finalize the menu by the end of the week."

Gracie sat in a corner of the sofa. She picked up the folder marked "Guest list" and flipped through the pages of names. "Where are you having it?"

"The country club," Vivian said with a grin. "I'm having a big outdoor wedding with lots of flowers and guests and dancing."

Gracie did a quick calculation, multiplying the number of guests by a per-head-cost for a meal, then swallowed hard. "Gee, things must be really great at the hardware store," she murmured more to herself than anyone else.

But her mother heard her and shot her a look. Gracie didn't know if it meant they weren't supposed to talk about such things or if her mother appreciated her concern.

"What time is the wedding?" Gracie asked.

"Four," Alexis said as she walked into the family room carrying a tray filled with drinks and cookies. She set it down on the ottoman and passed out cans of diet soda.

Gracie took hers, then popped it open. "I worked on a wedding once where instead of a sit-down meal, they had tons of appetizers. Not only were waiters circulating with trays, but there were various stations with fun things like melted chocolate for dipping and a mini sandwich bar. The savings for the bride's family were enormous."

Her mother picked up a folder marked menus and opened it. "Aren't appetizers pretty expensive?"

"They can be, but they're still cheaper than a meal. Plus, people are circulating more, so there's a lot of opportunities for conversation, which the guests really like. They're not stuck with the same six people at the table all night. On the savings side, you don't have to have such fancy table settings or decorations. At a cocktail party, no one expects the chairs to be covered. You can even serve a signature drink that matches the wedding colors, plus beer and wine."

Vivian narrowed her blue eyes. "Thanks for making my wedding into an experience on the same level as going to the outlet mall, Gracie. You know, another way we could save money is have everyone pack a lunch. Wouldn't that be too, too stunning for words?"

Gracie stiffened. "I'm sorry. I was trying to help."

"Yeah, well, don't. The wedding is in less than five weeks and I'm not changing anything. I want a big sit-down dinner. I want a band and I want lots of dancing. The signature drink idea is a good one, though. I'll talk to Tom about that."

Alexis smiled sympathetically at Gracie. "It wouldn't hurt to save a little money," she told Vivian.

"Why should I? You and Zeke eloped. Oh, and Gracie's never getting married, so why shouldn't all the money be spent on me?"

Alexis shrugged. "Always the baby of the family. You're spoiled."

"Whatever." Vivian grabbed a cookie. "Look, I'm paying for my own wedding dress. Isn't that enough?"

"It's fine," her mother said. "I appreciate you helping out. Let's talk about the dresses. Yours is ready, isn't it?"

"It's in, and I have my first fitting next week." She turned to Gracie. "It's so beautiful. Strapless, with lace and a drop waist. The bridesmaid dresses are a similar style, but really simple and elegant. They're black, edged with white. I can't wait for you to see them."

Vivian seemed to have forgotten her explosion from fourteen seconds before, but Gracie hadn't. The sharp words still stung.

Maybe the problem was she didn't know her role here. Despite all her experience with weddings, she was the odd sister out. If her presence was simply a courtesy, then she should remember to keep her mouth shut.

Still, she wanted to protest that it was unfair of Vivian to assume Gracie wouldn't get married. She was only twenty-eight and the last time she checked, that didn't mean love was out of her life forever. Sure there wasn't anyone special right now, but that could change.

"Alexis's dress has a matching little shrug that's so cute."

Vivian's previous outburst had been a painful twinge. This revelation was a full-on stab.

Gracie took a swallow of her soda. "It's important to have the maid of honor stand out a little."

"Exactly." Vivian beamed.

Alexis said something about flowers, their mom pulled out yet another folder and Gracie did her best to act normal.

It wasn't that she minded Vivian asking Alexis to stand up with her. They'd grown up together, they were close. It was that when Vivian had first told her about the wedding, she'd made it clear she was going to ask her friends to be in her wedding, and not her sisters. Apparently she'd only meant not Gracie.

Gracie understood intellectually that while she might technically be a member of this family, she wasn't in any other way. She'd been gone for the past fourteen years. Things had happened, people had changed. She'd changed. This wasn't her world. Oh, but it still hurt to be excluded.

"You seem to have everything under control," she said when they'd finalized the flowers for the bouquets and the tables. "I'm going to head out. I have some baking to do."

"When are you going to make me some sketches for my wedding cake?" Vivian asked. "I want it huge. I mean really, really big and spectacular. Every inch decorated."

Which described a cake that would not only go for several thousand dollars, but would take weeks to finish. Not that Vivian would care about that.

"I'll put something together in the next couple of days," Gracie promised. She rose.

"I'll walk you out," Alexis said and followed her to the front door.

"Well?" she asked when they were alone. "Are you going to find out what's going on with Zeke and Pam Whitefield?"

"Yes. Riley and I are going to follow her tonight and see what happens."

"Don't lose her like you lost Zeke," Alexis said.

"Thanks for the tip. I wouldn't have thought of it on my own."

She left the house and walked to her car. She felt uncomfortable, as if she had a bad taste in her mouth. The house where she'd lived for so long looked exactly as she remembered, but everything else was different, and those changes made her sad.

Riley pulled into Gracie's driveway and found her waiting just outside the front door. The storm had moved on, leaving the sky clear, which would be both a help and a hindrance to their evening plans. It was already twilight, but there were plenty of stars and a good-sized moon to provide light.

Gracie waved when she saw him and walked toward the car. He watched her, noting something was different. Something he couldn't figure out.

Not her clothes. She'd dressed casually, in dark pants and a long-sleeved T-shirt. Her blond hair had been fastened back in one of those fancy braids women seemed to love. She even had her damn camera with her.

108

"What's up?" he asked when she opened the door and slid onto the passenger seat.

"Hi," she said with a smile that seemed more forced than genuine.

He left the car in park. "I was asking a question, not offering an urban greeting."

"What? Oh. You mean what's up with me?" She shrugged. "Nothing. I'm fine."

Fine had been the bright, cheerful, glowing woman who had delivered the cake to his office earlier that day. This was not fine.

"Are you sure?" he probed, then could have kicked himself. Did he really want to *know* what could be up in Gracie's life?

"I don't want to talk about it." She let the smile fade. "Can you be okay with that?"

"Absolutely."

He backed out of her driveway.

"We'll swing by Pam's house and see if she's there. If she is, we'll wait and see if she goes out." He glanced at her. "Sound like a plan?"

"It's great. When I saw Alexis, she reminded me not to lose Pam this time. Good advice, huh?"

There was something in her voice. Something sharp, but also broken. He gripped the steering wheel and told himself to think about sports.

Fifteen minutes later, he slowed as they

turned onto Pam's street. Her house was on the far corner — a modest single-story structure with a big garden and bay windows.

"She's here," he said, pointing to the lights on in the house and the car — a white Lexus GS300 — in the driveway.

"Do you know why she's here?" Gracie asked, speaking for the first time since they'd left her house.

"She lives here."

"No, I mean why is she in Los Lobos? I would have thought she would head out for the big city."

"I have no idea." Nor did he care. Pam was firmly in his past and he was happy to keep her there. She'd lied her way into their marriage and as soon as he'd learned the truth, he'd been gone.

"It's just I don't know why they even asked me to be at the meeting," Gracie said as she stared out the side window toward the house. "Obviously my opinions weren't welcome. I don't get it. I just don't get it. Mom can't be making that much at the hardware store. I'm sure she owns the house outright, but still.

"Vivian's acting as if money is no object. A sit-down dinner at the country club? That's insane."

Riley didn't want to ask. He held in the question as long as he could, but it finally escaped. "What are we talking about?"

Gracie sighed. "Nothing. My sister. My *younger* sister. She's getting married in a few weeks. That's why I'm back here. They said they wanted my help. But they don't. Oh, Vivian wants a wedding cake, though. A big, heavily decorated one. Sure, I'm happy to give her that, but it's as if she has no idea what she's asking. We're talking hundreds of hours. Plus, there's the whole wedding party. I'm okay with it, but I don't know why she lied. All she had to do was tell me the truth. So she wants Alexis in the wedding and not me. What do I care?"

Her pain was a tangible creature in the car. Riley wished he was wearing a tie so he could loosen it. Instead he touched her arm.

"It's okay," he said, feeling like a complete idiot as he spoke the words. How the hell did he know if it was okay or not?

She turned to him and he saw a hint of tears in her eye. In the glow from the streetlight, she seemed more frail, somehow.

"I'm telling myself I'll be fine, but so far I know I'm lying. I'm not even a part of this family anymore. She and Alexis are close. That's okay. I have to accept it. It's just . . ." She swallowed hard, then drew in a deep breath and released it. "None of this is my fault. If I'm not a part of things, it's because my mother sent me away. I never wanted to go."

He felt both uncomfortable and awkward. Gracie being upset made him want to fix things, which was unfamiliar. But all these *feelings* — he didn't like them at all.

"Go where?" he asked.

"After that summer." She looked at him. "When you found out Pam wasn't pregnant, you took off. But you weren't the only one leaving town. I was sent away, too."

"Right. I remember. To some relatives. Iowa, was it?"

The corners of her mouth turned up in an almost smile. For a second he wanted to move in and kiss one of those corners, which was insane. He leaned back against the door.

"My grandmother's. I was sent away so I wouldn't ruin your wedding. But after that, I didn't come home." She looked out the front window. "My mother said I had some issues, probably because my dad died when I turned twelve and that's an impressionable age and you moved in next door and I fixated on you. She said I couldn't stay in Los Lobos, even after you were gone. That people wouldn't let me forget what had hap-

112

pened and I deserved a fresh start and maybe some help. So she sent me to live with my aunt and uncle in Torrance."

She pressed her lips together and blinked several times. "I didn't want to go. I felt like I was being permanently punished. I know what I did to you was wrong and twisted. I saw somebody, a counselor, for a while. She really helped me put things in perspective. But even after that, my mom said I couldn't come home. So then I decided to stop wanting to. And now they've asked me to come back, and I thought it was because they missed me, but it's just to do work on the wedding and it's like losing my family all over again."

It took him a second to realize she was crying. The tears fell silently down her cheeks. Riley felt a combination of compassion and anger. He knew all about being forced to do something he didn't want to do. The only reason he'd married Pam fourteen years ago was because his mother had guilted him into it. But he knew that even if he'd refused, she wouldn't have turned her back on him. At least not for long.

"I'm sorry," he said, feeling stupid for the useless words.

She nodded, as if she couldn't speak right then.

Riley reached out a hand toward her, then let it fall on the console. He swore silently, cursed himself for getting into this position in the first place, then leaned forward and pulled Gracie against him.

She resisted at first, then she sagged against him. He'd always thought of her as larger than life, but as he held her he realized she was kind of on the small side.

Her body felt warm against his. Her hands clutched at his shirt and her forehead pressed against his shoulder. He could smell the sweet scent of her body, along with a hint of maybe vanilla from her baking.

"I'm sorry," she whispered as she trembled. "I'm actually more together than this."

"I believe you."

And he did. She'd grown her business from nothing, which meant plenty of hard work and talent on her part.

He rubbed her back and felt the smooth length of her hair brushing against his hand. She shifted and wrapped her arms around his waist. Then she was looking at him with tears in her eyes and her mouth was swollen and the need to kiss her got so big that he —

"Pam," he said as some movement caught his attention.

"What?"

"Pam. She just got in her car."

"Oh. Oh!" Gracie straightened, brushed her checks, then turned to look out the window. "We have to follow her."

"Already on that."

He waited until Pam had pulled out and driven down the block before going after her. He nearly caught up with her at the stop sign, then drove more slowly as she headed into town.

"She could be going anywhere," Gracie said. "I hope she doesn't get on the freeway. It's already dark and I don't think I could take losing her."

"We won't lose her. Pam never paid much attention when she was driving. I doubt that has changed. I'm going to stay close enough to keep her in view."

They drove through Los Lobos, coming out on the ocean side. When Pam pulled into the parking lot of a small motel, Riley pulled up on the street in front of the low, one-story building.

"Why would she come here?" Gracie asked.

Riley just looked at her. Her eyes widened and her mouth dropped open.

"No," she moaned. "Don't even think that she's meeting Zeke here. A motel? It's tacky.

Plus, why couldn't he just go to her house?"

"His car would be recognized."

"Oh, right. Because no one will notice it here?"

Gracie had a point. Still, there had to be a reason Pam had gone inside.

"We need to check it out," he said.

Gracie nodded. They stepped out of the car and moved toward the long, skinny building. He noticed Gracie had her damn camera with her, but he knew better than to suggest she leave it behind.

They moved slowly, cautiously, staying in the shadows and stopping to listen before stepping through the carport to the main office. Pam's car sat at the far end of the parking lot, but she couldn't be seen.

"She's gone into one of the rooms," Gracie whispered. "We have to find out which one."

Riley debated going to the manager's office and bribing the guy into giving them the information. But with him running for mayor, he wasn't sure that was a good idea.

"We could go look in all the windows," Gracie said. "A lot of them have open curtains."

"I'm guessing Pam's in one where the curtains are closed."

"Oh. Good point."

Before they could make a decision, there was a loud pop and all the lights went out. Darkness descended with a suddenness that disoriented.

"Don't move," Riley said, instinctively reaching for Gracie's hand. "We need to get back to the car. Stay close."

His fingers closed around hers. He felt her other hand on his back.

"Lead on," she said quietly. "I'll be . . ." Her hand tugged his and he heard a thunk. "I'll just be tripping behind you."

Despite their pressing need to get out of here, Riley wanted to turn around, pull Gracie close and kiss her until she went boneless. If he hadn't had a bad feeling about the sudden blackout, he would have given in to the urge. Instead he walked in the general direction of the car.

"It's through here," he said and rounded a corner.

Just then the night exploded with a brilliant flash of light. Riley instinctively raised his arm to ward off the attack, only to realize whoever had been there was gone. He heard the sound of someone running, then a car door slammed. All the lights in the complex came on just as the car raced out of the parking lot.

"What was that?" Gracie asked.

"Someone took our picture. What I want to know is who would do it and why."

CHAPTER SIX

"It wasn't me," Gracie said quickly, waving her Polaroid.

"I know that," Riley said with a tone of impatience that made her wonder how much she really bugged him. "The flash came from in front of us."

He frowned, as if considering possibilities, then led the way to the car.

She wondered if he noticed they were still holding hands. She liked the way his fingers laced with hers and how warm and strong he felt. If she was interested in him, this could be a significant development and more than a little thrilling. Except she wasn't intrigued or thrilled. She was mildly interested in how nice he was to her and occasionally thought of him as good-looking, but that was it.

They drove back to her place. Riley followed her inside without being asked, which could have been another mark in the thrilling column, but, of course, wasn't.

"I want to know what that was," he said as they moved into her kitchen and she put on a pot of coffee. "Were we set up? Was it some jerk out for a good time by turning off the lights and taking pictures?"

She pulled out a small cake very much like the one she'd taken to Riley earlier that day only this wasn't decorated. "Both sound really crazy. How could we be set up?"

"Maybe Pam led us to the motel for a reason. It's the picture. It has to be. But so what?"

He paced the length of her kitchen and came to a stop in front of the schedule she'd taped up on the wall. "What's this?" he asked, then read aloud. "Three hundred and sixty point-two dots. Seventy gum paste roses, seventeen small, twenty-three medium, thirty large."

"What I have to do for a cake I'm making this week." She walked into the dining room and came back with a large portfolio, then pulled out a sketch of the cake. "It's really simple. Just three tiers with these little dots scattered and a wreath of roses at the base of each tier. I make all the decorations in advance, even the dots." She smiled. "To be honest, making the cake is the least of it. All the time is in the decorating."

"Speaking of your cake," he said with a smile as he moved toward the one she'd left on the counter. "Are you saving that for a special occasion?"

She grinned. "Knives are in that drawer." She pointed. "Help yourself."

She grabbed a couple of plates and two coffee mugs, then pulled out two forks.

"You seem calm," he said when they both had dessert and coffee and were seated at the small table in the corner.

"About what happened?" She shrugged. "I'm not sure there's anything to get upset about. The Pam thing is weird, though. Why would she go to a motel in town? I still think she could meet the guy at her house. It was dark. If he pulled into her garage and they shut the door, who would have known he was there?"

"Maybe this had nothing to do with Zeke. Pam talking to him earlier could have meant she needed insurance."

"Try telling that to Alexis," Gracie said with a sigh.

He took a bite, chewed, then swallowed. "Want to tell me the secret to your success?" he asked. "I've never tasted cake this good."

"Sorry, no. Besides, you don't strike me as the baking type."

"You're right." He pointed at the article

from *People*. "You didn't tell me you were famous."

"I'm not yet, but I'm becoming better known. That's nice. More work, but I can handle it." She glanced over at her schedule. "At least for now."

"Have you thought any more about expanding?"

"I haven't had time. I think it would be exciting to be a big company doing wedding cakes all over the world. Then I remember how much I enjoy talking to my customers, figuring out the perfect cake for them and then making it myself. Do I want to give that up? Plus are couples really interested in a cake from a big company?"

"There are a lot of options between doing everything yourself and being multinational."

"I haven't decided what I'm going to do."

He finished his cake and reached for his mug of coffee. Gracie took a moment to mentally pinch herself. Riley Whitefield was in her kitchen, visiting. Just talking and smiling. After all the years she'd had a crush on him, and then even more years of completely not thinking about him, it was strange to be here now, with him. What would her mother's octogenarian neighbor have to say about it?

She winced. "Maybe we should have pulled *your* car into the garage," she said.

He raised his eyebrows. "Worried about your reputation?"

"Pretty much. This *is* Los Lobos and I'm who I am and you're, well, you know who you are."

"I have for a long time now."

She laughed. "Good point. I'm just saying that if people knew you were here. . . ."

"They'd talk."

"Right. And you don't want that any more than I do. For me, it's just a matter of everyone questioning my mental capacity, but you have an election to win."

"Are you kicking me out?"

He looked good sitting in her kitchen. Handsome, masculine. She got a little shiver in her belly every time she looked at him. Which meant if she was actually *attracted to* him, she would be in big trouble. But she wasn't.

Still, when he stood and said, "Why don't you walk me out?" she couldn't help the flicker of anticipation that rippled through her, and as she trailed after him, she took a moment to appreciate the great butt Jill had mentioned on their lunch date.

He stopped by the front door and faced her. "We don't have any answers. Not about

Zeke or Pam or who took the picture."

"There were always rumors of alien landings up on the bluff. Maybe they're responsible."

"I'm sure that's it."

As he spoke, he stared deeply into her eyes. There was an intensity to his gaze that made her swallow hard. She felt unable to look away — like a small creature trapped by a predator. Only she had a feeling her fate was going to be a lot more thrilling than any field mouse.

"Were you always this pretty?" he asked as he reached out and cupped her cheek and jaw. "Weren't you skinny back then, with braces?"

"Oh, yeah. I had quite the ugly duckling phase. It lasted six long, painful years."

His fingers were warm and gentle against her skin. Her heart rate had increased to a beat per second far more normal for a hummingbird than a twenty-eight-year-old woman who knew better.

"You used to watch me," he said, moving a little closer. "I remember those big, blue eyes following my every move. You scared the hell out of me back then."

"I'm really sorry about that."

"Apology accepted," he murmured right before he bent down and kissed her.

A part of Gracie's brain refused to comprehend this was happening. There was no way Riley was in her house, kissing her. The cosmos simply didn't work that way. Yet she felt the tender brush of his lips against hers, along with the accompanying tingles as her body responded. She felt his hand leave her cheek as he wrapped both arms around her and drew her close.

She went because she wanted to and found herself pressing against him.

They'd hugged before. In the car when she'd lost it and he'd been so kind. But this was different. This was body against body, her arms around his neck, breasts flattening, thighs brushing and her tilting her head to make the kiss go on forever.

He read her mind — or maybe he wanted it, too — because he settled his mouth on hers as if he had no intention of moving. Heat blossomed inside of her and seeped into every cell. She breathed in the scent of him, felt the smooth texture of his shirt beneath her fingers and the thick, strong muscles that tightened.

When he teased her bottom lip with his tongue, she had the sudden thought that this was destiny. As she parted for him, she told herself it was closer to insanity. But when he swept inside to claim her, she couldn't think at all.

He moved with the confidence of a man used to pleasing a woman. He tasted of coffee and sugary frosting and something else even more delicious. As he explored her mouth, he rubbed his hands up and down her back, drawing her closer, making her want to arch against him and purr.

One hand slipped down to her butt and cupped the curve. When his fingers squeezed, she suddenly wanted more than just a kiss. Need swept through her, making her swell, making her weep, making her want him. And just like a man, he decided that was the moment to stop kissing her.

He pulled back a little and looked into her eyes. "That was something," he said.

She liked that he sounded a little breathless, as if he'd been caught off guard by the passion as well.

He brushed a loose strand of hair off her forehead, then kissed her lightly. "You're not in my plan," he said.

"You have a plan?"

"Always."

"Want to tell me what it is?"

"Want to tell me the secret ingredient to your cake?"

"Okay. No. So how do I get in the way?"

He cupped her face in both hands and

pressed his mouth against hers. Instantly liquid desire made her want to melt.

"That's how," he said as he withdrew. "We can't do this, Gracie. I have rules and one of them says the woman in question is easily forgotten. We both know you're not that."

She pressed her hands flat against his chest. "Are you referring to my stalker girl past? Haven't we talked about you letting that go?"

"This has nothing to do with your past. Good night."

He opened the door and walked away. She stood there for a good three minutes as she replayed their conversation, and the kiss. Then she shut the door and twirled through the small living room.

In the words of Sally Fields (sort of) at the Academy Awards — He liked her. He really liked her.

Doing her best *not* to think about the kiss interspersed with castigating herself *for* thinking about it had kept Gracie up most of the night. The good news was she completed all the dots and roses she needed for the wedding cake. The better news was the kiss had been about a million times more fabulous than what she'd imagined all those years ago, and she sure had done her share of imagining. The bad news was she was dead on her feet by the time dawn arrived and she heard the *thunk* of the local paper being tossed onto her porch.

She tightened the belt on her robe and opened the front door. After pushing her hair out of her face, she shuffled to the edge of the porch and picked up the paper. She was back inside before she'd pulled it out of its protective plastic wrap and flipped it open.

Her shriek was involuntary, as was her anger and sense of disbelief. This could not be happening! It was impossible. It was grossly unfair. It was there in black and white.

The front page of the *Los Lobos Daily News* showed a somewhat grainy but very viewable picture of Riley and herself standing in the middle of the motel parking lot and holding hands. They both looked incredibly startled — which was about the flash, not getting caught, but no one looking at the picture would know that.

Just as bad as the picture, was the headline. "Mayoral Candidate Caught in Love Nest." Even worse was the note that a reprinting of the fourteen-year-old "Gracie Chronicles" could be found starting on page nineteen.

Gracie rolled up the paper and pounded it against the wall. "Why? Why? Why? What is going on?"

She didn't have any answers, which only made her more frustrated. She paced the house, then, with sleep impossible, showered and dressed for the day.

A quick glance at the clock told her it was barely after seven. What time did Riley get up? She didn't know his number so she was going to have to head over to his house. She wanted to catch him before he left for the bank. But she wasn't excited about the thought of her car being parked in his driveway. Not now. Not when —

Her cell phone rang. Wary about who could be calling at this hour, she let it ring twice more before answering with a cautious, "Hello?"

"It's Riley. Did I wake you?"

"No. I haven't been to sleep yet."

"Did you see the paper?"

They spoke at the same time. Gracie sank onto a kitchen chair.

"I can't believe it," she moaned. "This is horrible. What's going on and who's behind it?"

"We have a whole list of suspects," he said, sounding grim. "Everyone from the mayor to Pam."

She processed that information. "I agree Pam could have something to do with it, having lured us to that motel in the first place, but why would she bother?"

"Haven't a clue. Maybe she's secretly hated me all these years. Yardley has to be annoyed I'm up in the polls. Of course after this morning, that may change."

The mayor? Gracie didn't know anything about him. "Are you saying the mayor could have convinced Pam to drive to that motel, then turned the lights out and while putting a photographer in place, all the while hoping we would follow her, get out of the car, walk around and be in exactly the right place for an incriminating photo?"

There was a moment of silence followed by a chuckle. "You've cut right to the heart of the matter. That sounds pretty improbable."

"Of course that doesn't leave us with many theories." She grabbed the paper and smoothed it out on the table. "I can't believe this happened. I'm involved in a sex scandal. Do you know what my mother is going to have to say about this?"

"Somehow I doubt that's the worst of your problems. Did you read the description of me?"

"No." She quickly scanned the short

article. "Riley Whitefield, a man who wears an earring. Are you kidding? There's no mention of you running the bank or anything nice. I'm guessing the newspaper editor isn't a fan."

"Apparently not. Plus the 'Gracie Chronicles' dig up the past. Anyone who didn't know the story does now."

"This can't be good." She propped her elbows on the table and rested her forehead on her free hand. "Do you have any idea of how people are going to run with this?"

"What do you mean?"

"This town." She felt her stomach start to churn and looked around for her bottle of Tums. "Everyone is going to think we're getting together after all these years. Don't forget, I'm a legend."

"Which makes me what?"

"The object of my affections. Oh, God, this is so humiliating."

"Tell me about it."

Franklin Yardley enjoyed his mornings. The quiet, the perfect cup of coffee and the fact that his wife, Sandra, rarely came downstairs before ten.

This morning, however, had been particularly invigorating. The picture on the front

131

page of the paper had put a bounce in his step.

"Good morning," Holly said as he entered the reception area outside of his office.

She rose, took his coat and briefcase, then followed him into his office where a fresh pot of coffee awaited.

"Did you see the paper?" he asked.

"Yes. What was Whitefield up to? I read the whole article," she said. "Gracie Landon was one scary teenager."

"I know." Franklin rubbed his hands together. "An odd girl. But she very well may turn out to be an unexpected asset. With the 'Gracie Chronicles' reprinted, everyone will want to take her side in whatever happens with Riley."

Holly frowned. "She sounds mentally unstable."

"It doesn't matter. She's recently returned to town, she and Riley have become an item. I'm going to have to think how to use this to my advantage."

He settled into his custom-made leather chair. Holly perched on the desk, the skirt of her navy suit sliding up to the top of her thigh. He allowed himself a moment of distraction as he rubbed his hand against her smooth, young, warm skin.

"Lunch?" he asked.

"I'd like that."

So would he. Not that either of them would be having a meal.

She picked up the paper. "If this Gracie person had a thing for him and she's a legend, does that mean people won't like him if he isn't interested in her?"

Franklin leaned back in his chair and let the moment of contentment wash over him. Of course. It could be just that simple.

"You're even more intelligent than you are beautiful," he said sincerely. "I'm a lucky man."

"You can use that?"

"Absolutely. I can challenge Riley Whitefield to a debate and insist we discuss the family values that are so important to the good citizens of this town."

Gracie slid the cake into the oven and set the timer. She'd barely begun collecting her dirty utensils when she heard someone knocking on the front door.

Her hormones immediately sent up a "yes" vote for it to be Riley. Most of her body agreed. But the sensible part of Gracie's brain knew that seeing him again so quickly after last night would be nothing but a mistake. She needed time to come to terms with what had happened. She needed to put it behind her, to focus on her future and not on a dark, handsome, former bad-boy who made her toes curl.

Fortunately, when she opened the door, she realized that worrying about Riley wasn't going to be a problem. Unfortunately, the visitor was her mother.

Lily Landon stood on the wrong side of fifty, but she had great genes and a fabulous hairdresser who kept the gray at bay. She worked hard and worried, which showed around her eyes, but the rest of her could easily pass for a much younger woman. Gracie thought about mentioning how great her mother looked in her trim jeans and brightly colored T-shirt, but the other woman's forbidding expression told her to keep her compliments to herself.

"Grace Amelia Louise Landon, how could you?" her mother asked as she stomped into the house. "I'm speechless. I've had the entire morning to figure out what I was going to say to you and I still can't think of a single thing."

Gracie hated the disappointment in her mother's voice more than the actual words themselves. She was still feeling frail about the whole not-being-asked-to-be-in-the-wedding thing and she didn't need this.

"It's not what it looks like," she said,

knowing it sounded totally feeble.

"I see. You *weren't* sneaking around at some motel last night with Riley Whitefield."

Gracie closed the front door and led the way to the kitchen. "We were, but it was because of Alexis. Have you talked to her? She's convinced Zeke is having an affair with Pam and asked me to help find out if it's true."

"What does that have to do with anything? Alexis has been crazy about what Zeke does with his time since they got married. So don't use that as an excuse."

"But I . . . She didn't . . ." Gracie felt like a fish gasping on a dock. "Are you saying Alexis made it up?"

Her mother dismissed the question with an impatient shrug. "I don't know. She's always been overly concerned. Zeke adores her, although sometimes I question how he can stand her, what with her dramatic proclamations."

Gracie sank into the nearest chair and tried to take it all in. This couldn't be true, could it? "I've been running around like a crazy person in a misguided attempt to help my sister and you're informing me that she's making the whole thing up?"

"That isn't my point."

"Maybe not, but it's mine. The picture in the paper, trying to follow Zeke. . . ." If this was her new life, she wanted a chance to exchange it for someone else's. She clutched her suddenly churning stomach. "Riley's going to kill me when he finds this out."

"He'd better find it out from someone else."

"What?"

Her mother glared at her. "It's been fourteen years. I had hoped with all the time away and some therapy that you'd get over him. Obviously that hasn't happened."

The unfairness of the accusation cut Gracie like a knife. "That's not true. I'm not chasing around after Riley."

Her mother pointed at the newspaper on the counter. "All evidence to the contrary. You never had any sense where he was concerned. It was bad enough we had to send you away so he and Pam could have a normal wedding without anyone worrying that you would somehow destroy it. But that wasn't the worst of it. You were all anyone talked about for weeks. You were a joke. That's why I sent you away. The newspaper isn't helping by reprinting those old stories. Do you want to have to go through that again? Haven't you learned anything?"

Gracie felt small and broken. She wanted

to curl up and disappear. Instead she stood and reached for her bottle of Tums.

"I've changed," she said quietly. "If you'd spent any time with me in the past fourteen years, you would know that. Of course if I'd grown up here, I would have known that Alexis is a drama queen and not fallen in with her plans."

Her mother's gaze narrowed. "I see. Now it's my fault. That's just so typical. When in doubt, blame the mother. I did what I did *for* you. Not that I expect any gratitude. That would be too much, I know. But maybe, just maybe you can have a little compassion for my position in town here. Do you know what it's like to go to the store day after day and listen to my customers making fun of my daughter? It's humiliating."

Lily turned and walked toward the front door. "I mean it, Gracie. Stay away from Riley. Give the poor man a chance to live his life without you always getting in the way. It was sad enough when you were fourteen, but now it's just pathetic."

CHAPTER SEVEN

Gracie went to bed. It seemed the safest place. So for two days she didn't get dressed, shower or even answer her phone. Aside from the occasional scoop of tuna salad and using the bathroom, the only time she got up was to pack up the wedding cake she'd just finished for the delivery guy late Thursday.

But on Friday morning, she couldn't stand herself anymore. Self-pity had never been all that interesting and she'd just put in her limit for the decade. So she cleaned up, ate a good breakfast and headed out to the brightly painted offices of Dr. Rhonda Fleming, DDS.

Dr. Fleming specialized in pediatric dentistry, so the waiting room was filled with several anxious children and their reassuring moms. Gracie ignored them, the underwater mural and the shiny copies of *Sports Illustrated for Kids*. She walked to the reception desk and asked to speak to her sister.

Two minutes later she'd been shown back into Alexis's tiny office where she spent her days battling with insurance companies and assuring coproviders that little Johnny did indeed need braces.

"What's up?" Alexis asked.

Gracie studied her sister's face looking for similarities and differences. At one time she and Alexis had been the close sisters. Vivian had seemed young and not very bright, so the two older girls had always played. But after Gracie left, that had changed. Somewhere along the way, she'd become the odd one out.

"I spoke with Mom a couple of days ago," Gracie said, doing her best not to remember how horrible and humiliated she'd felt after that visit.

"She's really fried about that newspaper picture," Alexis said. "Honestly, Gracie, it was really stupid of you to get caught."

Gracie held on to her temper with all her will and did her best not to lose track of her purpose for being here.

"Let's not talk about that right now. What interests me is that Mom told me you've always been high-strung where Zeke is concerned. That you've been worried about him having an affair for years when, in fact, he adores you."

She watched emotions skitter across her sister's face, as if Alexis couldn't decide what to say.

"I'm tired," Gracie said. "So far my visit back here makes me wish I was an orphan. Just tell me the truth."

Alexis pressed her lips together. "There are some charges on e-Bay, and I did see him with Pam."

"But. . . ."

"There could be another woman. He's always gone and —"

Gracie grabbed her sister's arm. "Dammit, Alexis, be straight with me. Were you just off having a tantrum?"

"Of course not."

Gracie waited.

Her sister tugged free and folded her arms over her chest. "Okay. Maybe sometimes I sort of overreact, but not this time."

Gracie groaned. "Great."

"I mean it. I really think there's somebody else."

Gracie stood. "Whatever. I'm not going to help you anymore. Don't ask me, don't even hint at it. If you have a problem with your husband, take it up with him and leave me out of it."

Alexis sniffed. "You're my sister. I would

think you'd be more understanding."

"Then you'd be wrong."

One of the best parts of being the boss was that nobody screwed with him. Riley knew he could walk through the bank without hearing a whisper directed at him. He figured all his employees were having a field day with the newspaper picture behind his back, but he didn't care about that. As long as they didn't say anything to his face, he was fine.

The one person who might have the balls to confront him hadn't said a word in the past two days. But when Diane appeared in his office late that morning, he wondered if his good fortune had run out.

"Good news or bad news?" he asked, pointing at the folder in her hand.

"I'm not in a position to claim either," she said. "Zeke Bridges sent this over. Mayor Yardley is challenging you to a debate."

"Really? Could be fun." Riley took the folder and flipped through the contents. He scanned the mayor's press release.

"Mayor Yardley thinks we should discuss the issues, along with the morals so near and dear to the hearts of our citizens."

Respectability. Why was that always at the

center of everything?

He looked at his secretary, taking in her stern expression and unyielding posture.

"Think I have a chance?" he asked.

"People around here would like you more if you'd donate the money for the new children's wing for the hospital."

He grinned. "You don't give up, do you?"

"Not when it's this important."

He held up a hand before she could get on a roll. "Spare me the lecture on the needy children and how they could all be saved."

Her response was a disapproving sniff. Chances were he had not won the heart or vote of the fair Diane.

"Thanks for bringing me this," he said and set the folder on the desk.

She turned to leave, but he called her back before she could.

"I have a question," he told her. "I would like you to be honest with me."

She nodded regally. "I always am."

"Good. Did you enjoy working for my uncle?"

"He was a fair employer."

"Did you like him?"

Her gaze narrowed. "Liking or not liking isn't part of my job."

"Agreed, but you still have feelings and

opinions. What did you think of him?"

"That you're more like him than you think."

It was the second time someone had said that to him in the past week, and Riley didn't like hearing it this time any more than he had before.

Gracie returned to her rental house to find her cell phone on the table, where she'd accidentally left it. There was one message, which she listened to.

"Hi, Gracie. It's Melissa Morgan from the Los Lobos Heritage Society. I'd really like to talk to you. Give me a call."

The woman left her number, which Gracie reluctantly wrote down, before calling her back. Melissa Morgan had sounded far too chipper in her message and Gracie didn't trust that for a second.

The woman picked up on the first ring and Gracie identified herself.

"Oh, you're a doll for calling me back," Melissa said in one of those high-pitched voices that could easily crack glass. "Here's the thing. We all know your mom and have heard about your little cake-baking business and we were thinking it would just be so incredibly sweet if you made our cake for us. She suggested it, actually. We're having a fund-raiser for the Historical Society. The old Strathern place has been completely redone, back to its original elegance. You know the Stratherns, don't you. The judge and his daughter Jill. Of course she's Jill Kendrick now that she's married the sheriff and all. What a beautiful wedding they had. Anyway, about the cake. We were thinking something simple to serve about three hundred. How many sheet cakes would that be?"

Gracie felt her chest tighten in sympathy. The woman had barely stopped for breath. Then the reality of what she'd said sunk in. No, no, no. She didn't want to do this. Yuck.

"You want sheet cakes?" she asked, hoping she didn't sound as horrified as she felt. "You know I make wedding cakes, right?"

"Oh, sure. That's what your mom said. But a little round cake wouldn't serve very many, would it?"

A little round cake? Gracie thought about pounding her head against the wall until she caused enough brain damage to create amnesia. Wouldn't it be great if she forgot this entire town existed? Because saying no wasn't an option.

"I can do something a little nicer than a sheet cake and still serve three hundred," she said. "Why don't you let me work up some sketches."

"Oh, you don't have to do that," Melissa said. "Just something simple and yummy." There was a slight pause. "Did you want us to pay you for this? Your mom said you wouldn't and we don't want to be rude or anything, but our budget is kind of tight."

Of course it was, Gracie thought, eyeing the wall. Her mother might be disappointed by her Gracie's behavior, but she thought nothing of volunteering her daughter's time and energy. "Don't worry. It will be my contribution."

She would keep detailed records of her supplies and more importantly, her time, then submit it as a charitable deduction on her taxes.

"Aren't you just the sweetest thing. The event is Sunday, June 5th. Oh, that's only a couple of days before the election." Melissa laughed. "I know this was ages ago and your mom really doesn't like anyone talking about it, but I have to tell you that I was in Riley's grade in high school. We all got a real kick out of some of the things you did. You sure knew how to get your man."

Gracie was grateful not to have to fake a smile. She thought about pointing out that she'd never in fact *gotten* her man and that she'd probably emotionally scarred

145

him for life.

Instead she made a few polite noises and quickly got off the phone.

"I have to kill myself now," she murmured when she'd dropped her cell into her purse.

Instead of reaching for a sharp knife, she crossed to her baking schedule and figured out how, exactly, she was going to squeeze in a cake for three hundred right in the middle of wedding season. Despite Melissa's desire for a sheet cake, Gracie simply couldn't do that. She would have to come up with a simple, yet elegant design that would. . . .

Someone knocked on her front door. Gracie glanced over her shoulder and thought about not answering it, but with her luck, the person in question wouldn't go away.

She braced herself for another attack from a family member or an adorable child asking her to bake something for the local orphanage and pulled open the door.

It was worse than she'd imagined.

Fourteen years ago Gracie's one goal in her small, teenaged life had been to get Riley to notice her. She hadn't liked it when he'd dated all kinds of girls, but she consoled herself with the fact that no one had ever caught his attention. Until Pam. Once

146

he'd started going out with that beautiful, blond cheerleader, he'd stopped dating the masses. Gracie had been crushed and had launched her campaign to keep the young lovers apart.

Obviously their getting married had proved how unsuccessful that campaign had been. Their divorce a few months later had been too little, too late.

Since then she'd done all that she could to put her past behind her. So coming face-to-face with it now didn't make her want to hula for joy.

"Wow! Gracie. Hi!" Pam Whitefield grinned like a Cheshire cat. "You look great. Welcome back to Los Lobos. How are you?"

Pam's obvious delight and bright, cheery voice made Gracie want to turn around and see who stood behind her, because there was no way Pam could have all this enthusiasm for *her.*

"Uh, Pam. Hi."

"Can I come in?" Pam asked, breezing past her and walking into the small living room. "How have you been? Oh, I saw that article in *People* magazine and I was just thrilled for you. You're famous. Isn't that fabulous?"

"I was excited."

Gracie spent her life in the kitchen and

she dressed casually — khakis, polo shirts, comfortable shoes. Pam was four years older, but didn't look it. Her elegant tailored slacks fit her in such a way that she seemed to be about as big around as a pencil. A silk sweater clung to a narrow waist and slightly oversized breasts.

Gracie fit right in with the California cliché of a blue-eyed blonde, but compared with Pam's gleaming hair and perfectly made-up face, she was positively dull. Pam's short blond hair moved with the easy elegance of a movie star's. There wasn't a wrinkle anywhere — not on her face or her outfit — and her shoes screamed designer. If Pam was the ideal, then Gracie fell right in line to be the cautionary tale.

As Gracie had spent enough of the past two days feeling badly about herself, she decided the best way to break the mood was to get Pam the hell out of here.

"So you stopped by why?" she asked with a smile, trying not to think that there was a very small chance this woman was having an affair with her brother-in-law. Gracie still didn't completely believe Alexis, but she couldn't dismiss the fact that Zeke had lied about where he was and had disappeared for long periods of time with no explanation.

"I have a proposition for you. I know you probably have dozens and dozens of cakes to bake. I know you're just back for a few weeks and I thought. . . ." Pam squeezed her Coach bag and shrugged. "It's a long story."

It was the cue to invite her to sit down and serve refreshments. Gracie resisted as long as she could before motioning to the sofa and excusing herself so she could dash into the kitchen and rustle up a slice of cake and some diet soda.

"I'm going to be opening a bed-and-breakfast in a few weeks," Pam said. "I had to do a lot of remodeling, which is nearing completion. I started with the kitchen and it's finished now. Not that I have any use for it. So I was thinking, if you want to come out and take a look at it, that would be great."

Gracie stared at her. "Why would I be interested in your kitchen?"

Pam, who had only moved crumbs around on her plate and had yet to take a bite, laughed. "Oh, silly me. I didn't get to the proposition part. I want you to rent my kitchen. I have two industrial ovens and plenty of counter space. With all the cakes you have to bake, I thought you might be interested. I won't be opening until after your sister's wedding, so you could have the run of the place at all hours."

Gracie's first thought was to ask how Pam knew about Vivian's on-again, off-again wedding. Then she remembered this was Los Lobos, where everybody knew every little thing about everyone else.

Her second thought was complete oven-envy at the thought of new large appliances that didn't cook hot and never quite got the left side of the cake exactly right without her turning the pan every ten minutes.

"How much do you want?" she asked.

"Why don't you come take a look and if you're interested, we can negotiate terms."

Pam smiled with just the right amount of casualness, as if willing Gracie to trust her. Gracie didn't trust anyone who wouldn't even take a bite of her cake. Okay, yes, there were calories, but a taste wouldn't hurt. Still, new ovens and a chance to keep a close eye on Pam really tempted her.

"I'd like to take a look," she said. "What time is good for you?"

"I'm sure there's an explanation," Jill said as she slid into the booth at Bill's Mexican Grill.

"For almost everything except those magic twenty numbers they're always talking

150

about in string theory, and why socks can escape from the dryer," Gracie told her.

"I was actually talking about this."

Her friend put a copy of the newspaper on the table.

"Oh, that," Gracie said. "I wondered why I didn't hear from you when it came out."

"I thought you might be flooded with well-wishers." Jill raised her eyebrows. "Please tell me you weren't in a motel with Riley Whitefield."

"We weren't technically *in* anything except their parking lot. You can see from the photo that we're clearly outside."

"You know what I mean."

"It's complicated." Just like her life.

"I don't have any appointments until three," Jill said, leaning back in the booth. "I had Tina clear my calendar."

"Lucky me."

Gracie quickly filled Jill in on the ill-fated attempt to follow Pam.

"So you followed Pam and the guy with the camera followed you," Jill said after they'd placed their order. "Who sent him?"

"No idea. I want to say Pam because I never liked her, but why would she care? The mayor, of course. If he's trying to discredit Riley in the election by stirring up the past. But how would the mayor know where we were going to be or that we'd be doing *something* photo-worthy? It's so confusing. To complicate the situation, Pam came to see me."

Jill paused in the act of picking up a chip. "You're kidding."

"Nope. She wants to rent me her kitchen in the new bed-and-breakfast she's building or refurbishing. I can't remember which. I'm supposed to go see her this afternoon. She says she has professional-grade appliances and I can rent from her while I'm here."

"Do you want to?"

"Have anything to do with her? No. Have access to her kitchen? You bet. I can barely fit my largest pan in the oven I have now. The heat isn't even, it runs hot. Sure, I'm tempted, but this is Pam. I don't like her and I don't trust her. Is she setting me up? Did she set Riley up?"

"You know what they say — keep your friends close and your enemies closer."

"Good point. I'm not sure I can work around her, though. She creeps me out."

"You could overfeed her and make her fat. That would be fun."

"Ha. She sat in my house with a slice of cake in front of her and didn't take a bite. That's just not natural."

"Agreed. What are you going to do?"

"Look at the kitchen and see if I can be bought. I suspect I can be."

Jill watched her. "There's something else. What aren't you telling me?"

"Nothing. I . . ." Gracie shook her head. "Except for seeing you, I'm really sorry I came back. There's so much family stuff."

"Like?"

"I feel weird, like I don't fit in." She reached for her diet soda. "Makes sense, I know. I've been gone forever and Vivian and Alexis grew up without me. We've had different life experiences, different memories. Technically, I'm still their sister, but emotionally I don't think I'm a real member of the family."

Jill looked distressed. "I don't think that's true. They care about you and you care about them."

"True. Although I'm rapidly losing patience with both of them. Sometime while my back was turned, Alexis turned into a drama queen and Vivian seems to be following in her footsteps."

Gracie told her about the on-again, off-again wedding. "Vivian's fighting with Tom every fifteen seconds, apparently Alexis has been crazy, and not in a good way, about what Zeke does with his time since they got married. My mother seems borderline normal, but she came over and read me the riot act after she saw the newspaper picture."

Gracie didn't go into detail about what her mother had said — she was still dealing with that herself.

"My life has become complicated."

"Sounds like." Jill leaned forward. "What can I do to help?"

"You're already doing it. Having you to talk to is great. And I'm now officially bored with me being the topic of conversation. What's going on in your world?"

"Emily is counting the days until school is out. I think there are officially thirty-four, but I would have to check the calendar in the kitchen to be sure. We're making all kinds of plans for summer, including a trip to Florida to visit my dad. He and Em get along great. I'm not sure which is more exciting to her — a visit with her favorite, and only, grandfather, or a chance to go to Disney World."

"Ah, tough choice."

Jill picked up her iced tea, then set it down. She traced a pattern on the brightly colored paper placemat.

"What?" Gracie asked with a smile. "You have a secret you're dying to spill. I can tell.

154

Come on. You can trust me."

Jill nodded. "I know. It's not that, it's just . . ." She bit her lower lip, then blushed. "Mac and I are thinking we'll start trying for a baby."

Gracie laughed. "Really! That's so cool. Is there a timetable?"

"We're going to start this month. I'm excited, but a little nervous."

"You'll be a great mom. You're terrific with Emily."

"I adore her," Jill admitted. "But by the time I met her, she had all the basics down. I'm not sure how I'll handle a baby."

"Pretty much like every other new mother. With a lot of love, patience and fear."

"Good point. Mac's hoping for a boy."

"Typical."

"I could go with either. So I'm excited and scared, which is an interesting combination."

Gracie held up her glass. "Congratulations."

Jill grinned. "I'm *not* pregnant yet."

"I know, but you will be. Yeah. I finally get to be an aunt."

Lunch with Jill had gone a long way to brighten Gracie's spirits. Even a visit to Pam's bed-and-breakfast and a fast-paced negotiating session hadn't upset her mood. She thought about driving directly back to the rental house, but she still had one thing she needed to do, even if she would rather have a root canal.

But it couldn't be put off much longer, so she drove to the center of town and parked her car on a side street. After locking it, she walked down First Avenue, past the bank building. She eyed the well-kept building, noted the entrance and carefully ignored it.

Over the next five minutes, she paced in front of the bank three times more, trying to gather the courage to actually go inside. She'd been here once before, but this was different. Just when she'd convinced herself to deliver the information by phone, a well-dressed woman in a tweed suit walked out of the bank and directly up to her.

"Gracie Landon?"

Gracie froze in midstep. Oh, please, oh, please let it not be someone wanting to talk about her, or her past or the newspaper picture.

"I'm Mr. Whitefield's secretary. He asked me to come out and escort you into his office."

Gracie winced as she glanced up at the square three-story building. "Let me guess — his office faces this way and he saw me

156

loitering."

"Exactly."

She sighed. Wasn't that just her life?

She followed Riley's secretary through the bank and up the elevator to the top floor, where she was shown into a large office dominated by a massive painting of an older gentleman in an uncomfortable-looking suit.

Gracie figured it was safer to keep her attention on the portrait, rather than the man sitting behind the desk in front of her. She pointed.

"Your uncle?" she asked.

"Yes. I'm told I'm a lot like him."

"That can't be good." She gave up on her mini art-appreciation course and looked at Riley. "I know what you're thinking."

"I doubt that."

"I wasn't stalking or doing anything like that. I was nervous about coming to see you so I was trying to make up my mind."

"What did you decide?"

"That it would be better if I phoned."

"You're here now."

"I know." She sank into the leather chair in front of his desk and set her purse on her lap. She dug around inside until she found her travel bottle of antacids, then popped two in her mouth and chewed.

He looked good, she thought mournfully. She didn't know if it was the elegant suit, the contrast between his dark hair and his white shirt, or the power tie, but he was definitely the man in charge.

"You take a lot of those," he said, pointing at the small bottle in her hand.

"I have a sensitive stomach. It reacts to stress."

"Have you seen a doctor about the problem?"

She dropped the bottle back into her purse. "Are you kidding? Any doctor would want to do all kinds of really gross tests. Plus, what if there's something wrong? I don't want to *know.*"

"But then you could get it fixed."

"Or I could find out I have some horrible, disfiguring disease."

"How could this be disfiguring?"

"Not a clue, but if it's possible, it will happen to me." She set her purse on the floor. "Look, this isn't why I stopped by. Can I talk about that?"

He leaned back in his chair. "Be my guest."

"Good." Although now that she had his attention, she wasn't sure what to do with it. "I just . . ." She drew in a deep breath. "I thought. . . ."

He pushed a pad of paper in her direction. "Would it help to write it down?"

"No. Okay. I have a couple of things. First, about my sister. I found out that she tends to exaggerate things. Especially where Zeke is concerned. I'm not sure anything is going on with him."

"Of course there is."

She'd expected Riley to be annoyed or accuse her of making the whole thing up, not that he would disagree. "How do you figure?"

"He told me. When I confronted him about what he was doing, he admitted being up to something but swore it had nothing to do with his marriage and that it wasn't illegal. He said there wasn't another woman."

"Oh. Right." She'd forgotten that. "But the no-affair thing means we don't have to follow him anymore, right? Or if you want to, that's fine. I just don't want to. I hope he's not sleeping with Pam. That would be too . . . Yuck. And speaking of Pam, she came to visit me today and offered to rent me her new industrial kitchen in the bed-and-breakfast and even though I really don't want to be involved in any of this anymore, I figured I could use the kitchen and maybe keep an eye on her. From a distance. Sort of."

Riley stood and walked around his desk. He might not have understood half of what Gracie said, but he recognized a bruised spirit when he saw one. Someone, somewhere, had done a number on her.

He perched on the edge of the desk close to her chair. "Tell me about Pam."

"She knows I bake cakes and she offered me her ovens. For a price. I went over and saw the layout. It's pretty fabulous. So we agreed on rent and I'll be baking there. I can sort of keep an eye on her."

"Okay. Sounds like a plan. Who rained on your parade?"

She looked at him. Pain tightened the lines around her mouth and darkened her eyes.

"No one. I'm fine."

"Gracie, don't bullshit a bullshitter. Something happened."

She swallowed. "I just . . ." She sighed. "My mom came to see me a couple of days ago. She wasn't happy about the picture in the paper or the article rehashing our past. She said it was going to start up talk again and that me chasing after you when I'd been a teenager had been bad enough, but now it was just pathetic."

160

She dropped her chin and stared at the ground. "I was thinking it would better if we didn't try any more investigating together. You know. So people won't talk. I can handle a lot of things, but pathetic isn't one of them. Between being back here and my cake orders and my sisters and everything. . . ."

She wound down like an old-fashioned music box. Riley did his best to avoid emotions — especially those belonging to Gracie, but he could no more ignore what she was going through now than he could have run her over when she'd thrown herself in front of his car fourteen years ago.

He leaned down and grabbed her hands, then pulled her to her feet. Before she could speak, he drew her close and wrapped his arms around her.

"Families will screw you every time," he murmured into her hair. "Look at what my uncle's doing to me."

She shuddered, then rested her forehead on his shoulder. "I never thought that before, and I don't want to think it now, but maybe you're right."

"Of course I'm right."

That made her chuckle.

As much as he liked holding her close, he let her go and reached up to cup her face in both his hands.

"You're not pathetic," he said. "No one thinks you are. If your mom is telling you that, she's wrong. I don't know what bug got up her ass, but it's not your problem. Understand?"

She nodded without speaking. He had a really bad feeling she was seconds from bursting into tears. He tried to be strong, but like every other guy in the universe, he would do just about anything to keep a woman from crying. So he did the only thing he could think of to distract her.

He kissed her.

162

CHAPTER EIGHT

This was so not a good idea, Gracie thought, even as she wrapped her arms around Riley. She was supposed to be pulling back, staying away from him, being strong and. . . .

Screw it, she thought as she closed her eyes so she could give herself over to his kiss. He smelled good, he felt good and he tasted good. What kind of idiot walked away from that?

His fingers caressed her face even as he tilted his head and deepened the kiss. She parted for him, wanting him inside, claiming her in such a way that she could forget the rest of her world. His tongue brushed against hers, sending shivers shooting down her spine.

The warmth of his body made her want to crawl inside of him and never be cold again. He felt strong, she thought hazily as she rubbed her hands up and down his back. Strong and solid.

Desire ignited — little flames of need that consumed her common sense and left her thinking about possibilities. The desk was big and she would bet there was a lock on the door. No doubt an hour or two in Riley's arms would cure most of her ills.

She moved closer, rubbing herself against him, wanting them to touch everywhere. Her breasts ached. She wanted him to feel her there, and between her thighs where the need was most intense.

He swore against her mouth, then dropped his hands to her hips where he pulled her against him. He was hard. The realization excited her. She closed her lips around his tongue and sucked gently.

He stiffened, then surged against her. When she released him, he pulled back enough to kiss her jaw, then down her neck. Her skin erupted in goose bumps, her legs began to tremble. If she hadn't been hanging on to him the overwhelming need would have caused her to collapse.

It was then she felt them — the one thing that had been missing from all her other relationships for as long as she could remember. Sparks.

They erupted like renegade fireworks, arcing through her brain, blinding her and making her want to run for safety. Sparks?

With Riley?

She wasn't sure if she pulled back or he let go, but suddenly there were a good two feet between them.

Her mind raced in a thousand different directions. She felt disoriented, as if she'd been drugged, or had slept too long during the day and couldn't quite wake up.

"Gracie?"

"I'm fine," she said. She turned in a circle, frantically searching for her purse. She spied it under the chair.

"This was a bad idea," she said as she crouched down to grab it. "Really, really bad. Super bad. Bad, bad, bad."

"I'm getting that," he said as she straightened. "You seem a little upset."

She gave him what she hoped was a bright, happy, I'm-fine smile. "I'm fabulous. Great. Gotta go. You have a good day."

She practically ran from his office, all the while not wanting to acknowledge the truth.

Sparks. Bright, shiny, glow-in-the-dark sparks.

Not with Riley, she told herself as she hurried to her car and practically threw herself inside. Anyone but Riley. It wasn't fair. It wasn't even reasonable, and it certainly wasn't nice.

She tried to put the key in the ignition,

but her hands shook too much. Instead she simply leaned her head against her steering wheel and let the irony of the situation wash over her.

After years of less than interesting romantic relationships she'd finally felt the one thing she'd always wanted to feel. Unfortunately, it was with the only single man on the planet she absolutely couldn't, under any circumstances, ever, ever be with.

Why was she surprised?

Riley looked through the weekly numbers, but his mind wasn't on the task. Not with thoughts of Gracie filling his mind and blood filling other parts of his body. She'd gotten to him. Somehow, when he wasn't looking, she'd managed to squeeze past his defenses and make him curious about her. He wanted to know what she thought, what she liked. He also wanted to see her naked and make love with her, but oddly enough, that was almost less interesting than the rest of it. Which scared the crap out of him.

He couldn't forget his rules, not to mention his goals. He was passing through this town, biding his time until he could claim his ninety-seven million. No woman was worth forgetting that, not even one as intriguing as Gracie. He didn't do relationships. Ever. And she was a happily ever after kind of woman.

One who sure knew how to kiss. And she felt damn good in his arms. He smiled as he remembered how she'd rubbed against him. If they'd been anywhere but his office. . . .

"Stop right there," he told himself. He and Gracie weren't an option. She was the kind of trouble he didn't need.

He turned his attention back to the reports and forced himself to concentrate. Thirty minutes later, he finished with his notes. His phone buzzed.

"Sheriff Kendrick here to see you," Diane said. "Shall I send him in?"

"Sure."

Riley rose and walked around his desk. He hadn't seen much of Mac since he, Riley, had moved back to Los Lobos. His one-time friend had dropped by to warn him not to make trouble, but since then they hadn't crossed paths more than a couple of times.

Mac Kendrick walked into the office. He stood a couple of inches taller, wore a sheriff's uniform and a gun. He was married, happily, Riley had heard. But in his mind, Mac would always be his best friend, the guy he'd gotten in trouble with, had chased girls with and had generally had a hell of a good time with until the night Mac had stolen the judge's Caddy and taken it on a joyride, only to get caught and hauled into jail.

Mac had never talked about what had happened, but he'd changed then. He'd stopped messing around and had gone into the military. Riley had not only lost his best friend, he'd lost the other half of his family.

"Is this an official visit?" Riley asked as Mac closed the door behind him.

"No." Mac glanced around the office. "Nice. Never thought I'd see you working behind a desk."

"Me, either. But it's not so bad." He motioned to the two sofas in the corner of the room. "Have a seat."

Riley waited until Mac had settled before sitting in the wing chair opposite. "What brings you here? Do you need a donation for the sheriff's retirement fund?"

Mac grinned. "I wouldn't say no to that, but it's not why I came to see you." His steady gaze settled on Riley. "I hear the election is going well."

"My campaign manager tells me we're up in the polls."

"Wilma, the woman who pretty much runs my department, says you're going to win. She knows that sort of thing."

"I appreciate the tip and I hope Wilma won't be insulted if I keep on polling."

Mac grinned. "I won't tell her."

"Good."

"I'm surprised you're interested in running for mayor."

Riley made a mental note to thank Jill Strathern-Kendrick, his attorney, the next time he saw her. Not only had she kept the terms of the will secret from Gracie, her best friend, she kept them from her husband — Sheriff Mac Kendrick.

"I never did like Yardley," Riley said.

"You're not alone in that. Maybe change would be a good thing." Mac glanced around the office. "I thought you'd be moving on for sure, but you're making your life here."

"Trying." Riley didn't mention that as soon as the election was over, he would be gone.

Mac turned his attention back to him. "It's been a long time," he said. "I always felt bad about how things ended."

Riley touched the faint scar on his upper lip. The one Mac had given him when they'd fought about Mac suddenly wanting to walk the straight and narrow.

"Me, too." Riley shrugged. "It was a long time ago."

"Yeah. You want to get a beer sometime?"

The question surprised Riley. He hesitated. Mac wasn't going to like his plans for the town. But until then . . . "Sure. You know where I live."

Mac grinned. "I cruise by on a regular basis to make sure you're not making trouble."

"Good to know I'm being protected by Los Lobos's finest." Riley looked at his friend. "I'm glad you came by."

"Me, too. Let's set up something soon."

"Come *with* me," Alexis said, her voice low.

"No." Gracie grabbed her headset and clicked it into her cell phone so she could keep working on her gum paste leaves. She quickly drew in the veins and point on the tiny leaf, then draped it over a cornstarch-dusted former to dry in a curved shape.

"Please. Just go with me. That's all I'm asking. Do you want me to beg?"

Gracie heard the tears in her sister's voice and tried to stay strong, but it was tough. She wasn't cut out to say no to people, especially not to someone who was family. Even if the relationship seemed to only run one way.

"I want you to leave me out of this," Gracie said, although she could feel herself weakening.

"I swear there's something going on. I know I've been crazy before, accusing Zeke of things and I'm running low on credits with you. I'm the boy who cried wolf, but I swear there's a wolf in my house now."

Gracie couldn't help smiling. "If I remember my preschool reading, I believe the wolf was in with the sheep."

"Whatever. You know what I mean."

She did. Her humor faded. "Alexis, you put me in a really bad position. Mom is convinced I'm turning back into stalker girl. My picture's on the front page of the newspaper and the legend of the 'Gracie Chronicles' is alive and well."

"I know. I'm so, so sorry. Please. Just come with me. You don't have to say anything. Just hover in the background and give me moral support. If he's really not there, I'll need your emotional support."

Gracie shook her head and stabbed the leaf she'd been forming. She knew she was going to regret this, but she couldn't seem to say the *N* word again. "Fine. What time do you want me to pick you up?"

"The numbers aren't just good," Zeke said with a grin. "They're amazing. If the election were held tomorrow, I doubt Yardley's own mother would vote for him."

Riley reached for his beer. "What happened?"

"Near as I can tell . . . Gracie. Your numbers shot up after that picture of the two of you in the paper. Along with the old articles about her crush and what she did to get her man."

Riley shook his head. The world was a twisted place. "So they love me now because of Gracie."

"They love you because Gracie loves you. Or she did. Everyone enjoys a good romance. Los Lobos wants yours with Gracie to work out."

"There is no romance."

Zeke raised his eyebrows. "You might want to get to work on that."

Riley looked at his campaign manager. "Let's make this really clear. I'm not faking a relationship with Gracie for the sake of votes."

"But. . . ."

Riley kept his gaze steady. Eventually Zeke turned away.

"But if you were seen together, around town, that would be okay."

Riley swallowed the rest of his beer. Talk about a strange situation. He'd gone slowly, doing his best to win over the good citizens of Los Lobos. He'd let them get used to him being around. He'd bought candy for Little League, sponsored the new jerseys, supported the local high school football team and the girl's basketball team. He'd sent the church band to some damn parade in Italy, and he'd done it all with a smile. Now they wanted him to have a relationship with Gracie to prove himself.

Why did the idea bother him? Spending time with her wasn't a hardship. He liked her and he wanted her in his bed. He should be grateful his plan was coming together and he would soon be in possession of his uncle's bank and the ninety-seven million dollars.

"We're going to have to start prepping for the debate soon," Zeke said. "How's next week?"

"Fine. Have we decided on a format?"

Zeke snorted. "I don't think the evening is going to be that formal, but I'll ask."

"Are you sure helping me won't interfere with your secret life?"

"I told you. I'm not having an affair."

"As long as Alexis believes that," Riley said, just as the doorbell rang.

He placed his beer on the coffee table in front of his chair, then stood and walked into the foyer. Zeke followed. When he opened the front door, he stared at the two women standing there. One made him want to grin. The other made him want to reach for one of Gracie's antacids.

"It's for you," he told Zeke.

"I'm sorry," Gracie said for possibly the forty-seventh time in less than two minutes.

"It's fine," Riley told her and meant it.

"It's not fine. It's terrible. I need to leave you in peace."

He and Gracie stood together at the far end of the foyer while Zeke and Alexis had a heated, although whispered, conversation.

"I didn't want to come," she told him. "Basically she guilted me into it. I'm a complete wiener dog who can be guilted into anything."

"That doesn't surprise me." He could imagine her giving in to a request from a friend or a family member, even when it wasn't in her best interest.

"He said he was going to be here tonight and she wanted to be sure."

"I gathered that."

Gracie stared at the black-and-white tiles. "Did I say I was sorry?"

"You did and you can stop now. None of this is your fault."

"I know, but I still feel bad. I was really

trying to stay out of your way. If you'll notice, you haven't seen me in two days. I figured that would be best for both of us."

He'd noticed. What he wouldn't admit to anyone and barely wanted to believe himself was that he'd missed her.

"You still getting flack about the newspaper picture?" he asked as he tucked a loose strand of hair behind her ear.

"What?" She looked at him, then away. "No. I've been avoiding all contact with my family. Pretty much with everyone. I thought this would be a good time to lay low. Then Alexis came looking for me."

"We're going to go."

Riley turned and saw Zeke with his arm around Alexis.

"Maybe we can finish this up tomorrow," Zeke added.

"Sure."

Alexis looked at her sister. "Gracie, I'll call you tomorrow, okay?"

"Sure. Fine. Night."

The front door closed behind them. Gracie sighed.

"I can't decide if they're going home to have makeup sex or fight some more."

"I don't want to think about either."

He wasn't interested in anyone's sex life except possibly Gracie's and his own.

Memories of the last kiss they'd shared still lingered and while he knew it would be a damn stupid idea to pursue the matter, his brain wasn't necessarily in charge.

"You're being really nice about this," she said as she gazed at him.

He liked looking at her. He liked her blue eyes and the way the curve of her mouth, or lack of curve, gave away her feelings. He liked how she stared at his earring with equal parts fascination and fear. He liked that she made cakes, loved storms and could be bought for the price of a restaurant-grade oven.

"I'm glad you stopped by," he said.

"What?" She blinked. "Oh, yeah. Right. Me stopping by. With Alexis."

Her cheeks turned pink and she dropped her attention back to the floor.

"Well, Alexis is gone and I should probably head out, too."

He didn't want her to go. Even though they weren't going to have sex — despite how much he wanted her — he wasn't ready to be alone.

He frowned. No, that wasn't true. He was fine with being alone. He wasn't ready to be without Gracie. Not yet.

"Want a tour of the old place?" he asked.

Gracie had expected Riley to say a lot of

things, from "Get out of my house," to "Come upstairs with me and let's get naked." She hadn't expected him to want to play tour guide.

While she knew the most sensible course of action would be to leave, she smiled her acceptance.

"I'd love it."

He put his hand on her shoulder, then slid it under her hair so he cupped the back of her neck.

"This is the foyer," he said.

"I figured that. The tiles are a giveaway. It's big." She glanced up at the elegant, crystal chandelier hanging down from the two-story ceiling. "How do you dust that?"

"Not a clue."

His fingers moved against her skin, making her even more aware of him. The touching made it difficult to think or speak or do anything but purr and rub against him.

"Living room," he said, pointing to the left with his free hand.

She walked in that direction. He kept pace with her, although he dropped his hand to the small of her back.

Carved double doors led to a large room with hardwood floors and old, but beautiful, Oriental rugs. Old-fashioned furniture filled the space. Heavy velvet draperies covered the windows.

"How dark is this room during the day?" she asked. "Those drapes wouldn't let in a speck of light."

"No idea," he said. "I don't get in here much."

Beyond the living room was some kind of parlor, then a bedroom suite with a sitting room and bath.

"For the maid," Gracie said.

"I have a cleaner who comes in twice a week."

The massive kitchen hadn't been remodeled since the 1950s but was big enough to host banquets. Rows and rows of cabinets stretched to the ceiling — some of them fronted by the original leaded glass. There seemed to be about fifty acres of counter space. It was old, chipped tile, but if replaced with granite it would be beautiful. Double sinks stood on both sides of the kitchen and there was a walk-in pantry that would comfortably house a family of four. Talk about heaven.

"This needs some serious fixing up," she said. "Let me know if you need suggestions. I have been known to spend a whole afternoon drooling over appliance catalogues."

"I'm more into take-out or heating up something in the microwave."

She supposed that made sense, what with him being a guy and all, but the possibilities made her envious.

"I can ignore the however-many bedrooms this house has, and the library and the antiques, but the kitchen is tough to walk away from."

"Make me an offer," he said.

She leaned against the counter. "I don't think I have enough in my checkbook." She tilted her head. "You're not kidding, are you? You'd sell this place."

"Sure. It's not my home."

"Where *is* home?"

"Whatever rig I'm on at the moment." He pulled up a bar stool by the large island and offered it to her. He took the second stool for himself. "I'm used to sleeping in cramped quarters with six other guys working rotating shifts. An oil rig is a twenty-four-hour-a-day operation."

She couldn't imagine such a place. "You said something about the South China Sea. How did you get there from here?"

"When I took off, I headed north and ended up in Alaska working on a sports fishing boat. I met a couple of guys in a bar. They were looking to hire a crew for a rig they'd just bought from an oil company. The big guys said there wasn't any more oil.

These two didn't agree."

"You went with them just like that?"

He grinned. "For a piece of the action. Lucky for me, they were right. The work is damn hard, but it's worth it. I learned all I could and took over the second rig they bought for a bigger share. Ten years later I was a partner and we were a company to be reckoned with."

"Bad boy makes good. You must be proud."

He shrugged. "It's how I make my living."

"But you're running the bank now."

"Right. The bank."

She glanced around at the large kitchen. "This isn't anything like you're used to, is it?"

"There's a lot more square feet. I don't know. The old house is pretty empty. There are dozens of rooms I've never seen." He rubbed his fingers across the island countertop. "My mom would have liked it, though. She grew up here."

"Really? I didn't know that. Why didn't. . . ."

Gracie pressed her lips together. Not her business, she reminded herself.

Riley looked at her. "You can ask. The reason she and I didn't come here when we moved back to Los Lobos is that her brother, my uncle, never forgave her for marrying my father. Her parents had passed away when she was pretty young and her brother, Donovan, had raised her. She ran off with my father when she was maybe seventeen. Donovan told her to come back or she would be cut off without a cent. She chose love over money."

She wanted to say that sounded so romantic, but there was something in Riley's voice. Something that made her hold back.

"What happened?" she asked.

"She got pregnant and lived in a run-down house in some dusty town in Arizona for ten years. The love of her life never bothered to marry her and one day, when I was nine, he disappeared. We came back here. I think she wanted to reconcile with her brother, but good old Donovan wouldn't have any part of it."

His expression tightened and his mouth thinned.

"You can't forgive that," Gracie said softly.

"It's one item in a long list."

"I'm sorry."

"It all happened a long time ago."

"But still." She slipped off the chair and moved close enough that she could rest her hand on his forearm. "I wish I could make it better."

In a matter of seconds, everything changed. Gone was the wounded guy and in his place was a predator. His eyes darkened, his body tensed and she would swear that the temperature in the room climbed about twelve degrees.

Riley stepped down and reached for her, but instead of pulling her close, he coiled his hand around her hair.

"Not a good idea," he told her.

She had to swallow before she could speak.

"Um, what's not a good idea?"

"Making me feel better. You're not my type."

He wasn't pulling her hair, but he wasn't letting her go, either. She felt completely in his control, which was kind of thrilling.

"So what is your type?"

He raised his eyebrows. "Volunteering?"

"Curious."

"Sure you are. Okay — I like women who are easy. What I call the three *F's*."

"Three *F's*?" What? "I can probably figure out one of them," she said, assuming it had to be the *F* word. "What are the other two?"

His dark eyes seemed to invite her closer. She felt compelled to move toward him until they were almost touching. Almost, but not quite. Funny how Riley had been so nice to her that she'd forgotten he could also be dangerous.

He leaned into her until he could whisper in her ear. "Are you sure you want to know?" he asked, his breath tickling her.

She nodded.

"Find her, fuck her, forget her."

"Oh." She didn't know what to say or even what to think.

"You're not someone I could forget," he murmured. "You're the kind of woman men buy flowers for, and rings. You're the kind of woman a man wants to make love with. That's not my game, Gracie. Never has been."

He straightened and released her hair. "You should probably go now."

"What?" Go? Leave? She shook her head and stepped back. "Right. Good idea. Excellent idea."

She felt like a small bird being charmed by a swaying snake. The side of her brain in charge of personal preservation told her to run. But the rest of her wanted to find out how it would feel to be seduced by the likes of Riley Whitefield.

She stared into his eyes. He was so gorgeous, and a great kisser. Maybe he could just kiss her one more time. Maybe . . .

"If I start, I'm not going to stop," he said flatly.

She jumped with the realization that he could read her mind, then turned and dashed out of the kitchen.

The trip home happened in record time. She longed for some quiet and a cup of tea as she sorted through what had just happened. But when she pulled into the driveway of her rental, she saw it was not to be. Vivian stood on her front porch.

CHAPTER NINE

"Another fight with Tom?" Gracie asked as she got out of her car and walked toward the front door.

Vivian actually looked shocked. "How did you guess?"

"Gee, I don't know. I guess I took a stab in the dark."

She figured her comment was sarcastic enough, although what she really wanted to say was "I knew something was wrong because the only time you ever bother with me is when you want something."

Gracie opened the front door and led the way inside. While her rental was light and bright and more than served her needs, she couldn't help remembering Riley's amazing house. Ah, well. One day, if she was ever rich and willing to live in Los Lobos again. Of course she figured the odds of the latter happening were even more slim than winning the lottery.

"So," she said as she filled the kettle with water, then set it on the stove. "What happened?"

Vivian sat at the kitchen table where she immediately poked at several decorative flowers drying there.

She picked up a rose and promptly crumbled it in her fingers.

"Sorry," she said, and set the bigger pieces back on the table. She rubbed her fingers on her jeans. "It's Tom, like you said. He's graduating with his MBA and we're getting married."

"I think I knew that," Gracie said as she pulled out a plastic container filled with loose tea and set it next to two mugs.

"He's interviewed for a few jobs in L.A. and I thought he was going to take one, but I just found out he's thinking about accepting a position at the bank."

There were several banks in town — branches of large multinational conglomerates, but when a local referred to "the bank" there was only one. Riley's.

"That's interesting," Gracie said, wondering if Riley knew. She doubted he worried about entry-level hiring, even in management, so he might not know about Tom.

"It's not interesting, it's horrible," Vivian wailed. "I don't want to stay here for the rest of my life. I want to leave and see other places. You got to go. Why can't I? I can't believe he would consider the job after all we've talked about."

Vivian began to cry. Her sharp, high-pitched sobs competed with the whistle on the kettle and won.

Gracie didn't bother pointing out that she hadn't exactly wanted to leave Los Lobos, that instead she'd been sent away in disgrace. After all, Vivian wasn't looking for logic.

Gracie scooped tea into two steeping spoons and dropped one in each mug. She carried them to the table and sat across from her sister.

"So call off the wedding," she said, not all that interested in the outcome of the conversation.

Vivian dropped her hands to her side and stared at her. "What?"

"Call off the wedding. If you're so unhappy, don't marry Tom."

"But I have to marry him. We're engaged. We've ordered invitations. Do you know how much this is costing?"

Gracie had a good idea. "You're still at the deposit stage. Most of it is refundable."

Vivian looked at her as if she were a

complete idiot. "I'm *not* canceling the wedding."

"Then you need to talk to Tom about his plans. His job is about more than just him if it affects where you live."

Her sister shrugged, then touched one of the roses. "Will you make flowers like this for my cake?"

"If you'd like. I haven't decided. I'll sketch up something in the next couple of days."

"They're really beautiful. You must be super talented."

"I work hard."

Vivian sipped her tea. "Tom says I don't work hard enough. He says we both have to be saving to buy a house, but right now I'm saving to pay for my wedding dress. Teaching just doesn't pay that much, which is why I'm working part-time in the hardware store." She sighed as if life were too much for her.

"Would you teach if you moved to L.A.?" Gracie asked.

"I guess I'd have to. But if Tom got a good enough job, I could just stay home."

"You're going to start a family right away?"

"No. What does that have to do with anything?"

Gracie didn't have an answer for that. In

her world, husband and wife were partners, pulling equally toward a mutual goal. Obviously that wasn't Vivian's idea of a good time.

Maybe Gracie was old-fashioned and outdated. Maybe that was why Vivian and Alexis had men in their lives and she didn't.

"I'm not the right person to come to for advice," Gracie said.

"I guess I need to talk to one of my friends, then," Vivian said. "Mom is completely crazed about the wedding and Alexis is so self-absorbed she can't see anyone else but herself." Her baby sister leaned close. "You're not like that, Gracie. You think about other people."

Gracie didn't know what to say. "Gee, thanks. I'm so glad you think so."

"I do." Vivian patted her arm, then stood. "I gotta run. I still don't have the shoes to go with my dress and I'm going into Santa Barbara to check out that new bridal shop. Don't forget the family meeting tomorrow. We have a lot to discuss. Have a good one."

She practically bounced out of the room.

Gracie collected the mugs and carried them to the sink.

What had just happened? How could Vivian go from fighting with Tom to shopping for their wedding in less than five minutes?

Gracie might not be an expert on the subject, but she was willing to go out on a limb and say the girl wasn't grown-up enough to be marrying anyone.

Not that it was her decision.

She returned to the table and carefully moved the flowers, then pulled out her sketch pad. She might as well get the cake design done. Even if the constant on-again, off-again wedding ended up being officially off, she could always put the design in her portfolio.

The next afternoon Gracie drove to her mother's house. She had sketches for several wedding cakes, along with some ideas about pretty but inexpensive centerpieces. As she pulled up in front of the house, she wondered if she was trying too hard. Should she continue to participate, even when it was clear she was only free labor, or should she walk away? Riley had said that family would screw her every time, but she didn't want to believe it. With her aunt and uncle gone, her mom and her sisters were all the family she had. If she didn't belong with them, she would be well and truly on her own.

She collected her portfolio and stepped out of the car. She'd barely started up the walkway when she heard someone call her name.

"Gracie! Oh, Gracie!" Eunice Baxter walked off her porch with a speed that belied her eighty-plus years. "I saw the picture in the paper the other day."

Gracie's shoulders slumped. Of course she had. "Hi, Mrs. Baxter."

The old woman beamed. "You looked so pretty. And Riley, my oh my, he's a fine male specimen. That earring." The beam turned into a giggle. "Very sexy."

Gracie blinked. Mrs. Baxter thought Riley was sexy? Gracie didn't know if she should be impressed or completely grossed out. She figured she could decide later, and maybe use the information for ammunition.

"Are you going to listen to him talk?" Mrs. Baxter asked. "I'm thinking I will. Maybe go early and sit in the front row." She winked. "That way I can look all I want."

"He's speaking somewhere?"

"At the high school later this afternoon. Something about civic responsibility, not that I care about what he's saying. I generally vote for whoever is most attractive, and I have to say that Riley beats Franklin Yardley hands down."

Gracie didn't want to think about Eunice Baxter participating in their democratic system of government by voting based on looks, but there it was. The founding fathers would be so proud.

"You should stop by," the older woman told her, then winked.

Gracie was tempted, although the reality of her showing up in the same place as Riley wasn't something she wanted to consider. Talk about trouble.

"Thanks for the information," she said and turned back to the house. "I need to get these designs for the cake to my sister."

"That girl," Mrs. Baxter said with a dismissive wave of her hand. "She and her boyfriend go at it like cats and dogs. I don't give them a year. Alexis isn't much better. Mark my words, Gracie, you're the best of the lot."

The compliment brightened Gracie's morning. "I appreciate that, Mrs. Baxter." Even if right now she didn't feel all that special. She waved and hurried into the house.

Fifteen minutes later she was sorry she'd bothered. Vivian dismissed all her centerpiece ideas, saying they were too unimpressive and not one of the three cake designs had been approved.

"I like them," Tom said. "They're all beautiful."

Obviously the bride and groom had made up, Gracie thought, liking Tom even more for liking her designs.

Vivian looked at him and rolled her eyes. "Honey, this is girl stuff. I know you want to be involved in the wedding, but I've been planning this since I was six."

Gracie looked at Tom. He met her gaze and shrugged, as if to say, "I tried."

Gracie felt more than a little sympathy for the man. If he really wanted to marry Vivian, he was going to have his hands full.

"The cakes are just so . . . I don't know. Small, I guess," Vivian said with a sigh as she touched the pages spread across the dining room table.

"These aren't to scale," Gracie told her, speaking between clenched teeth. "They'll serve three hundred."

Vivian pointed to a simple, but elegant design, with a cascade of orchids trailing down one side. "What if it was more like this, but all covered with flowers. Like a giant bouquet."

"It's not very defined. You want your guests to know there's a cake buried under there."

"Do they have to?"

"I like the one that looks like a present," Alexis said, bending over the sketches.

"What if there were flowers instead of bows?"

"I could do that," Gracie said, reaching for her bottle of antacids.

She walked into the kitchen for a glass of water. Her mother followed.

"I'm sure Vivian will pick something," she said. "I'm glad Tom wants to help."

Gracie nodded and turned on the tap.

"It's nice of you to do this for free. I read that article in *People*. I know your cakes are really expensive."

Gracie felt some of her bad mood drain way. She smiled at her mother. "She's my sister. I'm happy to help."

"So we're both running our own businesses. Who would have thought."

Gracie wasn't sure where her mother was going with this conversation. She wanted to believe that it was a slightly awkward peace offering, but she wasn't sure.

"I think yours is more complicated than mine," Gracie said. "You have employees and inventory, while I just have myself to worry about."

"Still, you've made something of yourself. I'm not sure I understand how you can be so smart about everything else and so dumb about Riley."

The arrow sailed straight and true, landing right in Gracie's heart. She almost wasn't surprised. "It's probably best if we don't talk about him. We're going to have to agree to disagree."

Her mother moved closer. "You're not even trying. That's what doesn't make any sense. Your sister said you were over there last night."

Gracie felt her mouth drop open. "Did Alexis mention she *begged* me to go with her so she could check on what Zeke was up to?"

Her mother ignored that. "Gracie, I only want what's best for you. That's what I've always wanted. I wish I could make you see what you're doing. The whole town is laughing at you."

"You know what, Mom? I think you're wrong. I think the whole town is so busy with their own lives that they don't have time for me. It's been fourteen years and everyone needs to get over it."

"You're the one who can't let go. You've never had any sense when it came to that boy."

Gracie put down the water and crossed her arms over her chest. "Number one, he's not a boy anymore. He's a very successful man who's made something of himself. I didn't know him before, but I know him now. He's great. He's better than great. He's amazing. He's smart and sexy and fun to be with."

Her mother flinched. "Oh, God. It's worse than I thought."

"It's not anything," Gracie told her flatly. "That's my point. You're upset about nothing. I'm not obsessed with Riley. I'm a completely different person. I've grown up, gotten a life. I've dated, had boyfriends and lovers and two years ago, I nearly got engaged. If anyone is lost in the past in this room, it's you, not me."

"You can't see what's happening," her mother said, obviously distressed. "I don't know how to help you."

"Here's a newsflash. I don't need your help. Maybe I did, say fourteen years ago, but you weren't interested. You sent me away. You were never there for me, even when I begged you to let me come home. You never cared about what I wanted, what I needed. I was desperate to be allowed to return to my family and you turned your back on me. So I got over it. I grew up, no thanks to you. So guess what? I don't really care what you think about me or Riley or anyone else. The three of you asked me to come back for Vivian's wedding. I said I would help and I will, but when this is all over, I'm leaving and I'm not coming back."

Gracie walked out of the kitchen and back into the dining room.

"I think I know what I want," Vivian said.

"Draw me a picture," Gracie said as she grabbed her purse.

"Where are you going? Wait. I need to talk to you. I'll tell you what I want and you can draw it. Gracie! Wait!"

But Gracie didn't look back. She walked to her car, started it and drove away. Her heart pounded so hard she was afraid it would break. She felt shaky and sore, as if she'd just been run over.

Ever since she'd moved in with her aunt and uncle, she'd fantasized about what it would be like to come home. She'd waited and waited for her mother to call and say it had all been a mistake — that of course she was welcome to return. But the call had never come and eventually Gracie had stopped expecting it.

In time she'd told herself she'd stopped caring. She'd never come home for the holidays, instead meeting her family in L.A. or somewhere else. It had become a tradition.

Now Gracie wondered if the real reason she'd avoided Los Lobos, was the possibility of disappointment. If she came back, she would have to face what had happened. There wouldn't be any room to hide.

Now that she was in the thick of it, she knew that staying away had been a fine idea.

She stopped at the red light and considered what to do next. There were several possibilities, including packing up her stuff and returning to L.A.

"I'm not going to run away," she told herself, trying to sound fierce rather than broken.

She thought about going back to her rental house, but she didn't want to be there, either. In the end, she found herself parking at the high school and walking into the auditorium to hear what Riley Whitefield had to say about civic responsibility and maybe join Eunice Baxter in ogling his earring.

Instead of heading for the front row, Gracie slipped in a side entrance and headed for a back corner. While she might want to convince her mother that no one in the town really cared what she did with her life or with Riley, she wasn't willing to put that theory to the test.

She sat low in her seat and did her best to avoid eye contact. The strategy seemed to work and she didn't even get a second look.

Thirty minutes later she found herself actually hanging on Riley's every word. He spoke about the town and how each citizen was responsible for the direction it would go. How everyone could be an example, by supporting local businesses instead of chain stores, and throwing away trash instead of leaving it on the beach. He talked about how the tourists provided necessary income, but that they could not be allowed to define what the town would be.

Gracie found herself caught up in his words and actually wanting to get involved. She sat up straighter and applauded with her neighbors . . . right up until she heard someone whisper, "Is that Gracie Landon? The girl from the newspaper?"

She glanced around and saw several people looking in her direction. Wives nudged their husbands. Older people leaned in to neighbors, then turned back to her.

Gracie felt trapped and in the spotlight. Should she run out of the auditorium? Pretend she didn't notice? Smile and wave?

Riley wrapped up his speech before she could decide and everyone stood to applaud. As the meeting broke up, Gracie tried to duck out a side door, but the crowd carried her down to the stage where she found herself in line to shake hands with the man himself. They were face-to-face before she could slip away.

"I shouldn't have come," she said when he turned to her and raised his eyebrows. "I didn't think anyone would notice."

"You're welcome, as long as you promise to vote for me."

"I'm not registered in this county."

"We could change that."

She was aware of several interested listeners moving close enough to overhear every word. She knew people would talk and report back to her mother. Maybe some of them were even silently laughing. But in her heart, at that second, she didn't care.

"I liked what you had to say," she told him honestly. "You're right about the local citizens defining what Los Lobos will be rather than letting the tourists do it."

"Thanks."

She tried to figure out what he was thinking, but she couldn't. Not with so many people trying to get his attention. She excused herself and stepped away, only to run into Zeke.

"What are you doing here?" he asked.

"Listening to your candidate."

Her brother-in-law was a good-looking guy with an easy smile. He seemed nice and funny and she understood why Alexis had

200

married him.

Zeke glanced around. "You're making a bit of a splash. We should probably get you out of the way, so folks will concentrate on Riley and the campaign rather than your legendary past."

She allowed him to lead her out a side door and into the parking lot. Gracie told herself none of this was her business, but she couldn't help grabbing his arm before he went back inside.

"Why won't you tell Alexis what you're up to? She's making everyone crazy with her concerns, and I'm guessing you're getting the worst of it."

"I'm not doing anything wrong."

"But you are doing something."

"Why is this your business?" he asked.

Gracie stared at him. "You're kidding, right? Your wife has had me following you around town, sneaking around, taking pictures and showing up where I'm not wanted, just to find out what you're up to."

Zeke shuffled his feet. "Okay. Fair point. The thing is —" He shrugged, then turned away. "I'm not doing anything bad. I'm not cheating on her or trying to leave, or spending money or any of that. I just need a little more time. I swear I'll tell her soon."

It wasn't good enough, but it would have

to do. "I can't make you tell me," she admitted. "I wish I could."

"Your sister is a little high-strung. I'm not saying I haven't been acting weird in the past few weeks, but before that if I took an extra five minutes at the grocery store, she was convinced I'd run off with a checker."

Not exactly Gracie's idea of perfect happiness. "Does that worry come from her or from you?"

"I haven't a clue. Honestly, I love your sister more than anything. She's crazy, but she's also sweet and caring and never boring. You know."

His warm smile made Gracie feel better about the situation, even if his words made her uncomfortable. She didn't know what Alexis was like. Not really.

"I gotta run and take care of my candidate," Zeke said. He bent down and kissed her cheek. "Thanks."

She wasn't sure what he was thanking her for. She stared after him as she thought about all he'd said about her sister.

The sense of having lost her family was still there, but for the first time she considered that while she'd been sent away against her will, she had chosen to stay away. She could have come back, if she'd wanted to. Yes, she'd felt rejected by her family, but it wasn't as if she'd bothered to reach out overly much.

Something to consider.

The next morning Gracie collected her various ingredients, baking pans and other supplies, loaded up her car and drove up to the bed-and-breakfast on the bluff.

She remembered this old place from when she'd been a kid. Rumors of an alien landing some time in the 1950s had made the location both irresistible and terrifying. Some of the high school kids used the place as a make-out point, while the younger ones tested their bravery by being willing to run up to the front door and knock.

In her youth, Gracie had made it all the way to the porch, which had been pretty darned impressive. Now she parked in back with the expectation of actually stepping inside and working. Aliens be damned, she had cakes to bake.

She knocked once as a courtesy, then used the key Pam had given her to let herself in.

As it had when she'd first seen the kitchen, her heart fluttered with all the foolishness of young love. This time, however, it wasn't a man who got her blood to racing. Instead it was gleaming stainless steel appliances, yards and yards of counter space and big windows that let the morning light spill in.

Gracie mixed up her first cake batch and carefully poured everything into the pans. She added the heating core to the larger pans and slid them into the waiting oven.

As she set the timer, she heard another car pull up next to hers and looked out in time to see Pam stepping out of her Lexus.

Unable to escape due to cake-bakeage, she plastered a smile on her face and hoped for the best.

"Hi," she said cheerfully as Pam entered. "How's it going?"

"Great." Pam dropped several books of wallpaper samples onto the counter. "I'm down to the details with the rooms, which is fun."

Gracie had sort of dressed for her day. She wore a cotton blouse over black pants, but felt frumpy next to Pam's Ultrasuede pants and matching jacket, with a little camisole underneath.

"I drove by the high school," Pam said. "There was a crowd there for Riley's speech."

"Really?" Gracie pretended she hadn't been there. "Is his campaign going well?"

"I hope so," Pam told her.

Gracie tried not to react, but the surprise must have shown because Pam grinned.

"I mean it," she said. "Hey, it's been years and years. I was young and foolish and I sure don't hold a grudge against Riley. Besides, Franklin Yardley gives me the creeps. He'd just been elected mayor when I was a senior and he was at graduation handing out some award. I swear he patted my butt when he gave it to me."

Gracie pressed both her hands on the counter. She remembered Jill telling her a similar story. "You're kidding! He did the same thing to a friend of mine. She was totally grossed out."

"Do you blame her? He was old and it was just too disgusting. I wanted to say something, but I didn't think anyone would believe me. So Riley gets my vote."

She sounded sincere and Gracie sort of wanted to believe her, but she couldn't. Not completely.

"You never remarried."

Pam leaned against the counter. "I know. I thought about it, but I really prefer being single. I'm seeing someone now. He lives in Santa Barbara, which is pretty perfect. We're close enough to get together on a regular basis, but he's not in my face all the time. I like that. I've been on my own for so long, I don't think I could get used to living with a man. What about you?"

Gracie was more than willing to get used to living with a man, but the only one who made her feel sparks wasn't interested in her. Besides, he was the last guy on the planet she should be with. It made no sense. And they wanted really different things. He might find her attractive and kiss like a dream, but she knew he wasn't the settling-down type.

She shook her head and realized Pam was staring at her. "I'm sorry. What did you ask me?"

Pam laughed. "Never mind. I can see you're distracted. I'll just grab my light reading and get out of your way."

Pam picked up the wallpaper sample books and left the kitchen. Gracie stared after her and wondered if maybe she'd been wrong to judge Pam so harshly all those years ago.

CHAPTER TEN

Riley stood outside in the late afternoon. He'd canceled his last two meetings with the intent of going for a drive. But instead of heading up the coast or even south to L.A., he'd traveled a short distance across town to find himself parked outside of Gracie's rental.

He knew she was home — her Subaru Forrester sat in the driveway and he could hear music. As he stood beside his car, he stared at the front door and wondered when he'd left the world of normal behind.

There were a thousand other places he could be and a handful he *should* be, and Gracie's house didn't fall into either category. She was nothing but trouble — not the way she used to be by stalking him and making his life hell. No, this trouble was worse. He liked her.

He enjoyed her company, her humor, her craziness and right now he wanted to be with her in every sense of the word.

He told himself he was only here to talk, that she wasn't his type and he was a man who was cautious about where he laid his head. He'd always been careful to pick women who were content to be part of the three *F*'s. Gracie wasn't like that.

If he had a brain in his head, he would walk back to his car and drive away. Instead he stepped forward and pressed the doorbell.

"Just a sec," she yelled from somewhere inside the house.

He heard something slam, some mild cursing, then running footsteps and the front door flew open.

She stood in front of him with a smudge on her cheek and a dish towel in one hand. She'd pulled her hair back in a ponytail. Her T-shirt fit snugly, emphasizing curves that haunted him, while her slightly loose khakis hung low on her hips. She was barefoot, not wearing a speck of makeup and he wanted her with a hungry desperation that made it impossible to speak.

She grinned. "Thank God you're not my mother or one of my sisters. I'm all familied out right now. I can't even tell you the forty-seven ways they're making me crazy."

She stepped back. "Come on. I have a

cake in the oven and I have to turn it every ten minutes to keep it baking evenly. I know, I know, I could have gone back over to Pam's but I was there before and she was actually nice and it kind of freaked me out."

She shut the door behind him and led the way into the kitchen. "So what's going on with you?"

The sway of her hips called him. He wanted to grab her, pull her close and take her right there in the hallway. He wanted to tug the rubber band from her hair, pull off her clothes and have her on top, wet, ready and panting his name as she demanded he give her more.

"I wasn't in the mood to work," he said instead. "Thought I'd stop by."

They reached the kitchen. She bent over the oven, pulled it open and used the dishcloth to protect her fingers as she gave the large cake pan a quarter turn.

"I appreciate the company. Oddly enough, you're the most normal person I know these days. Who would have thought?"

She straightened and walked to the refrigerator. "Do you want anything to drink? I have soda and milk and some sparkling water." She glanced at him. "Let me guess — macho guys don't drink sparkling water."

"Not unless we open it with our teeth first."

"Figures." She held up a can of soda. "This okay?"

"Yeah. Thanks."

He glanced around at the small kitchen. Even though she was a short-term tenant, she'd still made the space her own. There were cake pans and racks covering the space. She'd tacked up sketches of cakes, a calendar and the article from *People* magazine. The small table held all kinds of delicate-looking tools he couldn't identify.

The room felt lived in, comfortable. No ghosts here.

He settled on a bar stool by the counter and took the drink she offered.

"What terribly important meetings are you missing out on?" she asked as she set the timer for ten minutes.

"One about the direction the Federal Reserve will probably take. A recap on our lending ratios. Banking stuff."

She leaned against the counter across from him. "Are you enjoying being a banker? It has to be different from living on the oil rig."

"Shorter hours, and everyone smells better."

"That has to be nice. But do you find it

interesting or boring?"

He frowned as he popped open his soda and took a drink. "I never thought about the banking job as more than something I had to do to inherit." When he'd either satisfied the terms of the will or failed, he was walking away.

"Would you consider it as a career?"

"Maybe. There are aspects I like." He loosened his tie, then unfastened the top button on his dress shirt. "The clothes can be a pain."

"I know what you mean. I like baking days when I don't have to get all fancy for my meetings." She glanced down at her T-shirt and brushed a smudge of flour. "When I'm in the kitchen I make sure everything is washable. I seem to be the kind of baker who has a lot of accidents with ingredients."

He could smell her. Something soft and feminine that had nothing to do with the sweet scent of baking cake. Need nearly drove him to his feet, but he pushed it down and did his best to ignore it. After all this time, Gracie had turned out to be an unexpected pleasure in his life. They were friends, and he wasn't about to screw that up with sex.

"My secretary keeps pressuring me to give money for the new children's wing of the local hospital. She suggests it be in my uncle's name, which I'm not willing to do."

Gracie tucked a loose strand of hair behind her ear and glanced at the timer. "Give the money at all or give it in your uncle's name?"

"I don't want anything named for him."

"Then give it someone else's name. Or no one's. Why do wings always have to have names?"

"Good point. I may do it just to get Diane off my back. The woman defines stubborn." He picked up his soda and grinned. "There's a reason to give to charity."

"I doubt the hospital board will really care what drives you to donate. I think they'll just be happy to cash the check." She tilted her head. "Where exactly does the money come from? You don't have the inheritance yet, do you?"

"Thinking of asking me for a loan?"

"If I remember correctly, it was ninety-seven million dollars. If you had that kind of money, I'd be more on the lookout for a grant rather than a loan."

"Fair enough. This money comes from the bank. A certain percentage of profits are earmarked for charity." Riley couldn't escape the irony of his uncle being willing to give millions to charity, but leaving his own sister to die.

"And you get to pick where they go? That's kind of cool."

"Diane does most of that. I sign the checks." He smiled. "I have to admit, she's someone I wouldn't mind taking back to my other business with me. Talk about efficient."

"The other business being your partnerships in the oil business."

He nodded. "We have over fifty rigs now."

She straightened just as the timer dinged, then walked to the oven and rotated the cake. "Amazing how you left here with nothing and did so well. That's pretty cool. Your mom would be really proud of you. Did she know you were a success before she passed away?"

"Some. I sent her money when I could." Not that it had been enough. If only, he thought grimly. If only he hadn't still been angry at her for making him marry Pam. If only she'd told him the truth. If only he'd come back.

"So you're already rich," Gracie teased as she closed the oven and turned back to him. "That kind of makes you really attractive."

He shook his head. "You're not into guys with money. If they have it you won't say no, but otherwise you don't care."

She stared at him. "How do you know that?"

"Am I wrong?"

"No, but we've never talked about it. You barely know me."

"I know enough. Besides, I married someone who wanted my money. I learned to recognize the signs."

"Makes sense," she told him. "So now you keep your wealth a secret?"

"I never get close enough for them to know. As far as the women in my life are concerned, I'm just a guy who works on an oil rig."

"Women?" She raised her eyebrows. "Like a herd?"

"My own personal harem. But I'm always open to new applicants."

"As intriguing as that sounds, I'm not very good in a crowd."

He agreed. She was a woman who wanted a conventional life. "So why aren't you married with three kids?"

"I really only want two. Maybe a dog. I don't know. I never met the right one."

"Dog or guy?"

She laughed. "Guy. I've dated, I almost got engaged. Most of them were really nice men. Smart, good jobs, dependable."

"But?"

214

"It's dumb and ridiculous." She stacked several dirty bowls together then carried them over to the sink. "I want . . . sparks. You know? That wild, chemical attraction. I want my stomach to clench when the man in my life touches me. I want to hold my breath when the phone rings in case it's him."

"Passion."

She wiped her hands on a towel. "Exactly. I haven't felt that before. Plus, it's slightly possible that I might have some trust issues, given my whole family situation."

"Your mom sending you away." He stood and walked around the counter. "My dad walked out on me when I was a kid."

"So you know what I mean."

He stopped in front of her. "We could be on *Oprah*," he said, staring into her blue eyes and wondering how it was possible for them to be such a beautiful color.

"Or *Dr. Phil.* I'm sort of addicted to him."

They were close enough that she was all he could think about. Her mouth beckoned and tempted, her body seemed to sway toward him. The kitchen crackled with electricity. When her eyes dilated, he knew she felt it too.

"Oh," she breathed. "But this was supposed to be a bad idea."

"It still is."

"But it's why you came over."

Was it? He hadn't consciously thought about it, but she could be right. "Tell me no and I'll go away."

"Just like that?"

He nodded.

She looked at him for a long time, then reached up and rubbed her thumb against his lower lip.

"What is it about good women and bad boys?" she asked softly. "You're a kind of a temptation I've never had to resist before."

"Do you want to resist?"

Did she? Gracie wasn't sure she had an answer. Of course not being able to think was part of the problem. With Riley standing so close, staring at her as if he wanted her more desperately than he'd ever wanted any other woman ever, she found herself melting inside.

Her body ached. Every inch of skin longed to be touched by him. She wanted to feel him against her, in her. She wanted to lose control and take him with her. She wanted them both aroused, desperate, helpless in the face of their desire, then she wanted to be with him afterwards, when they touched and kissed in the wonderment of what they'd just done.

Of course this was Riley whose philosophy with women didn't exactly lend itself to tenderness. Was she prepared for him not sticking around? Was she prepared to be part of the three *F's*?

He lightly stroked her cheek. The soft brush of his fingers shouldn't have been all that exciting, but she felt her body respond to the flash of what could only be described as sparks.

And then she knew it didn't matter about after or what the neighbors would say or her past or his. Because the Riley she'd wanted fourteen years ago had been little more than a cardboard cutout. She hadn't known enough to make him real. While the man in front of her was pretty spectacular.

"You're going to hurt yourself with all that thinking," he said. "Look, Gracie, if you have to talk yourself into it, I'm not interested in —"

She raised herself on tiptoes and pressed her mouth to his, effectively cutting him off in midsentence. The hand by her cheek dropped to rest on her shoulder, but otherwise he didn't move.

Ah, so he was going to make her prove to him she wanted this. That was fine — she was more than up to the challenge.

As she moved her lips against his, she

217

grabbed his shirt and pulled it free of his slacks. Even as she stroked her tongue against his bottom lip, she slipped her hands under the shirt and rubbed them across his belly then up his chest.

She was prepared to do more — a lot more — to convince him, but it turned out to be unnecessary. His mouth parted and he claimed her in a kiss so deep, she thought she could get lost in it forever, even as his arms came around her and hauled her hard against him.

Her hands were trapped between them, but that didn't matter. Not when his tongue stroked hers, circled, danced and caused the sparks to explode into a whole fireworks show. He was warm and strong and when she shifted her hips, she found out he was already hard.

Instantly her stomach clenched, as did her thighs. Between her legs she felt both heat and dampness. Wanting exploded.

She pulled her arms free and moved her hands around to his back. She was still under the shirt so she could feel his bare skin. Muscles bunched as she moved over them. She slipped lower to his hips then his butt where she gently squeezed the tight, high curve.

Oh, yeah, this was good, she thought hazily as he surged against her. She rotated her pelvis, bringing herself more firmly in contact with his erection. Desire flowed hotter and faster.

He pulled back a little and lowered his head so he could kiss her neck. He lingered at the sensitive spot below her ear, nibbling and licking until her entire body tingled. He reached for the hem of her T-shirt and tugged at it. She released him long enough to let him pull it over her head.

When he'd tossed the garment aside, he stared into her eyes. She looked back at all the passion swirling in his and felt herself surrendering more.

"I want you," he breathed as he set his hands on her waist and began to move them higher.

Anticipation swelled within her. Her breasts ached, her nipples tightened. *Touch me,* she screamed silently, but what she said was, "I want you, too."

"Yeah?"

As he asked the question, he brushed his thumbs across her nipples. Sparks moved past fireworks and became an entire electrical storm. She arched her head back and silently begged him to do more, to never stop, to keep —

He bent down and took her nipple in his

mouth. Even through the fabric of her bra, she felt the heat and moisture, the light grating of his teeth. She clutched at him, as much to keep her balance as to hold him in place. He couldn't stop. Not ever. It felt too good.

He reached for the two hooks on the back of her bra. When it slid down her arms, she released him long enough to shove it away. Then he was back, his mouth on her bare flesh and it was all she could do not to scream.

"Oh, yes!" she moaned, eyes closed, breathing shallow.

He circled her nipple, then sucked on it. He caressed the other breast with his fingers. It was incredible. No better. It was need and heat and wanting all merging and growing until she could only gasp with the pleasure.

She ran her fingers through his hair, then over his shoulders. Suddenly she wanted him naked. She wanted to touch him.

"Riley," she whispered as she reached for the button on her khakis. "Take your clothes off."

She liked that she didn't have to ask twice. He straightened and immediately went to work on his shirt. After unfastening the cuffs, he simply pulled it over his head, tie and all. He kicked off his shoes, pulled off socks, then dropped his trousers and boxers in one easy movement.

She'd managed to shed the rest of her clothes and enjoy the view for all of three seconds before he moved in and claimed her with a kiss that stirred her down to her soul. They clung to each other, holding, rubbing, reaching, grasping.

He started nudging her backward. She couldn't stop kissing him to figure out where they were going. Then his hand was on her breast and it didn't matter.

She reached between them to caress his arousal just as she felt herself bump into the table.

Riley leaned around her and swept the surface clean. Pans and racks went flying to the floor. The crash of metal on tile reverberated in the room, but she didn't care. Not when he lifted her up onto the smooth wood of the table and positioned himself between her legs.

She opened herself wide for him, expecting him to claim her that minute. Instead he slid one hand behind her head and the other into the swollen wetness of her desire. His fingers found that one spot she liked best and began to circle it.

"Look at me," he said when she would

have closed her eyes. "I want to see if you like it."

She smiled. "I like it a lot."

"Yeah? What about when I do this?"

He gently squeezed his thumb and index finger around the sensitive flesh, moving up and down in a quick motion that took her breath away.

Speech became impossible as she lost herself in sensation. Her body tensed as liquid pleasure poured through her. She couldn't breathe, couldn't think, couldn't do anything but stay impossibly still and silently beg him to never stop.

He didn't. He kept on touching her until her release became as inevitable as the tide. She slowly closed her eyes, then held on to his shoulders as she got closer and closer until —

He stopped. She opened her mouth to protest. She'd been seconds from —

He kissed her. At the same moment he claimed her mouth, he pushed deep into her, replacing his fingers with something far larger and more impressive. She groaned, then wrapped her legs around his hips to hold him in place.

Even as their tongues mated, he moved in and out of her. She felt his thickness rubbing her, pushing her already aroused body past any reasonable limit to that place where pleasure is the only possibility. She clung to him, wanting, needing, straining until at last she lost herself in the wildness of her climax. Muscles contracted, released, then contracted again. She gasped as it went on and on. He continued to fill her, getting harder and thicker until at last, when she'd nearly finished, he shuddered and pushed into her one last time.

Gracie would swear she'd actually lost consciousness for a second or two. When her brain resurfaced she found herself leaning against him, breathing heavily. His arms held her tightly against him as if he would never let go. His heart thundered in her ear.

She raised her head and smiled at him. "Not bad."

He chuckled, then cupped her face in his hands and lightly kissed her. "I was going to say that."

"So you've had worse?"

"Oh, yeah."

"Better?"

He kissed her again. "Not possible."

"Good."

She felt relaxed and comfortable and just a little squishy inside. Why was there never a box of tissues around when you needed them? Usually she did this sort of thing in her bedroom where there were supplies, like tissues and condoms and —

Oh . . . my . . . God. She pushed him away and slid down until she stood on the floor and faced him.

"What?" he asked. "Did you get a leg cramp?"

"We didn't use any protection."

Good humor faded as if it had never been. "You're not on the Pill?"

"No." Several things happened all at once. The smell of burning cake suddenly filled the kitchen just as she noticed the smoke pouring out of the oven. Riley took several steps back, as if to put physical distance between himself and what they'd done, and someone started pounding on her front door.

Gracie shrieked and reached for her clothes. "I'll accept anyone but my mother," she said as she pulled on her panties. "And don't you give me that look. I didn't do this on purpose."

"I know."

"Not every woman in America is on the Pill."

"I know that, too."

"Then you have no right to be mad at me."

"I'm not. I'm mad at myself."

She didn't think that was any better. The pounding continued, along with a faint cry of "Gracie? Gracie? Are you home?"

"I think it's the woman who lives next door," Gracie said.

She fastened her bra, then stepped into her pants. Riley had already pulled on his slacks.

"Could you get the oven?" she said. "I don't want the smoke detector coming on."

He did as she requested. She grabbed her shirt and shot out of the kitchen. After tugging the T-shirt in place, she smoothed her hair, then pulled open the door.

"Hi," she said, smiling brightly and hoping her neighbor, whose name she couldn't remember, wouldn't notice anything was wrong.

"Oh, Gracie. I'm so glad you're here. It's Muffin. She fell in the pool and I can't get her out. She won't come to the steps. She's just swimming around and it's been so long. Please. Please come help me!"

The woman, late sixties with the wrinkled appearance of someone who had lived hard and was now tired, actually wrung her hands together. It was already dark and there was a cool breeze off the ocean. The last thing Gracie wanted to do was jump into a cold swimming pool, but she forced herself to nod.

"Let me grab my shoes," she said. "I'll be right there."

She turned back to find Riley in the hallway. He finished tucking in his shirt.

"The neighbor's dog fell in the pool," she said.

"I heard. I'll take care of it."

She blinked at him. "Excuse me?"

"I'll do it. It's cold out there. I'd appreciate a towel or two, though."

He walked past her before she could say anything. Her neighbor — Gracie still couldn't remember her name — clutched his arm.

"Oh, thank you so much. I don't know what I was going to do. Little Muffin seems to be losing strength. Plus the water is so cold and she's so small." The woman gave a sob.

Gracie was about to head after them when she remembered the towels. She dashed into her bathroom, pulled out three, then hurried to the front of the house and over to her neighbor's.

By the time she got there, Riley had already pulled off his shirt and shoes and waded into the pool. Muffin, a very small and wet Yorkie, paddled furiously, but not in the direction of her rescuer. As Riley approached the dog growled and paddled toward the deep end.

"Muffin, no!" the older woman cried. "The nice man is trying to help you. Go to him, honey. Go on. Mommy says it will be fine."

Gracie crouched by the edge of the pool. Riley shot her an unamused glanced.

"Don't say it's my fault," she told him. "You volunteered."

"Next time stop me." He muttered something under his breath that sounded fairly unrepeatable in mixed company, then he moved out toward Muffin.

The Yorkie might be tiny but she was a fine swimmer who zipped across the pool like a missile. Every time Riley moved within grabbing distance, she darted away.

In the lights from around the pool Gracie saw Riley shiver in the freezing water. She stuck her fingers into the pool, then quickly pulled them back. Okay, maybe it wasn't a good idea for both of them to get chilled to the bone.

Riley finally cornered the small dog by the ladder in the deep end. As he treaded water, he reached out for Muffin. The dog moved left. Riley grabbed her and pulled her close. Man and dog instantly yelped, but he didn't let go.

Still cursing under his breath, he swam the foot or two to the side of the pool and tossed Muffin to safety, then started climbing the ladder. Gracie hurried around to hand him a towel. It was only then that she saw the little dog had scratched up his chest.

"I'm so sorry," she said. "I'm sure she didn't mean it."

"It hurts as much as if she did."

The neighbor wrapped her dog in a fluffy white towel and cooed. "There's a good girl. There's a pretty girl. You need to stay away from the big, bad pool." The woman looked up. "I don't know how to thank you."

"It's fine," Riley said. He started to the gate that would take him out of her yard. "Good night."

"Oh, wait. I could pay you something."

Riley waved and kept walking. Gracie hurried after him.

"We need to get you cleaned up," she said. "Those scratches look —"

She never got to finish her sentence. As Riley stepped out onto the driveway there was a huge flash of light. Seconds later Gracie heard the sound of running feet, then a car door slammed, an engine started and the vehicle sped away.

CHAPTER ELEVEN

"This is *not* happening," Gracie said in a voice that was uncomfortably close to a shriek.

Rather than respond, Riley grabbed her hand and pulled her back inside her house. When the door was firmly closed and locked, he glanced down at the oozing scratches on his chest and swore.

"Damn dog."

Gracie spun toward him. "Yes, the dog was really bad, but did you see that? Did you see the guy with the camera? What's going on? Who's doing this? And why? I'm totally creeped out. Some man was lurking outside my house. He was obviously following one of us and —" She looked at his chest and winced. "Bathroom. Now."

He followed her down the short hallway into an old-fashioned bathroom decorated in various and unappealing shades of green.

Gracie dug around in the cabinet, then

229

straightened and held out a tube of something. "I don't think this will hurt too much, but we've got to get something on those scratches. Should we wash them first?"

"I think the pool took care of that. It was cold as hell, but I could smell the chlorine."

She glanced down at his soaked and dripping trousers. "So those will be ruined."

He figured his clothes were the least of his concern. He didn't much care about the marks on his chest either — what had his full attention was the man taking pictures. Gracie's life hardly supported the idea of her having a lot of angry enemies trying to ruin her, which left only one alternative. Someone was setting him up.

But for what reason? Was someone unhappy about him running the bank? He figured that was possible, but not likely. Which left Franklin Yardley, mayor of Los Lobos — a man determined not to lose his election.

"Deep breath," Gracie said as she opened the tube of ointment.

"I promise not to scream like a woman," he said dryly.

"Good to know."

As she smoothed on the medication, he considered possibilities. The only way the asshole photographer could have been there at the right moment was if he'd been hanging around, watching. So he was following Riley. Or someone had tipped him off.

He looked at Gracie as she worked. Of everyone in town, she knew the most about his comings and goings. She'd hesitated before coming to the door. Could she have made a phone call?

Even as he considered the question, he wanted to dismiss it. There was no way Gracie would set him up.

His refusal to seriously consider her as a suspect told him two things — first, that he was in more trouble where she was concerned than he'd first realized. And second, that she was probably guilty as hell.

Gracie stood in the center of her driveway and told herself to keep breathing. It had been one of those nights, where the churning in her stomach had kept her up past midnight and her whirling thoughts had taken care of the rest of the hours. She felt sluggish and crabby and completely and totally furious.

There was a huge "above the fold" picture of Riley on the front page of the local paper. He had a towel over his head, as if trying to hide from the camera, when she knew darned well he'd just been drying off his hair. Worse, there were scratches on his chest. In the picture, they didn't look as fresh and angry as they had in person. Instead they looked as if they could have been caused by a night of wild sex.

The headline didn't help: Mayoral Candidate's Secret Life.

Gracie wanted to stomp her foot and scream. She did neither, mostly because it was very early and she was barefoot.

So now what? Where could she go to complain? A letter to the editor? A banner across Main Street? Could she just find Mayor Yardley and smack him upside the head?

She squinted at the picture again, then groaned. She was there. In the background, but still clearly visible, looking shocked and more than a little disheveled.

Gracie crumpled the paper in her hands and slowly made her way back to the rental. She did *not* need this in her life. She had cakes to bake and a meeting at lunchtime at her mother's to discuss a wedding that may or may not still be on and . . . . "I need a vacation," she mumbled as she stepped back into the house and slammed the door behind her.

Gracie hovered on the front porch of her

mother's house. She didn't want to be here. After what had happened just a few days ago, she never wanted to walk inside again.

To be honest, she wasn't sure how she'd found herself agreeing to yet another planning meeting. Alexis had called and insisted and somehow Gracie had said yes.

"Talk about stupid," she muttered, then stepped up to the front door and knocked.

The door opened instantly. Alexis smiled. "Good. You made it. Come in."

Gracie followed her inside. Her sister moved into the living room where Vivian sat by the window.

"Where's Mom?" Gracie asked.

"She's not coming," Alexis said, turning toward her and folding her arms across her chest. "She doesn't know about this."

Gracie didn't like the sound of that. "Want to explain yourself?"

Vivian stood and smoothed the front of her flower print dress. "You really hurt her feelings the last time you were here. She wouldn't tell us what you two fought about, but she's still upset. You can't do this, Gracie. You can't make everything about yourself."

"You're right," Gracie said, unable to believe they'd set her up to attack her. "That's your job."

233

Vivian's mouth dropped open. "That is so not true. Alexis, can you believe she said that? Make her apologize."

Gracie shook her head. "I'm out of here."

"No." Alexis grabbed her arm. "Gracie, wait. We have to talk about this. Please. We're worried about you."

Which sounded great, Gracie through grimly, but she'd learned enough about her sisters in the past couple of weeks to be wary of just about everything her family had to say.

Gracie pulled free of Alexis and walked to the sofa where she perched on the edge of a cushion. She had a bad feeling she knew what was coming. Vivian sat across from her, while Alexis took the other end of the sofa.

"We're worried about you and Riley," Alexis said.

"I knew it." Gracie wanted to spring to her feet and run screaming from the room. "I knew that was exactly what you were going to want to talk about." She glared at her sister. "I'll accept it from my mother, because of who she is, but there is no way I'm going to take it from you. Need I remind you that *you* are the reason I had to deal with him in the first place. You're the one who had me sneaking around his house

234

and taking pictures."

"I understand that I had some small part in it," Alexis said primly.

"Some small part?" Gracie had the sense of being in an alternate universe where logic no longer existed. She turned her attention to Vivian. "Are you here to lecture me about Riley, too, or do you have something else?"

"No. It's Riley."

"Great. Then let's get one thing straight. I don't care what you think or say. I'm going to do what I want. But for the record, we are not involved. There is absolutely nothing between us. We're —"

Sleeping together. Oh, yeah. In her outrage, she'd forgotten that one simple fact.

"Then explain this," Alexis said, pulling the newspaper out from under the coffee table and slapping it on the surface. "What exactly were you two doing?"

"My neighbor's dog fell in the pool. She came over in a complete panic. Riley went in after her dog, despite the fact that the water was freezing cold. Unfortunately Muffin didn't understand the whole rescue concept and scratched him. I can get you her phone number if you'd like. She'll confirm everything."

Alexis didn't look convinced. "Why was he at your house in the first place?"

Interesting question, Gracie thought. She realized she had no clue what had made him stop by.

"Why does that matter? You don't get to tell me who my friends are."

"Are you friends?" Vivian asked. "Or is it just the illusion of friendship?" She leaned forward and lowered her voice. "Gracie, honey, we're so worried. You're in a really fragile state right now."

"*I'm* fragile?"

Vivian nodded. "I feel your pain. Despite the fact that we should really be talking about me and my wedding, I have enough compassion to know what you're going through. I'm sorry you never fit in."

Gracie narrowed her gaze. "What are you talking about?"

"In high school. I know you were unpopular and a misfit. You've never had any friends. No one liked you and now you're back here, reliving your youthful crush on Riley."

Gracie stood. "Okay, that's it. I'm tired of being used and insulted."

Vivian rose. "I'm trying to help."

"I don't think so, but if this is your idea of help, I don't want it or need it. You don't know anything about my life. How dare you make judgments? For your information, I

236

did fine in high school. I got good grades, I had friends, I was a cheerleader and gosh, I was elected to the Homecoming court. Oh, my boyfriend even expected me to sleep with him after prom. Sounds pretty traditional to me, but then I didn't grow up here. I don't know what your expectations are."

Alexis sighed. "Vivian, you're not helping. Sit down and shut up."

"What do you mean I'm not helping? I'm trying to make her understand."

"What do you want me to understand?" Gracie asked. "What exactly is your point?"

Vivian's eyes filled with tears. "This is all about you and Riley. What about me? What about my wedding?"

"Is the wedding back on this week? Wow. Color me surprised."

Vivian glared at her. "So you're not just pathetic, you're also a bitch."

Gracie looked at the two women. "Fine. You guys win. Think what you want. If your opinion of me is that I'm a bitch obsessed with the man from my youth, I can live with that."

She turned to leave.

Alexis jumped to her feet. "Gracie, don't. We have to work this out. We're family."

Were they? She thought about her aunt and uncle. She'd barely known them when she'd moved in with them, but they'd loved her and cared about her. They'd always been supportive and loving. When they'd been killed in that car accident, she thought she would never recover.

"Don't bother," Vivian said as she wiped her face. "She's just mad because I didn't ask her to be in the wedding. And I'm glad, Gracie. You hear me? I'm really, really glad."

Gracie walked to the door, then glanced back. "Me, too," she said softly and left.

Gracie climbed into her car and pulled out her cell. The little message envelope flashed, but she couldn't think of a single person she wanted to talk to right now. She shoved the phone back in her purse and considered her next destination. She didn't really want to go back to the rental. Too many memories.

She started the car, then made a U-turn and headed across town. As she pulled into the parking lot of the bed-and-breakfast, she noted Pam's car.

Still, the potential to get lost in her baking seemed more enticing than her worry that she would run into the other woman, so she parked and went inside.

Twenty minutes later she had a preheated oven, plenty of batter in large bowls and the measurable lifting of her spirits. She'd just started to pour when Pam walked in.

The slender blonde looked stunning, as usual. She smiled as she leaned against the counter and set down several fabric samples.

"Can I lick the bowls when you're done?" she asked with a grin.

"Raw eggs. I doubt you want to risk it."

"Hmm, good point. Still, I love the way your cakes smell. If I could find a way to bottle the scent, I could make a fortune. Instead I'm knee-deep in fabric samples." She held up two dark prints covered with flowers. "What do you think?"

"They're both really nice."

Pam laughed. "Let me guess. Decorating isn't your thing."

"Not really."

"I enjoy it. I think the B&B is going to be a lot of fun." She sighed. "I would be happier if there really had been an alien landing like we all thought in high school."

Gracie finished pouring and carried the pans to the oven. "I can't see extraterrestrials flying all the way to earth only to land in Los Lobos. Don't you think they'd want somewhere with better shopping and more restaurant choices?"

"Good point. Although I can think of a few people I'd like taken away by aliens."

"Oh, me, too," Gracie said as she straightened. "We could start a list."

"Can I go first?" Pam grinned.

Gracie carried the bowls over to the sink. "Do you have a grand opening date yet?"

"I'm thinking the Fourth of July weekend. Plenty of tourists looking for a place to stay. I've put out the word and I'm already getting reservations. Of course that puts the pressure on for me to finish, but hey, I can manage. Sleep is highly overrated."

Gracie nodded as she ran water in the bowls. This all felt so weird. She was standing here having a perfectly normal conversation with Pam Whitefield, whom she had always hated. But Pam seemed to be completely nice while Gracie's own sisters were acting mean enough to be candidates for demonic possession. What was going on?

"Are you getting a lot of flak about the picture in the paper?" Pam asked. "I confess I saw it this morning."

"Not a surprise," Gracie told her. "It was on the front page. Hard to miss."

"I'm sorry. It's a real drag for you. But Riley looked good. He always did have an impressive body."

"He was helping my neighbor. Her dog fell in the pool."

"So that explains the scratches."

240

"Exactly. Little Muffin wasn't as grateful as she could have been." She finished with the bowls, wiped her hands, then turned back to Pam. "Then some guy takes the picture and suddenly Riley's in the middle of a scandal. Poor guy."

Pam's kind expression didn't change, although Gracie thought she might have seen a little sharpening around the eyes. Or was that just her looking for trouble?

"So you're not . . ." Pam shrugged delicately.

Not sure if she was being set up or no, Gracie sighed. "I swear, there was a pool, a trapped Yorkie and a frantic neighbor." Yes, there had also been sex, but she wasn't about to spill that.

"Just as well," Pam said. "Riley looked great, but he never really grasped the whole 'pleasing a woman' thing."

Gracie had to bite her tongue to keep from defending him. "Bummer," she said instead.

Pam tilted her head. "It would be kind of sweet if you two got together after all this time."

That made Gracie choke. "You've got to be kidding. Aside from the fact that you're about the last person who should want that, I can't imagine any universe in which it would be considered normal."

Pam looked away. "Sometimes you can't fight fate."

Gracie returned to her rental late that afternoon feeling as if she'd run a marathon, or at least a half one. She was weary to the bone, slightly beat-up and more than a little out of sorts.

She couldn't make sense of her world, which was unlike her. In the past few years, she'd prided herself on living smack in the middle of normal. Coming back to Los Lobos had changed all that. Okay — coming back to Los Lobos and getting involved with Riley had changed all that.

While she didn't mind the Riley part of her life, the rest of it wasn't so easy to deal with. She didn't like fighting with her family. She'd had the fantasy of a warm and loving reunion in mind, but the reality was about as far from that as it was possible to get. She hated the lectures, the assumptions, the judging, the rejection. Worse, without them, she was truly alone.

Gracie tried to tell herself that she'd been alone since the death of her aunt and uncle. The only difference was now she knew it whereas before she'd hoped she had more.

Only the news didn't make her feel any better.

Fighting a headache, she pulled into the driveway of her rental only to see a familiar car parked next to her spot. The gleaming Mercedes made her heart beat a little faster, but that was nothing compared with the rapid tap dance it took up when Riley stepped out and nodded at her.

Man, oh man, did he look good. She liked the way the sunlight caught the earring he wore. How many bank presidents claimed that slightly sexy, slightly dangerous look? She liked that he was strong and determined and someone she could count on. She liked how he made her feel inside. Okay, she liked how he made her feel on the outside, too. She wanted —

Gracie stopped her car and turned off the engine. In the second it took her to drop her keys into her purse and open the door to step out, she reminded herself that not only was she in town for a few weeks, but that she couldn't seriously think about getting involved with Riley.

No, no, no, no, no. Not him. Remember? Anyone but him. He was her past, her scary obsession. He was a man going in one direction and she . . . she was going somewhere else.

"Hi," she said as she got out and slammed her door shut.

"Hey."

"Have you been waiting long?"

He shrugged. "About fifteen minutes. I was about to call your cell."

"I was at Pam's. Baking. So what's up?"

"We have to talk."

She couldn't help smiling. "Riley, that's the girl's line. I thought guys took an oath to never say it."

"This time it's true. We have to talk about last night. We didn't use a condom. If you're not on the Pill, we have to discuss what could happen."

CHAPTER TWELVE

Riley watched closely as Gracie reacted to his statement. Her eyes widened slightly, her mouth twisted and her shoulders slumped. Obviously this was not the topic she'd hoped they would discuss. But did that mean she was guilty of setting him up in more ways than one?

He couldn't decide, and he hadn't been able to come to a decision all day. He wanted to say he knew Gracie, but did he? She was funny and smart and led with her heart and her chin, but he'd been used by women before. Was she any different or was she just better at it?

"Come on in," she said, and led the way into the house.

He followed her into the kitchen where she put down her purse and turned toward him. She folded her arms over her chest.

"It was just one time," she said, sounding more defensive than angry. "The odds of anything happening are really, really slim."

What he didn't understand was how it had happened at all. Ever since he'd been a kid and thought he'd gotten Pam pregnant, he'd been obsessively careful. But last night. . . .

"I agree it's unlikely," he said. "But I want to know."

She nodded and walked to the large calendar on the wall. Stickers of cakes had been placed on various dates with the names and locations next to them in black felt pen. She counted out the days twice, then sighed.

"My period is due in twelve days."

Riley figured he knew as much or as little about the inner workings of the female reproductive system as the next guy. He prided himself on being good in bed, but the baby-making stuff was more of a mystery. Information reluctantly learned in high school sex-ed drifted through his brain. If he remembered correctly, midcycle was the most dangerous time. Well, shit.

"How long after that can you find out if you're pregnant?" he asked.

She winced. "I don't know. A couple of days. I've never used a pregnancy test myself, but I've heard they're fast and you don't need to be very late."

She turned to face him. Her eyes were

wide and troubled. "Don't you think it's a tiny bit premature to be having this conversation? Can't we just wait and see what happens?"

"Sure."

He had the information he needed now. He would bide his time until she either got her period or he had proof she was pregnant. While he didn't want a repeat of Pam's performance, he also wasn't willing to walk away from his responsibilities. His father had walked out twenty-one years ago, but Riley still remembered everything about the day. He wouldn't do that to any kid of his.

"It's just the odds are so against me being . . . you know." She swallowed. "Honestly, I can't take on one more thing. I've got wedding cakes, my family, you, whoever is following one of us, the newspaper pictures. I just can't deal with any more."

As she spoke, she reached for her purse, then dug out her bottle of antacids. After popping two and chewing them, she sighed.

"I'm such a rock, huh?" she asked softly.

"You do okay."

"I'm not so sure. I thought coming back here would be easy, but it's not. Who was that guy last night? Is he after me or you? I'm guessing you, because of the election. Plus you have the debate in a couple of days. But it's creepy. And I hate the newspaper thing. The picture. I feel so bad about it, but it wasn't my fault. Still. . . ."

She pulled up a bar stool and sat down. She rested her elbows on the counter and her head in her hands.

"I'm being a lousy hostess," she said. "There's cake in the cupboard and stuff to drink in the refrigerator. Help yourself."

She didn't look like someone planning his demise, he thought. If he had to put money on it right now, he would say Gracie wasn't involved. But was that his gut talking or his dick? Because even now he wanted her. Slumped shoulders and pouty expression, it didn't matter.

"Don't you have any real food?" he asked.

She turned her head so she could stare at him. "What?"

"You're always offering me cake. What about a sandwich or meat loaf?"

She straightened. "I don't keep bread in the house. What kind of insanity would that be?"

"But you have cake."

"I make cakes. It's tough not to have them in the house when I actually bake them. But I don't really cook, so you're not going to find meat loaf ever. I think I have a few cans of soup. And my tuna salad. That's a staple in my life."

"Do you eat anything other than cake and tuna?"

"Sure. Salads. Fruit. I have some soy-based granola in the cupboard."

He grimaced and claimed the stool next to hers. "No thanks."

"It's really good."

"You're really lying."

"A little." She turned so she faced him. "You still mad at me?"

"I was never mad."

She sighed. "Yeah, you were. When I first got here. Are you thinking. . . ." She shrugged. "I guess I don't know what you were thinking, but it can't have been good. I didn't. . . . I'm not the one doing all this."

"I know," he said, because he wanted to believe her. "I hired a private detective from L.A. He's coming up in the morning and he'll find the photographer. Once we know who's taking the pictures, we'll find the person behind it."

He watched her as he spoke, looking for hints of panic or concern. Instead she held his gaze and when he'd finished said, "I can't wait to get to the bottom of this. We'll both feel better with some answers."

Which meant what? That she wasn't the one setting him up? He wanted Gracie to be innocent, which bugged the hell out of him. He didn't get involved — not ever. He'd yet to see the purpose of anything longer than a night with a woman. Keeping his distance meant he didn't get betrayed. So why was he still here?

"My sisters had an intervention today," she said. "It was pretty horrible. Alexis thinks I'm obsessing about you. She seems to have completely forgotten that I only got involved because of her. Vivian is convinced I had a completely horrible time in high school, that I was a social misfit with no friends and no boyfriend. Where do they get that? I was normal. I was a cheerleader."

"Yeah. I can see that shallow perkiness in you."

Her gaze narrowed. "I'm not shallow and I'm not especially perky."

"You're a little off beat."

"I can accept that. My world view is slightly skewed, but I like that about me." Her shoulders slumped again. "Pam is confusing."

"Pam? My ex-wife?"

"That would be her. I've been using her kitchen at the bed-and-breakfast, which means I run into her. She's been really . . . nice."

He'd expected a lot of words, but that

250

wasn't one of them. "Are we talking about the same Pam?"

"Sure. Tall, skinny, blond. Great clothes." Gracie leaned back on the bar stool. "It's annoying, let me tell you. But the thing is, she's been really sweet. Saying nice stuff about you, even."

"What a humanitarian."

"It's kind of creepy. I almost want to like her, but I can't. Still, I don't know why she's acting this way. Jill told me she was still really bitchy, but she hasn't been to me. You think she's up to something?"

"You don't want to take her at face value?"

"I should, huh? I mean it's totally horrible of me to judge her, but I can't help it. I want to like her but every time I try a little voice in my head starts screaming. Which means either she's faking me out or I'm a really bad person."

"You're not a bad person."

"You don't know me well enough to decide."

"Sure I do."

He stood and reached for her hand, then pulled her to her feet and drew her into his arms.

"It's okay not to like Pam," he said, his lips pressing against her forehead. "I won't tell."

"Thanks." She snuggled closer, pressing her body against his.

She felt good, he thought. Warm. Soft.

"You're not supposed to be doing this," she told him. "What about the three *F's*?"

He stared into her blue eyes. At that moment he would swear he could see down to her soul. There weren't any secrets, any dark places. Which meant one of two things — either he was a complete sap and she was a great actress, or he was messing where he didn't belong.

"I already told you, I can't forget you," he said.

Her gaze held his. "We didn't do the other *F* either. You know that, right? We made love last night."

It wasn't something he liked to think about, but he nodded in agreement. "Yes, Gracie, we made love."

The words came from a place deep inside. He wasn't sure he'd ever said them before and he knew he'd never meant them. Until Gracie.

What the hell was he doing?

He released her and stepped back. "I gotta run," he said.

"Okay. Thanks for stopping by."

He waved, then turned on his heel and stalked out of the room.

Priorities, he told himself. He had them and he couldn't forget them. He didn't get involved, he didn't care, he didn't stick around. Nothing was going to change that. Not this town and certainly not Gracie.

Riley spent the morning of the debate in his office at the bank. The loan department had just sent up its weekly report, which Diane handed to him.

"Business is up," she said as he flipped through the file. "A lot of home loan refinancing."

"I can see that," he said, aware she was making a point that he was just as determined to ignore.

"Those people — the customers — are going to expect to have the thirty years to repay. What's going to happen to them?"

Riley didn't answer. They both knew what would happen. If he closed the bank, the loans would be recalled. Every single customer would have less than three months to secure new financing. If they couldn't, they would lose their house.

"I know you think your uncle was a bastard, Riley, but are you sure you're making the right person pay for that?"

The soft words couldn't have been more shocking if Diane had written them in blood. He stared at his secretary, wondering which was more surprising — that she'd called him by his first name or that she'd used foul language.

"You're walking a thin line," he told her.

She smiled. "Are you going to fire me?"

"No."

"Then I fail to see the danger." Her smile faded. "You could do some good here," she told him. "You've taken to the work. You like it. This is much bigger than your grandfather. This is about the community."

"Want to know that I don't give a rat's ass?"

She stared at him for a long time. "Then expecting more from you was my mistake."

She left without saying anything else. When he was alone again, Riley turned in his chair and stared at the portrait of his uncle.

"Sorry, big guy," he said. "I'm not interested in saving your town. You thought you'd won this round — that I would do what you said to get the money. But things aren't going to turn out the way you expected. I'm going to win — my only regret is that you're not alive to watch me screw you."

Gracie arrived at the community center just

before three. She had a lot of memories of the old building — many school events had been held there, along with her Girl Scout meetings. There were smaller classroom-size spaces on the second floor and a larger open area on the first. She knew the debate would be held in the largest space, but she didn't head in that direction. Instead she circled around back and came in a rear entrance, so as not to cause a stir. She found Jill hovering by the heavy door. Her friend waved her in.

"I saved us a couple of seats," Jill said in a low voice. "Hurry. They're about to start."

Gracie followed her inside. The lights over the audience had dimmed a little, leaving the two candidates in bright light up on stage. People were still settling and talking.

Jill led her to two seats on the far right side, three rows from the back. Gracie let Jill go in first, so she could be on the end and duck out quickly if she had to.

"It's a big crowd," Jill said quietly as she glanced around. "I doubt anyone will notice you're here."

"That's the plan," Gracie said. "I didn't expect this many people."

"Me, either. They're broadcasting the debate live on the radio."

Gracie slumped down in her seat and tried

not to make eye contact with anyone. "I probably should have stayed home and listened to it there."

It would have been the sensible decision, but in truth, she'd really wanted to see Riley. Being around him seemed to set her world back on its axis. She supposed she should be upset about them making love, but she wasn't. It had felt too right to be in his arms. And last night . . . when he'd held her . . . she couldn't help wanting him to never let go.

She did her best to ignore the red flashing Danger signs in her head. Yeah, yeah, she knew the drill. Getting involved with Riley was a mistake on too many levels to count. Even if she was willing to ignore the humiliation of falling for a guy she'd once stalked, there was the whole two different lives thing. His idea of a long-term relationship was one that lasted two nights. She wanted forever. Until recently he'd lived on an oil rig and traveled the world and she rarely left her neighborhood. They had nothing in common and. . . .

She frowned. Except for his seeming inability to commit to a woman for more than twenty-four hours, what was the problem? He was a great guy, she liked him, they had fun together. Was she overanalyzing this?

256

Was there —

"So what's going on with you?" Jill asked, keeping her voice low. "How's the cake business?"

"Good. Busy. It's that time of year. The Pam thing is difficult."

Jill grinned. "Are the cakes taking one look at her and falling?"

Gracie chuckled. "Actually not. It's more creepy than that. She's . . . nice."

Jill raised her eyebrows. "Not possible."

"I know. That's my feeling, too. But it's true — she's pleasant and friendly and accommodating. She even said nice stuff about Riley. I can't decide if I should just accept her at face value or continue to be wary."

"You know what my vote would be."

"Yeah. To keep my distance and carry a cross at all times."

"Exactly. Everything else okay?"

Gracie nodded. As much as she would like to talk about her family, this wasn't the place. Nor could she tell Jill what had happened with Riley. Eventually she would come clean, but not in a crowd.

Maybe she should regret what had happened, she thought. But she couldn't. The pregnancy thing was a little troubling. She pressed a hand to her stomach and told herself it wasn't possible. Statistically, the odds were seriously against it. Although she had to respect the irony of the situation if she *was* pregnant, what with Pam faking her pregnancy all those years ago so Riley would marry her.

Gracie had a feeling that even if she turned up pregnant, he wouldn't be making an honest woman of her. She wasn't sure how she felt about that. While she'd never planned to be a single mother, she wouldn't turn her back on her baby. If Riley wasn't willing to participate, that was okay. But it made her sad to think he would walk way from his own child. Still, getting married just because of a pregnancy seemed like a recipe for disaster. She didn't want a relationship based on "have to." She wanted heart-stopping, bone-melting, forever and till death do us part love.

"What are you thinking about?" Jill asked. "You have the strangest look on your face."

"How did you know Mac was the one?"

Jill sighed. "I just did. At first we were just friends." She smiled. "Okay, *he* was just friends and I was crazy about him. He's so sexy. Anyway, we spent time together and it was always great. The more I got to know him, the more I wanted to know him. One thing led to another and then I was in love with him. Why do you ask?" Her gaze narrowed. "Are you —"

"Good evening, ladies and gentlemen," the moderator said. "Welcome to our first and only mayoral debate between our current mayor, Franklin Yardley, and his opponent, Riley Whitefield."

"Don't think I'm going to forget what we were talking about," Jill murmured in her ear as she turned her attention to the front of the room.

Gracie figured she would simply appreciate the interruption and deal with her friend later. She listened to the introduction of both candidates. Franklin Yardley looked as slick and polished as ever, but he was much older than his rival. Riley had the advantage of youth, size and mystery. There was something very appealing about the dark-haired stranger sitting on the mayor's left. Gracie had a feeling she wasn't the only woman in the audience who felt the pull.

The moderator explained the format. Each candidate would make an opening statement, then they would answer questions from the panel of newspaper reporters and professors from U.C. Santa Barbara. Finally, there would be a four-minute closing statement. Before the debate, the two men had drawn straws and Riley would be going first in the opening and closing statements.

He stood as he was introduced. Gracie found herself leaning forward, as if anticipating what he was going to say. He looked good, she thought. The dark suit flattered his strong, hard body. He wore his hair relatively short and brushed away from his face. His diamond stud glittered in the harsh overhead lighting.

Would the good citizens elect a man with an earring? Gracie wondered.

"Mayor Yardley has served our community for sixteen years," Riley began with a smile. "That's half my life. He's seen Los Lobos through good times and bad, strong tourist seasons and weak ones. He's learned the ins and outs of the job. I would guess after this many years, there aren't any surprises. He's a professional and a man of many talents."

He looked around the room. For a second, Gracie would have sworn their eyes met, but she was pretty sure she was sitting too far back for him to see her.

"I've spent the last fourteen years traveling around the world," he continued, "but in the end, there was only one place I could call home. While the sentimental side of me appreciates that Los Lobos has barely changed in all that time, the businessman inside of me wonders if that's really for the best. If we want our children to have a superior education that allows them to have a better standard of living, we need money to pay for schools. If we want a community that can stand on its own and not always be at the mercy of the tourist dollar, we have to come up with a thoughtful, innovative plan that will take us forward without forcing us to lose touch with the very values and philosophies that make us what we are."

"He's good," Jill whispered. "I'm impressed."

"Me, too."

Riley might have started his bid for mayor because it was a condition of his uncle's will, but he'd obviously embraced the idea and made it his own.

Riley finished his opening statement to the sound of loud applause. Mayor Yardley spoke, outlining his accomplishments in office. Next to Riley, he looked uncomfortable and out of place — as if he'd overstayed his welcome at a party.

The trend continued through the questions. Riley seemed to have a fresh take on every issue, while Yardley reiterated what he'd done before. Even from the back of the room, Gracie could see the older man starting to sweat.

"Riley's going to win this," Jill murmured. "He's really going to pull it off."

Gracie felt a fierce flush of pride, as if she had something to do with Riley's success. When he finished his closing statement, everyone in the room rose and cheered. It took several minutes for the crowd to settle down enough for Franklin Yardley to speak.

"You seem taken with my opponent," the mayor said slowly. "I can see why. He's new and shiny. Lots of big ideas. But it takes more than ideas to keep a city running smoothly. It takes practice and experience. And it takes character. You all know me. You're my neighbors, my friends. You've served on committees with my wife, gone to school with my children, played golf with me."

Yardley stared out at the crowd and smiled. "You know my secrets — the good and the bad about me."

A few people chuckled. "You're lousy at poker, Franklin," someone yelled.

The mayor nodded. "That I am. I've never had a good face for it. I can't tell a lie to save my soul. Things matter to me. My family. This town. I've been here all my life. Four generations of Yardleys have served in Los Lobos."

He paused and drew in a deep breath.

"Maybe it's time for a change. Maybe I've done all I can do. But is Riley Whitefield really the man you want? He's young. Inexperienced. He's been traipsing all over the world when he had business right here in town. Most of you know he took off to make his fortune while his own mother lay dying of cancer. Never even came back to see her. Not the example I want set for my children."

Gracie stiffened. "That's not what happened," she whispered to Jill as people began to stir in their seats. "He didn't know."

"You think Yardley cares about that?" Jill asked.

Gracie stared at the stage, looking for some reaction from Riley. He remained seated, his expression calm.

But the mayor wasn't finished. He leaned forward at the podium. "Riley was just a boy then. Barely eighteen. He'd had a difficult time, getting a local girl pregnant, marrying her, then divorcing her. But people grow up. The boy becomes a man. They change. Well, some do. I'm not so sure about Riley."

Gracie felt her stomach start to churn. She had a feeling this was going to be very, very bad.

Mayor Yardley glanced at Riley, then at the crowd. "Who do you want as the leader of your community? A man you know and trust? A man who has never lied or misled you? Or Riley Whitefield who is a stranger to us all? Not only did he walk out on his dying mother, he's returned to take advantage of our own Gracie Landon. She has loved him faithfully for years and he has repaid her with betrayal and scorn. Not only is she pregnant right this minute, but Riley is refusing to make an honest woman of her."

CHAPTER THIRTEEN

Gracie felt the room tilt. For a second she thought she might faint for the first time in her life. A rushing sound filled her ears, her body felt both too heavy and too light and she couldn't seem to focus on anything. Then her vision cleared and she watched Riley spring to his feet and stare at her in fury and shock.

"Gracie?" Jill asked. "Did you —"

Gracie didn't wait for Jill to finish her sentence. She could feel people looking at her, pointing, staring, talking. But none of that mattered. She didn't care about anything but Riley and what he must be thinking.

"I have to go," she said as she stood and ran to the door. She heard someone calling her name, but she didn't stop, didn't turn around.

"Is it true?" someone yelled. "Did Riley knock you up?"

Gracie felt burning in her stomach, but this pain had nothing to do with her usual acid issues. Instead this ache came from the realization she had gotten very close to something special and it had all just been ripped away from her.

Riley considered returning to the bank. It was just after five so he could easily head home, but for some reason he didn't want to be alone.

The debate had been a disaster. Yardley had been so damn cheerful at the outset that Riley had begun to suspect he was up to something. But he never would have guessed what. Yardley had struck hard and in exactly the right place. The good citizens of Los Lobos might be willing to overlook a lot of flaws but no one would forgive him messing with a town legend.

How had Yardley known? Had he taken a few facts and put them together? Or had someone told him what had happened? He hadn't said a word to anyone and he doubted Gracie had been spreading rumors. Which meant the information could only have come from her.

He parked in his designated spot behind the bank, then climbed out of his car. There were still a few people heading inside to conduct their business before closing. He saw a woman pushing a stroller along the sidewalk. The air was warm, the sky clear. Everything was completely normal. Yet he felt as if he'd been beaten up and left on the edge of the road.

How could she have done that to him? Why? He would have bet a considerable portion of his soon-to-be-lost inheritance that Gracie didn't like Mayor Yardley. So why would she help him? Bitterness over the past? Was this all an elaborate plan of revenge?

As he walked into the building, he told himself it might not be her. That whoever had followed them and taken the pictures could have seen enough to know what had happened. Until he had the report back from the private detective, he couldn't be sure of anything.

Except he didn't want it to be Gracie. Fourteen years ago, he would have sold his soul, or even his car, to get her out of his life. Now . . . Now he didn't know what he wanted.

He rounded the corner and headed for the elevator. Several employees stood together, talking quietly. As he approached, one of them nudged another. They all turned to look at him.

"Good afternoon, Mr. Whitefield," a young woman said. She didn't quite meet his gaze.

He nodded and stepped onto the elevator. They were talking again before the doors closed and all he heard was "Do you think it's true that he really —"

Word travels fast, he thought as he walked onto the second floor. He would guess the live radio broadcast was responsible. Zeke was going to be screaming tonight. They were going to have to come up with a great recovery plan and he didn't have a clue as to what it would be. Beating up Yardley might make him feel better, but wouldn't help the election. Same with suing the old bastard.

Riley moved into his office and closed the door behind him. He stared at the portrait of his uncle.

"You're not winning," he told the long-dead figure. "Not now, not ever. I'll find a way."

He would do what he'd always done when the odds were against him. He would put his head down and work harder than everyone else around him. He wouldn't let anything get in his way. Not the town, not the past, not the damn mayor and not even Gracie.

He heard a knock on his door.

"Go away," he called.

"Mr. Whitefield, you have someone here to see you."

"Not interested."

"This is important."

Riley knew he'd cleared his schedule for the day of the debate, so she wasn't talking about a meeting. Had Yardley come by to gloat?

He figured that wasn't the mayor's style. Curious, and more than a little interested in a distraction, he crossed to the door and pulled it open.

"Who is it?" he asked, even as he found himself hoping Gracie had stopped by to explain herself.

Rather than answer, Diane stepped back. Riley looked behind her, expecting to see a familiar, curvy blonde with a quirky disposition and a ready smile. Instead he saw a man in his mid-to-late fifties, dressed in a worn suit and a stained white shirt. The hair was grayer, the lines in his face deeper. Somehow he seemed a whole lot smaller than Riley recalled.

It might have been over twenty years, but Riley remembered everything about the man who had abandoned his mother and himself.

The old man gave him a twisted smile. "Hello, son. How have you been?"

Gracie drove halfway to Los Angeles before pulling off the freeway in Ventura and turning around to head back to Los Lobos. She gave herself the "I am a grown-up" lecture and reminded herself she couldn't run away from all her problems, even if it seemed like a good idea at the time.

She even believed herself — sort of. But if someone had offered her a one-way ticket to help colonize one of the moons of Jupiter, she probably would have signed right up.

There were too many emotions swirling inside of her for her to know what she was feeling. Sick, mostly. Sick and sad and angry at whomever had betrayed her. Except she hadn't told anyone what was going on, so where had the mayor gotten his information?

Her cell phone rang again. She grabbed it and glanced at the display screen, then tossed it back on the seat. So far she'd had three calls from Jill, two each from her sisters and about six from her mother. She wasn't in the mood to talk to any of them, and she hadn't heard from the one person she wanted to. Riley.

What was he thinking? Did he know she

hadn't been the one to spill his secrets or was he right that second making a little doll that looked like her with plans to stick pins in it? Worse, did he hate her? Because she could stand him being angry, but not him turning away from her without giving her a chance to prove her innocence. Not that she had any kind of plan on how she was supposed to do that.

What she didn't understand was how this had happened in the first place. Who had set them up? And how? She had a hard time believing her neighbor had spied on her until she'd seen Riley come over, then waited until she was pretty sure they were having sex, only to throw her precious dog into a cold pool and then go pound on Gracie's door and beg for help.

Which meant it was someone else. Which left her back where she'd started, wondering who and why and how and all the other question words.

An hour later she saw the sign for Los Lobos and turned off the freeway. At the bottom of the off-ramp, she hesitated, then turned right instead of left and drove to the chichi side of town. She drove past Riley's house and carefully parked around the corner so as not to fuel the gossip mill, then walked back to his front door and braced herself. She might have to stand there pounding for a really long time before she convinced him she wasn't going away and that he had to talk to her.

"I'm going to make him listen," she told herself as she raised her hand to knock.

The door swung open.

The movement was so unexpected, she actually stumbled forward and nearly tripped over the threshold. Riley raised his eyebrows.

"Have you been drinking?" he asked.

"What? No. I didn't think you'd let me in. I was prepared to keep pounding until you did."

"Are you disappointed?"

"No."

He looked good. No, he looked great. Jeans, a plain white shirt and Nikes. Faint stubble darkened his jaw.

She wanted to step into his embrace and have him pull her close. She wanted to tell him that she hadn't been the one, that he could trust her, that she cared about him and would never betray him. She wanted to offer proof or at least a plan to get proof. She wanted him to say it was going to be all right.

Instead she opened her mouth, closed it, then grabbed the front of his shirt with both hands and did her best to shake him.

"It wasn't me," she said as he stood there as immobile as a rock. "I didn't tell anyone what we did and I certainly didn't say I thought I might be pregnant. I don't know where he got the idea. It wasn't me."

She still held on to his shirt. He raised his hands to cover hers. His dark eyes watched her.

"I know," he said simply.

She blinked. "Really? You believe me?"

He nodded.

"Why?"

One corner of his mouth turned up. "Can't you just accept it?"

"No. Not really. If I were you I'm not sure I'd believe me. Why do you?"

He shrugged, which wasn't a very satisfying answer, but it seemed to be all she was going to get.

He loosened her hands from his shirt and stepped back. "I'm going for a walk on the beach. Want to come?"

"Sure."

It was close to sunset when they arrived. Riley parked his Mercedes in one of the public lots, then took Gracie's hand as they crossed to the sand. She'd kicked off her shoes. Without the heels, she barely came up to

273

his shoulder. Her hair hung loose, her shirt was untucked. She should have been a mess, but he found her sexy as hell.

Was that why he'd told her he believed her? Because he wanted to sleep with her? He supposed it was as good a reason as any, because there wasn't any logic in the entire situation.

He didn't want her to be the guilty party. It was as simple as that. If it turned out he was a fool to trust her, it could cost him ninety-seven million dollars and the revenge he'd been after.

Later he would listen to his head, he told himself. Later he would come up with plans that would help him recover from what had happened at the debate. Later he would tell Gracie to get lost and forget her. But not right now.

"I used to come here a lot when I was a kid," Riley said. "As soon as I got my driver's license, it became one of my favorite places. I would walk along the beach and try to make sense of my life."

"I didn't think that was possible for a teenager."

He looked at her and smiled. "It's not."

"At least you made the effort. My way to try to make sense was to write really bad poetry. I mean seriously bad. Trees should come after me seeking revenge for their death so that I could have the paper to write my bad poetry."

"Trees aren't much into organizing."

"Color me happy."

She glanced at him as she spoke. A hint of a smile caused her blue eyes to crinkle at the corners. He nearly pulled her close and kissed her, but the smile faded and she sighed.

"How did he know?"

"The mayor?"

She nodded.

"He had us followed. Or maybe just me."

"Is that what your detective told you?" she asked.

"He's been on the job all of a day. I doubt he knows anything yet."

"Oh. Good point." She tucked a strand of hair behind her ear. "The guy the mayor or whoever hired did a much better job following us than we did following Zeke. Maybe we should have hired him."

Despite everything, he chuckled. "I like your logic."

"So the guy was just there to take pictures, but somehow he figures out what we're up to and tells the mayor?"

"Or Yardley takes a wild stab in the dark and gets lucky."

She squeezed his hand, then stepped in front of him.

"I didn't do it, Riley. I swear."

"Gracie, you don't have to keep telling me that. I believe you."

"I hope so. It's just it looks so bad. I'm the only one who knows we made love and I'm the only one who knows that we didn't use anything and that there's a teeny, tiny chance I'm pregnant."

"You're not the only one," he reminded her. "I know."

"Oh, right. Because you're the one telling the mayor." She squeezed his hand tighter. "I mean it. I need you to believe me. It's desperately important. I don't lie. I can be a little anal about getting my cakes exactly right and I don't have as much patience with my family as I probably should and I never get my checkbook to balance to the penny. I figure, hey if it's within five dollars, fine. But I don't lie and I would never set you up. I'm not afraid of the truth. Remember? I'm the girl who put a skunk in your car. I tend to do things out in the open so the world can see."

The sun had slipped below the horizon. As the light faded, her skin took on a luminescence, as if she glowed from within. At that moment, staring into her beautiful face, he would have believed anything. Not so much because he wanted her — although he did — but because she was there.

For the first time in as long as he could remember, someone was there for him. Someone who was interested in him, his day, his opinions, his feelings. Guy friends were never that involved and he didn't let women get close.

He believed Gracie because he didn't have a choice.

He reached for her free hand and laced his fingers with hers, then he pulled her close, so they touched from shoulder to thigh.

"How did we get here?" he asked.

"The highway and then Beach Drive."

He grinned, then he chuckled, then he started to laugh. She wiggled her shoulders.

"I've always had an excellent sense of humor," she said.

"Yes, you do."

He bent down and kissed her nose. Her mouth beckoned, but as much as he wanted to be in her bed, he wasn't willing to give this up. Not yet.

He released her left hand and tugged her along so they were walking again.

"Any other directional questions I can answer?" she asked.

277

"Not right now."

"You could get a GPS system."

"Yes, I could."

She drew in a deep breath. "I love the smell of the ocean. Where my aunt and uncle lived in Torrance, we were about five miles from the beach, so we could go there a lot. I've always lived close to the water. I'm not sure I could live anywhere else. How do people survive in the mountains or the desert?"

"It's what they know. I didn't see the ocean until we moved here when I was nearly sixteen."

She glanced at him. "Where *did* you grow up?"

"Tempe, then finally here." He remembered the trailer he and his mom had lived in. "I never asked her why we stayed so long after my dad left. Maybe she was waiting for him to come back." His mother had always been a dreamer.

"Six years is a long time."

"Too long. Then we moved here. She told me things would be better because her brother was here. Until then I hadn't known I'd had an uncle."

"What happened when you met him?" Gracie asked.

"I didn't. She left me at the motel and

278

went to see him herself. When she came back, I knew that she'd been crying, but she wouldn't admit it. She wouldn't say anything except she was going to find us a nice little house where we could be happy."

He led Gracie toward a cluster of rocks and sat down next to them. She settled beside him. He reached for her hand again.

"I put the pieces together over time," he said, not wanting to remember, but lost in the past all the same. "Her brother told her that she'd turned her back on the family when she'd run off to be with my father. As far as he was concerned, she didn't exist. Neither did I."

Gracie shifted closer so she could snuggle up against him. "I'm sorry your uncle was just a big old poop head."

Despite the ghosts and the ache of the past, Riley smiled. "I've been calling him a heartless bastard all these years, but I kind of like poop head."

"It's truc. How could he ignore his own family?"

Riley leaned back against the rocks and put his free arm around her. "Easily enough. I never did meet him. When I got in trouble around town, he'd send me a letter, reprimanding me for whatever I'd done."

"You were never that bad."

He glanced down at her. "I was wild."

She smiled. "I know. It was one of your best qualities. Your bad-boy ways made my little teenage heart beat so fast. You were dangerous and sexy." She gave him a teasing grin. "Did you know I had a crush on you?"

He chuckled. "Gee, really? You were so subtle about it."

"I know." She sighed. "That's me. Subtle gal. Did he come to the wedding?"

"No. My mom probably sent him an invitation, but I didn't care if he showed up or not. I'm sure Pam was hoping for a great gift, but he didn't bother with that, either."

"I know Pam's being really nice and all," Gracie said. "But it's hard for me to feel sorry for her."

"Me, either. I didn't want to marry her. Did you know that?"

She stared at him, her eyes wide. "You're kidding. I thought you were wildly in love with her."

"Lust," he said firmly. "There's a huge difference. At eighteen, I liked having her as a steady girlfriend, because she put out. When she told me she was pregnant, I was furious. She'd sworn she was on the Pill and I believed her."

280

Gracie shifted on the sand. "I never said I was."

He brushed his mouth against her hair. "Not the same thing. I told you, I don't blame you for that."

"But I —"

He pulled his hand free and pressed it against her mouth. "No."

"But —" He pressed a little harder. "What aren't you getting?"

"Okay."

He appreciated her worrying, but as far as he was concerned, the fault was his. He'd been the one so damned intent on having her, he'd forgotten to make sure they were both protected. He hadn't gotten successful by being stupid.

"What were we talking about?" he asked.

"You not wanting to marry Pam because you were secretly in love with me."

"Not exactly."

"But close."

"I didn't want to marry Pam."

"I'll take that if it's all I can get," she said. "And remind you — again — that I warned you about her."

"Yes, you did, but I didn't listen. Not that it would have mattered. My mother insisted. She said I had a responsibility." He grimaced as he remembered the fights he'd had with her. "She wanted me to be respectable and do the right thing."

"You just wanted out."

"Yeah. I'm not saying my mom was wrong. But at eighteen, I didn't see it. I married Pam, stayed around long enough to find out she wasn't pregnant, then took off. But first I told my mom she'd ruined my life and I would never forgive her."

He stared out at the dark ocean. The moon hadn't risen and he could barely see the white foam swirling along the beach.

"It was the last time we ever spoke," he said slowly.

"What?" Gracie pushed away and stared at him. "You mean because you left?"

He nodded. "I was angry. I took off and headed north. Eventually I ended up on those oil rigs in the South China Sea. I grew up a little and got some perspective. So I sent her a letter and a check. She wrote me back, asked me to come see her sometime. I said I would. But I never made the time."

He hadn't thought it was important and he'd still been angry.

"Finally she wrote me and told me she was sick. Cancer. So I made arrangements to come back. But she didn't say it was urgent and I didn't drop everything. A week before I was supposed to leave, I got a call from a nurse in the county hospital telling me my mother had less than forty-eight hours to live. It took me fifty hours to get back. She was already dead."

Gracie tightened her hold on him. "I'm so sorry."

"Don't be. It's long over. Technically Yardley was right today. I never did come back to see my mother while she lay dying."

"You didn't know."

"Is that a good excuse?" he asked, still staring at the ocean. "I don't think so. She was alone. That's the worst of it. She died in the county hospital by herself. Her selfish son couldn't be bothered to get his ass back in a timely fashion. And her own brother, who lived right in town, didn't bother going to see her."

Gracie rose to her knees and stared at him. "What are you talking about?"

"Donovan Whitefield kept his word. He never forgave his sister." Riley looked at Gracie. "I found her letters later. The ones he'd returned without ever opening them. She begged him for money to pay for treatment. What I sent her wasn't nearly enough and she knew that back then I couldn't have afforded medical treatments. So she asked him, and he didn't even bother to read them."

283

She made a noise low in her throat then threw herself at him.

"I'm sorry," she whispered, pressing against him and shaking.

He stiffened, not sure what to do with her sympathy, then he wrapped his arms around her.

"It's okay," he said.

"It's not." She raised her head and looked at him. He thought he saw tears on her cheeks, but he wasn't sure. "None of it is okay. You're carrying around all this guilt, but it's not your fault. You didn't make your mother sick and you didn't know you had to come back."

So Gracie wanted to make it all right for him. Didn't she know that wasn't possible?

"I did after she told me," he said flatly.

"But she could have made it more clear. You're not psychic. Okay, yes, you're guilty of not hurrying, but that's all. The rest of it. . . . How could your uncle have done that? How could he have turned his back on her? I might not like Alexis and Vivian very much right now, but I would never turn them away. Especially with something like that."

Riley doubted Gracie would turn away a rabid dog if it needed help.

"You need to understand I'm long past

saving," he said. "I've made my peace with the past." Although "peace" might be the wrong word. He'd accepted what had happened and decided how he was going to make it right.

She cupped his face in her hands. "You haven't found peace. You're still angry."

He liked that she could read him so well. "I'll get over it."

Gracie wasn't sure that was possible. How was Riley supposed to accept all that had happened and move on? She could feel the pain inside of him. It radiated from him and made her ache inside. She wanted to surround him and hold him until he began to heal.

She wanted to return to the past and prevent it all from happening.

He was good and strong and decent. He didn't deserve all this.

"I'm sorry," she whispered, still cupping his face. "I hate that Mayor Yardley took a very personal, painful piece of your past and used it to make himself look better. It's slimy and horrible."

"Is he a big old poop head, too?"

"He's on the poop head management team." She wiped her tears. "How could he do that? It's so horrible. And now people

285

are going to think badly of you. It's not right."

"I'll survive," he said.

"What you need is to win the election. Can I do anything to help?"

"I'll let you know if we come up with a plan that includes you."

"I don't mind knocking on doors and telling people I'm not pregnant."

One corner of his mouth turned up. "That would get their attention. Why don't we wait until we're sure you're not pregnant before heading in that direction."

"Oh. Right. Good point." She slumped down next to him. She didn't want to think about a baby right now. "I don't think I could handle one more thing."

"You mean between your sister who's getting married, the one freaking out about her husband, the cakes you have to bake, Pam, the mayor telling everyone we've had sex and the fact that you might be pregnant?" he asked.

She groaned. "Gee, when you put it like that, I barely have anything going on anymore. Is your list better or worse?"

"It's different. My father showed up today."

She didn't think there was anything else that could shock her, but she was wrong.

"Your father? Here?"

"At the bank," he said as he slid his hand into her hair and finger combed it to the ends. "It's been twenty-two years and I still recognized him. I guess that says something."

She didn't know what to think. "He wanted to see you?"

Riley gave a laugh that had nothing to do with humor. "No. He wanted money. There was no 'Hey, son, how's it going.' He just asked me to write him a check because he's running a little short this month."

She felt as if someone had drop-kicked her heart. Riley spoke as if it didn't matter, but she knew the pain of being abandoned by a parent. Maybe her situation was a little different, but the loss was very similar.

"I'm sorry," she whispered.

"It happened. I threw him out but he'll be back. Hell, I'll probably give him the money just to get rid of him."

"I'm sorry," she repeated and wrapped her arms around him. "I don't know how to make this all better."

"Not your job."

"I know, but I still want to fix it. Make things better." She reached up and touched his face. "Come home with me."

Nothing about his expression changed.

"That's a short-term solution."

"It's the best I have right now."

"I'm not complaining."

CHAPTER FOURTEEN

Gracie wondered if she would fight second thoughts on the drive back to his house. The night was dark, the car silent. Their only communication came from his hand holding hers, his thumb brushing against the back of her hand.

Her body was an odd combination of tension and relaxation. While the thought of them making love again had her quivering from the inside out, she also felt completely calm. As if this decision had been made a millennia ago and she was simply fulfilling her destiny.

"Want to stay at my place?" he asked quietly as they got close to the large mansion. "You could pull your car into the garage."

"That sounds good," she said.

He drove into the driveway and hit the remote control button. As the large double garage door opened, she slid out and walked around the corner to her car.

Five minutes later, she'd parked next to him and followed him into the massive kitchen. As it had before, the sight of the large, open space made her cake-baker heart beat faster.

"Kitchen envy," she said with a sigh. "I need a twelve-step program to recover."

"Can we take care of that later?"

"Sure."

He crossed to the refrigerator. "Hungry?"

She followed him and tried to peer over his shoulder. "You have food?"

"I have take-out leftovers." He grabbed a chilling bottle of champagne, then stepped back. "See anything you like?"

She couldn't seem to take her eyes off the champagne long enough to make a menu selection.

"Did you just happen to have that chilling in anticipation of the three *F's* or. . . ."

He coiled his free hand in her hair, tugged her head back, then pressed his lips against hers. The kiss was hot, quick and full of promise.

"I bought it yesterday."

Passion flooded her brain, making it difficult to concentrate. "You mean after we. . . ."

His dark gaze locked with hers. "After we

made love. Yes. This isn't generic, I-hope-I-get-lucky champagne. I bought it for you, Gracie."

Her bare toes curled. She didn't remember a man buying champagne for her before. Certainly not — she glanced at the label — Dom Perignon.

She closed the refrigerator door with a bump of her hip. "I'm not very hungry. For food."

He smiled. "Good."

He walked to a cabinet and removed two champagne glasses, then jerked his head toward the hallway.

"Shall we?"

"Absolutely."

She followed him to the wide, curving staircase. On her last visit to his house, the tour hadn't gotten this far. She noted several portraits on the walls. Previous generations of Whitefields, she wondered. But she didn't want to spoil the mood by asking.

The staircase continued up to a third floor, but Riley stopped on the second and made a left turn. They passed four or five other rooms before he pushed open the door of one and stepped inside.

Gracie wasn't sure what to expect. She didn't know if Riley wanted to sleep in his grandfather's bed to prove that he could or if he would choose another space. As she glanced around she saw that he'd apparently picked a more neutral space — what looked like a simply furnished guest room with a large bed, two nightstands and a dresser. The light from the hall spilled onto a pale carpet. The walls looked either blue or green — she couldn't tell.

Riley set the champagne on the dresser and unwrapped the foil. Seconds later, he popped the cork and poured them each a glass.

"I've never had champagne this fancy," she said as she took the slender flute he offered and then sipped.

The bubbles bounced off her tongue — the flavor was light, delicious, almost sweet and addictive.

"Do you like it?" he asked when she'd swallowed.

"Very much. Unfortunately, it's not going to fit in my budget."

"Save it for special occasions," he said as he took a sip, then set his glass on the dresser and moved close.

She started to say there was no point — that for the rest of her life whenever she saw the distinctive shape of a bottle of Dom Perignon, she would always think of him.

Instead she moved over so she could put her glass on the nightstand, then watched as he stepped close and took her in his arms.

The first time they'd made love, there had been a frantic quality about the joining. She'd wanted with a desperation that hadn't allowed her to do much more than feel. This time she was able to think as well as experience and she tried to pay attention to every detail so she could relive it later.

She noticed that even as he claimed her mouth in a soft, teasing kiss that promised so much more, he placed one hand on her hip and the other on the back of her neck. He kept the hand on her hip still while he moved the other through her hair. He'd done that before, she thought hazily as he bit down on her lower lip and made her want to squirm against him. He seemed to love touching her hair. He often —

His tongue touched where he'd nipped her and she parted instantly. As he swept inside, her stomach muscles clenched and her breasts began to ache. She rested her hands on his shoulders, enjoying the heat and strength of him.

He explored her mouth, touching, circling, enticing. When he retreated, she followed, wanting to know every part of him. He tasted of champagne, he smelled of ocean and night and desire.

When he shifted his mouth so that he could kiss her jaw, she leaned her head in the opposite direction to give him more room. He nibbled his way down her neck. Her skin puckered, her breasts swelled even as she felt her nipples get hard and sensitive. She wanted to rip off her clothes and have him take her right there. She wanted him to go slowly, so the moment never ended.

Indecision filled her as she clung to him. He sucked on her earlobe, licked the skin on her neck and then made a slow but steady beeline for her breasts.

Without thinking, she dropped her hands from his shoulders so she could unfasten her shirt and let it drop off her shoulders. He bent over her, moving closer and closer, making her work frantically at the hooks on her bra. The last one caught and she nearly broke it in her haste to bare herself before him.

At last the hook gave and she jerked the bra down and tossed it on the floor. But instead of touching her there, he straightened.

"You're so beautiful," he said as he stared into her eyes. "You make me want things."

"Good."

Although she wasn't all that interested in talking about them right now. If they were naked things, then doing would be much better than talking.

Unfortunately, he didn't seem to read her mind. Instead of reaching for her, he picked up his glass of champagne and took a long sip. Then he set the glass down, bent toward her and took her nipple in his mouth.

The combination of his heat, the cool champagne and the bubbles was a sensation she'd never experienced before. She grabbed for his shoulders to keep herself from falling. When his tongue swirled around, moving the bubbles over her sensitized skin, she gasped with pleasure.

He swallowed, then straightened and reached for his glass. "I need to take care of the other breast," he said with a grin. "It's important to be fair."

"You bet," she told him, already weak with anticipation.

He filled his mouth with the champagne, then caressed her with a tingling, exciting, bubbly caress. She wrapped both arms around his head in a silent plea that he never stop.

When he'd swallowed again, he licked her, then sucked until she felt her bones melt and her body turn to liquid.

He straightened and pulled her close, then kissed her mouth. She couldn't get enough of him. She couldn't be near enough, touching enough, feeling enough. There were so many sensations, so many promises between them. She wanted the chance to fulfill each other.

When he reached for the button on her jeans, she reached for his shirt. They managed to unfasten each other, then he shrugged out of his shirt and she stepped out of her jeans. She pulled down her panties while he took care of the rest of his clothes. Then they were both naked and heading for the bed.

He kissed her everywhere. As she lay on her back, he kissed and licked and nibbled his way from her ears to her toes. Sometimes he sipped champagne first and she experienced the erotic combination of hot, cold, smooth and bubbly kisses.

On the return trip, he nibbled her ankle before licking his way up to her knees. He bit down and made her giggle, he sucked and made her squirm. Then he moved higher, to her thigh.

His large hands kneaded her muscles, his thumbs sweeping closer and closer to the heat radiating from between her legs. He watched her as he touched her, his dark eyes bright with desire, his mouth curved up in a smile.

She let her gaze sweep over him, the broadness of his shoulders, the breadth of his chest, the dark hair swirling down his flat belly. He was hard and ready and she ached to have him inside of her . . . right up until he bent down and she felt his breath on her. She moved her legs farther apart and closed her eyes in anticipation. Then she felt it — the soft brush of his mouth and the long, slow lick of his tongue.

As he moved against her, he slipped a single finger inside of her and gently pushed it in and out.

The combination of sensations made her gasp for breath. She'd been prepared to like what he did but not to fall so hard and so fast. She could barely breathe. Her muscles tensed and she dug her heels into the bed. Good manners insisted that she wait at least a couple of minutes before losing herself in her orgasm, but she wasn't sure she could hold on that long.

He felt too good. When he stroked her, he seemed to know exactly the right speed. That relentless finger continued to move in and out, teasing, pushing, promising bigger and better things to come.

He circled her most sensitive spot, then

caressed it with the flat part of his tongue. He blew on her and made her shiver. He covered her with his lips and gently sucked until she knew her release was as inevitable as the tide they'd watched earlier.

He began to move a little faster. The finger, his tongue. Pressure built and built until she had no choice but to give way. She clutched at the sheets, raised her chin to the ceiling and gasped out her release.

The waves came one on top of the other. He continued to stroke her, to move in and out and she found herself carried along as the pleasure stretched out endlessly.

At last the need slowly died away. He drew back and kissed her thigh, then pushed up to his knees. She opened her eyes and smiled at him.

"I have another *F*," she said lazily. "Fabulous."

"I like that *F*."

"Me, too."

She patted the mattress and waited until he stretched out next to her before standing and walking to get the bottle of champagne from the dresser.

Riley gave himself over to enjoying the show. From the back Gracie was all swaying hips and graceful curves. From the front — he swore silently — she was a goddess.

Her long blond hair covered enough of her breasts to make him want to see more. Her narrow waist only emphasized the swell of her hips. He liked the fullness of her thighs, the length of her legs and that secret place between them that gave her all the power.

When she returned to the bed, she waved the bottle. "Mind if I ignore the glass?"

"Help yourself."

She knelt beside him and took a sip of champagne. He had to admit that a beautiful naked woman kneeling next to him, drinking out of the bottle just before they got to the next round was going on his top ten list of erotic moments.

After setting the bottle on the nightstand, she bent down and pressed her mouth against his belly. He groaned as he felt her warm mouth followed by the cool, bubbly sensation of the champagne. Her tongue swirled against his skin.

"I like this," she murmured.

"Me, too."

She picked up the bottle and took another small sip. This time she moved lower and he braced himself for what was to come.

But all the preparation in the world couldn't stop his body from reacting as she knelt between his parted legs, reached down to hold him still and then took him in her mouth.

He forgot to breathe through the sheer pleasure of her lips and tongue caressing him even as the cool champagne tickled and aroused and her long hair brushed his belly and thighs. She swirled her tongue around, then licked the very tip of him.

He swore out loud, grabbed for control and had a feeling his grip could slip at any second.

"Gracie, you can't."

She raised her mouth, swallowed the champagne, then tilted her head. "Technically, I can."

"Okay, yeah. I'm begging you not to."

She gave a heavy sigh. "Oh, all right. What would you prefer?"

"Me inside of you."

Her blue eyes widened slightly as she smiled. "I guess. If you insist."

"I do."

He reached for the nightstand and pulled open the top drawer. "Want to stay in control or want me to take you?"

She laughed. "I think I'd like to be taken."

"Consider it done."

He grabbed a condom and quickly slipped it on. When she stretched out next to him, he turned toward her and gathered her in his arms.

They kissed. She tasted faintly of champagne and mostly of herself. He claimed her, even as he stroked his hands all over her body.

She was sensitive, squirming as he brushed his fingers across her tight nipples. She was wet, moaning as he slipped his fingers between her thighs. She parted instantly and even though he'd thought to make it last longer, he couldn't help shifting so that he could kneel between her legs and push his way home.

As he plunged inside of her, she tightened around him. Her arms drew him closer. He drove in as deeply as he could, losing himself in the slick heat. He withdrew, then pushed inside again. This time he felt a quickening to the tightness, a tension in her muscles.

He braced himself, then bent down and kissed her mouth even as he began the steady rhythmic thrusting designed to take them both over the edge. She wrapped her legs around his hips and held him in place. Her hands grabbed for his butt and pulled him in deeper.

Faster and faster, pushing, reaching, needing, plunging until he felt her shatter beneath him. She broke the kiss and gasped for air, then screamed his name. As the contractions pulsed through her, he let go, shuddering as his climax claimed him and her body milked every drop of pleasure from him.

Later, when they were both lying curled up together under the covers, he buried his fingers in her hair and kissed her forehead.

"It's late," he said. "Want to sleep here?"

She stirred, lifting her hair from his shoulder and blinking sleepily. "You don't strike me as the sleepover type."

"I'm making an exception."

She put her head back and closed her eyes. "That would be nice. But get me up early so I can head out before your neighbors wake up."

"I thought you hated morning."

"I do, but I don't want to make things worse for you."

He rubbed his other hand along her bare back. "It's fine," he said. "You don't have to get up early for me."

"Okay."

She spoke slowly, as if barely able to stay awake. He squeezed her.

"Go to sleep."

"Mmm."

Her breathing slowed.

Riley reached up and turned off the light, then pulled the covers around them both. He stared up at the dark ceiling.

She'd been right. He wasn't a sleepover kind of guy. Considering all that was happening right now, including the fact that Gracie might be pregnant, he should be running for the hills. Funny how he didn't want to.

He wanted to stay right where he was — with her.

He continued to stroke her back, then moved higher to play with the ends of her hair. Had he ever spent the night with a woman before? Had he ever let one stay with him? He frowned as he tried to remember, then decided it hadn't happened since his brief marriage to Pam.

Why now? Why Gracie? He didn't have any answers. Or maybe he didn't want to find them.

Gracie Woke up as she usually did, slowly and with a great appreciation for having slept well. She stretched, rolled over and found herself in an unfamiliar bed.

"That can't be good," she said as she raised herself into a sitting position and pushed her hair out of her face. She spotted a note on the pillow next to hers and as she reached for it, memories flooded back.

"My mistake. It was better than good," she said with a smile. "It was amazing."

Riley sure knew how to make a woman's toes curl, she thought as she flopped back on the mattress and read the note.

"I had an early meeting and didn't want to wake you. There's coffee downstairs. Help yourself. Last night was great. Thanks."

She rubbed her thumb across the plain white paper, as if by touching it she could touch the man himself.

But there was no warm skin, no sexy scent, nothing but the memory of what they'd done together and it was a poor substitute for the real thing.

She rolled on her side and faced the spot where he'd slept. "Now what?" she asked aloud as she ran her fingers across the mussed sheets. Where did they go from here and what did they do when they got there? Who was this man who knew how to touch her heart and her soul?

Her stomach clenched. For once the tension had nothing to do with acid or even the thought she might be pregnant. Instead, it was all about her growing feelings for Riley.

"I can't," she whispered. "I can't fall for him."

He was her past. He was the root of every humiliation she'd suffered for years. To get involved with him now would be. . . .

She closed her eyes and heard her mother's voice telling her how everyone was laughing at her. She was the butt of jokes. Gracie winced at the thought. She wasn't willing to go through that again. Not when —

"Wait a minute." She sat up and stared at the opposite wall. "This is my life. Not my mother's. Not anyone else's. Mine. I decide."

Okay. That sounded very self-actualized. Now what? If she wasn't going to live to please faceless strangers or her mother, what *was* she going to do?

"See it through," she said firmly. She had no idea what was happening with Riley, what she felt for him or what he felt for her, but she would see it through. If there was something there, she wanted to know. If this was just some twisted trip down memory lane, then she had to know that as well. One way or another, she would figure it all out. Even if she found herself brokenhearted at the end, it beat spending the rest of her life always wondering.

Fifty-five minutes Later a freshly showered and dressed Gracie left her house with the intent of stopping by Jill's office. As of last count there had been eight messages from her friend. She wanted to reassure Jill that she was fine and maybe tell her a little of what had been happening. Since the mayor had announced the details of her private life to the whole town it seemed silly to try to keep secrets from her best friend.

As she turned at the stop sign, she noticed how close she was to her mom's house. Maybe she should swing by there and get her daily dose of stern talking-to. After that, she would tell her mother that while she loved her and appreciated her advice, she had to make her own choices. Right now she wanted to pursue things with Riley. Maybe it was a mistake, but the mistake was hers to make. If her family couldn't support that, she would do her best to understand.

"That sounds really powerful," she told herself as she pulled in front of the familiar two-story house. She had a feeling that actual rejection by her family would be pretty painful. It didn't seem to matter how badly they treated her, she kept coming back for more.

As she walked up toward the front door, she noticed Vivian's car parked in the driveway. Oh, joy, Gracie thought. A two for one.

She raised her hand to knock, then saw the door was partially ajar. She pushed it open as she called out, "Hi. It's me."

Silence followed her announcement.

"Mom? Vivian?"

She heard a sound from the back of the house and headed in that direction. As she entered the long hallway, she could hear voices.

"I can't believe you're doing this," her mother said, sounding more than a little angry. "What's *wrong* with you?"

"Nothing. I don't know why you're so upset," Vivian grumbled.

"I'm upset because this wedding is costing thousands and thousands of dollars."

Gracie stopped in the middle of the hall. She wasn't sure if she should announce herself again or simply leave.

"I'm helping with my wedding dress," Vivian said.

"It's over three thousand dollars. To date your contribution is all of two hundred. Honey, I want you to be happy and have the wedding of your dreams, but you can't

307

keep canceling it."

"I know. It's just Tom was really mean last night. I don't think I can be with him."

"Fine. If you want to cancel the wedding today, we will. But know that it's over. I'm not doing this anymore. As it is, I'll be out nearly five thousand dollars, and that's just for deposits. I don't have that kind of money. I've taken out a mortgage on the house to pay for this. I can put the rest of the money back, but where am I supposed to get the five thousand dollars I've just lost? I didn't mind when it was for your wedding, but I won't just waste the money because you can't make up your mind."

Gracie took a step back. She didn't want to hear any of this.

Why on earth would her mother take out a home loan to pay for a wedding? That sounded crazy, especially with Vivian not being sure about what she wanted. Between the expensive wedding gown, the country club location and the formal dinner, Gracie would bet the total bill would be well over twenty-five thousand dollars. You could practically put a kid through college for that.

"Mom, no!" Vivian began to cry. "I'm sorry. I know I'm making this hard. I don't want you to have to lose money and I know the wedding is too expensive. I'll work harder. I will. And I'll go talk to Tom. We'll work it out. Don't cancel the wedding. Please?"

Her mother sighed. "All right. But no more games. There's too much at stake."

Gracie turned and quietly walked out of the house. She didn't want to intrude on a private moment between mother and daughter and she didn't agree with what they were doing.

While she understood her mother's reluctance to give up the deposit money for a wedding that wasn't happening, she didn't agree with getting married just to have a wedding. Vivian and Tom seemed to break up every fifteen minutes. That didn't bode well for their future together.

"Not my rock to carry," Gracie muttered to herself as she got in her car and drove toward Jill's. But even as she tried to put the conversation behind her, she felt sad for the sense of being an outsider. The closeness she'd once felt with her mother and her sisters was gone forever, which meant she was well and truly on her own.

Riley found himself enjoying his day at the bank. After his night with Gracie he could easily ignore the stares and whispers of his employees. Let 'em talk — he knew the truth and in the end, he would win this battle.

Not that Zeke agreed.

"We're in big trouble," his campaign manager said as he paced in his office. "I'll have new numbers by this afternoon, but they're not going to be good." Zeke stopped in front of his desk and stared at him. "Everyone loved you for romancing Gracie and they'll hate you just as much for treating her badly."

"I'm not."

"It sure sounds like it."

Thanks to Yardley. Riley leaned back in his chair. "My personal life. . . ."

"Shit." Zeke glared at him. "Dammit, Riley, if you had to get an itch scratched couldn't you have picked some other —"

Riley was out of his chair before the other man finished his sentence. He reached across the desk, grabbed Zeke by the tie and twisted the fabric to tighten it around Zeke's neck.

"Don't talk about her that way," Riley said in a low voice.

Zeke nodded, then pulled back. Riley let him go. Zeke swallowed, then straightened his tie.

"Right. Okay. So we need new numbers." He glanced at Riley, his expression wary.

"Are you going to keep seeing her?"

"Yes."

"Gracie's terrific. My sister-in-law. I've always liked her. But you know that Yardley's claim is going to cost you votes. Maybe a few, maybe a lot."

"We'll deal with it."

"Right. Sure. I'll come up with a new strategy. Let me think on it for the next day or so." He took a step back from the desk.

Just then Diane knocked on the door as she pushed it open.

"I'm sorry to interrupt, but you asked me to let you know as soon as your father returned. He's here."

Riley wasn't even a little surprised. He nodded. "Let me finish up here."

Zeke's eyes widened. "Your dad. That's cool. Maybe we could use him in the campaign."

"No."

"I'm just saying it would make you seem more approachable."

"No."

Zeke opened his mouth, then closed it. "All right. I'll get back to you by end of day tomorrow. By then I'll have poll numbers and a new strategy."

"Fine."

Zeke gathered his folders and ducked out

311

of the room. Seconds later, his father entered.

"Morning, son," he said cheerfully. "How are you?"

"Great."

Riley studied the older man. Same suit, he thought. Different shirt. This one a little more worn than the one from the previous day. Riley didn't know where his father had been or what he wanted the money for. Honest to God, he didn't care.

"How much," he said before his father could speak again. "How much do you want."

The older man smiled. "I've been thinking about going into a couple of franchises. They seem to be doing well. Some of those sandwich shops really rake in the money."

He continued talking, but Riley wasn't listening. Instead, he studied the man who was his father and searched for resemblances.

The eyes, he supposed. Maybe the dark hair. Did they share a sense of humor? A taste for good Scotch? Obviously they both had no problem walking away from women.

At ten Riley had worshipped his father. The man's disappearance had cut out his heart and it had taken years to recover. His mother never had. Oh she'd been brave, living her life, smiling, laughing, but there'd been a sadness underneath. As if she'd risked everything she had and then she'd lost it all.

"How much?" Riley asked again, interrupting him.

The old man stopped talking and blinked. "Two hundred thousand?"

Riley opened the top desk drawer and removed the personal checkbook he'd brought in that morning. He wrote the amount without saying a word.

"I appreciate this, son. Your generosity means a lot."

Riley passed him the check. "Next time, don't bother coming by. Just send me a letter."

They looked at each other, then his father nodded. "If that's what you'd prefer."

"It is."

"Don't you want to know how I found you?"

"No."

"All right." The old man looked at the check. "Oh. How's your mother? Happy?"

Riley wanted to punch him then. Anger swelled inside of him until it threatened to burst out in a destructive wave.

"She's fine. Thanks for asking." He stared pointedly at the door. "I have a meeting."

"Of course. Thanks for the money."

The man who had been his father for the first ten years of his life walked out. Riley was fairly confident he would never see him again, although there would be a steady stream of letters requesting more money for more failed dreams.

When he was alone again, he pushed the button to ring Diane's phone.

"Yes?"

"I want to donate the money to the children's wing of the hospital," he said. "In my mother's name."

There was a brief pause. Riley imagined his unflappable secretary openmouthed in astonishment.

"I'll call them right away."

"Good."

He disconnected the call, then slowly turned in his chair. He still hated his uncle, he thought as he stared at the portrait of the man. He would never give an inch on his desire for revenge. But for the first time Riley understood what it must have been like to be one man who had the money to solve everyone's problems.

Gracie tapped the cooling pan twice for good luck, gave it a quick twist, then pulled it up in one, quick motion. The cake fell out perfectly.

"Impressive," Pam said with a sigh. "I can't even get muffins to pop out of the pan. I end up using a knife and they get all bent and scrunchy on the edges."

"Practice," Gracie said with pride as she stared at the bottom layer of an oval cake. "Practice and a little bit of prayer."

"How many layers will this one be?" Pam asked.

"Five, which means it's huge and it's heavy." She reached for the next cake pan and tapped it.

"How do you keep the layers from sinking into each other?"

"Dowels. I stick them into the cake to provide support." The cake pan lifted easily. She sighed. "I love it when a plan comes together."

Pam leaned over the cake and inhaled. "I don't know what it is you put in your mix, but your cakes always smell so good."

"Thanks." Gracie knew Pam wouldn't mention taste, what with never having eaten a single bite. Gracie wasn't sure she ate ever. She was unnaturally thin, which was very annoying.

"There are hundreds of flowers," Pam said, pointing to the carefully stacked trays of fondant roses. "But they're for the cake you made and iced yesterday, right?"

"Oh, yeah. That's what comes next. Assembly." She glanced at the clock. The groom's father would arrive to pick up the cake in six hours. Eek! "I have to let the cake cool completely or the heat will mess up the icing. That's the tricky part. Everyone gets married on the weekend, which makes it tough to stagger the work. I can prepare all the decorations in advance. In any case, it's easy because the cake I'm finishing today doesn't have any fancy trim or piping. I just have to put on the decorations I've already made. I'll decorate this one tomorrow."

She carried the cooling racks over to the far counter and lifted the protective box off the three tiered cake she'd frosted the previous day.

"It looks perfect," Pam said, sounding impressed. "It's so smooth."

"Thanks, I —"

Her cell phone rang. Instantly her body went on alert. She'd reached that unfortunate stage where every call was either Riley or not Riley. A quick glance at the display screen told her she didn't recognize the number.

"Hello?"

"Gracie Landon?"

"Yes."

"Hi. My name is Neda Jackson. I freelance for several bridal magazines and I've just been given an assignment to do a feature on you. They want me to come up and take pictures of you working, along with several of your cakes. We'll do an interview, I'll talk to former clients, that sort of thing. They're hoping for about a six- to eight-page spread."

"I . . . They . . ." Gracie forced herself to breathe. Six to eight *pages* in a bridal magazine? "I'm excited." More than excited. Giddy. Thrilled. Willing to do the happy dance in public.

"Me, too," Neda said. "Our deadline's tight. How's the first part of next week?"

"Great. I'll have two cakes in progress. Are you in L.A.?"

"Yes."

"Good. Let me get in touch with a couple of brides and see if you can take pictures this weekend."

"Perfect."

Neda gave Gracie her number, then confirmed the time of the meeting. When they hung up, Gracie shrieked as she twirled through the kitchen.

Pam laughed. "I take it that was good news."

317

"Better than good. In terms of career highlights, this is a grand-slam home run."

CHAPTER FIFTEEN

Gracie was still floating later that afternoon when she returned to her house. She had more decorations to make and she seemed to do those best in a quiet place without Pam watching.

She set up her supplies in the dining room, then pulled out sketches for the next three cakes she had to make. Five minutes later she had her list of decorations required, with a few extras for breakage. It was daunting, but she was sure she was up to the task. She was going to have to be, now that she'd hit the big time.

"A six-page spread," she said aloud, just to hear the wonderful words herself. Talk about a good life.

While the *People* magazine spread had made her known to the world, a feature in a major bridal magazine put her in front of her actual clients. With this free advertising coming her way, the decision to expand had just been made for her.

She started work on the leaves. After rolling out the gum paste to an even thickness, she used a tulip petal cutter, then trimmed each flower into individual petals. Using a sharp veining tool, she drew in lines and points on the leaves, then carefully placed them on a flower form dusted with cornstarch so they would dry in a curving shape. According to her calculations, she would need about three hundred and sixty leaves for the cakes. When those were done, she would start on the flowers themselves. Good thing she enjoyed working late into the night.

She'd just settled into a steady rhythm of making leaves when she heard a car outside. She stood and walked toward the front door just as someone rang the bell.

But it wasn't any someone, she thought as she opened the door. It was Riley.

"Hi," he said. "I was driving by and I saw your car."

She felt giddy and nervous and a little bit melty on the inside. "I'm glad you stopped." She stepped back to let him in. "What brings you to the low-rent side of town?"

"A couple of things."

He pushed the door closed, then pulled her close and kissed her. The melty sensation spread to her entire body. She closed her eyes and let herself get lost in the kiss. This was actually turning out to be a very good day.

"Feel free to stop by for that anytime," she said when he'd straightened.

He grinned. "I will. But that's not the only reason. I wanted to ask you out to dinner."

Her insides gave a little lurch. "Really?"

"Really. Mac called me earlier and suggested the four of us go out to eat tonight. I thought it would be fun."

Her first thought was that she'd never made it over to Jill's and that they could talk over dinner. Her second thought was. . . .

"Fun? Fun?" She stared at him. "Have you been taken over by those aliens from Pam's place? Fun? It won't be fun. The four of us in a restaurant together? Us on a date? In public? Have you forgotten the 'Gracie Chronicles'? Do you have any idea what people will say? The scandal? You're running for mayor and I'm trying to have a normal life here. That is *not* going to happen if the four of us go out to dinner."

He looked at her. "Is that a no?"

"What? Of course not. I'm just ranting. What time should I be ready?"

He narrowed his gaze. "You're doing this

on purpose, aren't you? You're trying to make me freak out."

"Not at all." She grinned. "Okay, maybe a little. But people will talk. Walk with me. I have to work. I'm falling behind and that's never good."

She led the way into the dining room and motioned to the chairs around the table. "Have a seat. I have to do leaves."

He settled across from her. "Making cakes is a lot of work."

"Tell me about it. Oh, guess what happened. You'll never guess, so I'll tell you. I got a phone call today." She told him about her upcoming interview with Neda Jackson. "I can't believe it. Do you know what this is going to do for my business?"

"Make it explode."

"Exactly."

"I've seen your calendar, Gracie. You're already stretched pretty thin. Does this mean you're ready to expand?"

"I don't know. If I get much more work, I'm going to have to hire some help. So I guess, yes. It's just I hate to give up the control. I love doing all the cakes myself."

"You can only put in so many hours a day. It sounds as if you're about to have to make a big career decision."

"Do I have to?" she asked.

"Not if you don't want to."

She sighed. She knew he was right. She'd been building her business based on word of mouth for the past five years. Things were about to get complicated. There was no way she could do more cakes — not during the busy wedding season of late spring through summer. Which meant she either started saying no or she got herself a staff.

"I guess I'm about to expand," she said slowly.

"Good for you. Where will you set up shop? Here?"

She made a strangling sound in her throat. "Not even for money. Los Lobos is not my idea of fun. I'll head back to L.A."

"I'm with you on that," he said. "At least on leaving Los Lobos."

"But you won't be. Once you win the election, you'll be mayor. Isn't it a four-year term?"

"The will says I have to win, not that I have to serve."

She dropped her veining tool onto the table. "You'll just walk away from everything? What about the bank? Will you sell it?"

That would be okay, she told herself. Her mother's loan would simply transfer to the next owner. No doubt the local bank would be bought out by some big multinational concern.

"I'd shut it down," he said.

"I don't understand."

He shrugged. "Once I own the bank, I can pretty much do what I want. I'll close the doors. That damn business was the only thing my uncle cared about. I want it to disappear, as if it never existed."

Revenge. Of course. She'd forgotten that's what all this was about for him. Getting back at his uncle.

"But if the bank closes, what happens to all the people who have money in it?"

"They get it all back. The accounts are cleared out, the loans called, debts paid. Then nothing."

Loans called? "What do those people do? The ones who owe the money?"

"Get other financing."

"What if they can't?"

"Not my problem."

But it might be hers. Although she was pretty sure her mother would be able to secure another loan. The house was paid for and she'd only borrowed enough for Vivian's wedding. At least Gracie hoped that was all she'd borrowed.

He smiled. "Pam's loan on her bed-and-breakfast is through the bank. That's got to be good news for you."

"I guess, but I'm worried about everyone else. Riley, I know you want to get back at your uncle and I completely understand that, but what about the town? You'll be destroying it."

"Again, not my problem."

She'd been so caught up in how he made her feel, how great he'd been to her, that she'd forgotten there was an angry man hiding inside. He'd been carrying his pain for so long, it had damaged his soul.

"I don't believe you can harm innocent people for revenge on one man," she said. "That's a lot of guilt to carry for no reason."

"I don't plan to feel guilty. Besides, why do you care? You can't wait to get out of here."

"I know, but I feel badly for everyone who's going to be affected by this."

"They'll get over it."

She felt badly for him, as well. He might think he could do this and walk away without any guilt, but she had her doubts. Was his revenge going to be worth all the regrets?

"Are we still on for dinner?" he asked.

"Of course. Why?"

"You're thinking too much. You don't approve."

"It's not my place to approve or disapprove. I just hope you've thought it all through and that what you're doing will be worth it."

"Don't worry. At the rate things are going, I won't win the election and inherit the bank. Then the town will be safe."

"You don't give up so easily. I would say you still have a good chance."

"You're right." He stood. "Can you be ready by seven-fifteen? We're meeting Jill and Mac at seven-thirty at Bill's Mexican Grill."

"Sure." She glanced at the clock. It was barely after four. She had plenty of time to work on her leaves, then dress to dazzle. If she was going to be the center of attention tonight, she wanted to give everyone something special to talk about.

"I'll let myself out," he said and headed for the door. "See you soon."

"Bye."

She heard the front door close behind him, then sighed.

While she understood why he felt he had to shut down the bank to get his revenge, she knew in her heart it was wrong. But how could she convince him of that?

Just one more thing for her to sweat. Oh, and that her mother could have her loan called. Of course Gracie could help out with that if necessary. At least she could let that worry go.

Which left her time to deal with her possible pregnancy, why Pam was being so nice, who was following her and/or Riley and taking pictures, the election, her sister's on-again-off-again wedding, her relationship with her sisters and her mother, and what kind of cake she was going to make for the heritage society. Oh, and the fact that she and Riley were going out on a date. In public.

Holly slid off the desk and adjusted her skirt. She bent down and kissed Franklin Yardley before straightening and walking out of his office.

Franklin leaned back in his chair. Damn, he was going to miss screwing her. Just knowing she walked around his office in those short skirts and no panties was enough to get him hard.

He'd always had willing assistants, from his first year in office. They'd fit the same profile — young, intelligent, sexual. He'd taught them everything he'd known and eventually they'd moved on with no hard feelings.

He would miss the variety, the youth, the

willingness to do anything, anywhere. But a promise was a promise and he'd vowed to give them up. The idea of sex with just one woman for the rest of his life was a little daunting, but it would be worth it.

He would also miss this office and the perks that went with it. After he won the election, he would clean up the books, close the private account he'd used to skim money from the city for the past fifteen years and make sure the paper trail went up in smoke.

He would divorce Sandra, of course, leave the country and settle into his life of luxury. His private line rang and as he reached for it he thought how much he loved it when a plan came together.

"Yardley," he said briskly.

"Hey, lover. How's it going?"

Franklin glanced at the closed door and knew Holly sat on the other side. Less than ten minutes ago, he'd been screwing her brains out right here on his desk.

"Great. You?"

"Good. Happy. You were magnificent at the debate."

"Thank you. I have to admit I was worried about Riley gaining in the polls. I thought we might have to hire our photographer friend again, but not anymore. Riley is going to lose the election without me having to try."

"I know. I can't believe he's stupid enough to mess with Gracie Landon." Her voice tightened. "What a bitch. But it's our gain. In a couple of weeks you'll be reelected and Riley Whitefield will have lost everything."

"Including his uncle's ninety-seven million dollars." Franklin sighed with satisfaction. "You know we won't be getting it all."

"That's okay," she said easily. "I can accept forty million as a consolation prize. It was so sweet of Donovan Whitefield to leave the bulk of his estate to the Grand Cayman Association for the Advancement of Orphans."

Franklin nodded. "He always liked to help those less fortunate than himself. Especially his friends. He's the one who suggested the Grand Cayman Islands. The rest of the estate will go to real charities to make everything seem on the up-and-up." He chuckled. "I wonder what Riley would say if he knew his uncle had set him up to fail?"

"He's never going to know," she said. "Instead he's going to lose the election and leave town with his tail between his legs."

"Then you and I will pack our bags and be gone."

"I can't wait," she breathed. "I want to be

with you."

"Me, too."

"I love you, Franklin."

"I love you, too, baby."

Bill's Mexican Grill had fabulous food, but it wasn't known for its ambiance. The restaurant was casual, bordering on tacky, which left Gracie in something of a clothing dilemma.

She wanted to look fabulous. After all, she and Riley were about to be the center of attention for the entire evening. People who saw them together would talk about it with their friends and she wanted to make sure that one of the things they said was how great she looked.

It was only fair. The last time she'd generated this much talk with her crush on Riley, she'd been fourteen and, as her mother's neighbor Mrs. Baxter had mentioned, unfortunate-looking. All arms and legs with a completely flat chest, hair that never looked good, no matter what she did to it, braces and acne that had defined her face. Yuck.

Time and growing up had changed all that. She might not be a beauty queen, but she had left "unfortunate-looking" far behind. She wanted to celebrate her curves, her glossy hair and perfectly blemish-free complexion.

She stared in the mirror, ignored the electric curlers piled on her head and considered the blue sleeveless dress she held in front of herself. While it was pretty and had a low cut front, she thought it was a bit too obvious. Sort of an "oh, look, I'm on a date" dress. But she did want to wear a dress or at least a skirt because pants just seemed too — something. Wrong, maybe. Plus she'd not only shaved her legs, she'd fake-tanned and the color had come out really nice.

"Khaki skirt?" she mused aloud. "Khaki skirt with my pale blue twin set?"

The twin set in question was kind of fun with a little beading and appliqué work. She'd bought it for pennies on the dollar at a consignment store up in Palos Verdes the previous fall when all the rich women were getting rid of their summer wardrobes.

She dug through her closet, searching for the skirt, then stopped when she heard someone pounding on her front door. A quick glance at her watch told her it couldn't be Riley. It was barely after six.

Gracie grabbed the skirt and tossed it on the bed, then headed for the front of the house. She pulled open the door and had to hold in a groan when she saw Vivian standing there.

Tears poured down her sister's face. She stood

hunched, as if she'd been battered one too many times.

Gracie's first instinct was to offer sympathy. Then she remembered this was the sister who wanted the uber expensive wedding, but refused to actually commit to getting married.

"What's up?" Gracie asked.

Vivian stepped into the house and choked on a sob. "It's over. With Tom."

"Again?" Gracie asked, then winced when she realized that sounded kind of unfeeling.

"You don't get it," Vivian told her through her tears. "Before, all those fights, it was me. I kept telling him the wedding was off and walking out. I j-just wanted some attention from him. He seemed to be so quiet and serious lately. But after last night, when I walked out again, he came by to s-see me this morning. He said it was over. For real. That I w-wasn't ready to be married to him or anyone."

She covered her face with her hands and continued to sob. Gracie moved close and patted her shoulder. She knew she should probably be hugging her sister, but that didn't feel right. They weren't that close anymore.

Vivian reached in her jeans pocket and pulled out a tissue. "He said I'm too immature, that he loves me, but he's not going to see me anymore until I grow up."

"I'm sorry," Gracie said softly.

Vivian shook her head. "I don't know what to do. He won't talk to me. He really means it. He said every time I called off the wedding I really hurt him, but that I didn't seem to care. He said I only thought about myself in all this. That I was wrong to make Mom take out a loan to pay for our wedding. He said I was a spoiled brat and that I should be ashamed of myself."

The tears started anew. Gracie hovered next to her, not sure what she should say.

"Have you talked to Mom?" she asked in desperation.

"N-no." Vivian sniffed and wiped her face. "She's going to be really mad about all this. She's told her friends everything about the wedding, and how great it's going to be. If she has to go back and say it's off, she'll just die."

Gracie had a strong feeling her mother would be far more upset about the money that couldn't be refunded. "I'm sure her friends will understand."

Vivian looked at her. "Are you kidding? They'll gloat about it. That's how they are. *Their* daughters' weddings didn't get canceled. Mom is going to kill me."

"I know this all seems really horrible right now," Gracie said as she rubbed her sister's back. "It hurts and there doesn't seem to be a solution, but it will get better. Now you have some time to figure out what you really want. Is Tom the guy you want to spend your life with?"

"Of course he is. That's why I wanted to marry him. I only said I was canceling the wedding to get him to pay attention to me."

"Why didn't you just ask for his attention?"

Vivian rolled her eyes. "Oh, please. Like anyone ever does that. Have you *ever* even *had* a boyfriend?"

"Lots. And I learned a long time ago that playing games was never smart. Vivian, did you listen to what Tom said to you? He wants you to be honest with him."

"No guy wants that." She straightened and squared her shoulders. "Okay, I can fix this. I'll just show up at his place wearing nothing. He'll have to let me in then. Once I've got him in bed, I can convince him of everything. Okay. Yeah. That's a good plan. It will be fine." She gave Gracie a watery smile. "I gotta go get ready. Thanks for listening. I'll let you know when Tom agrees to the wedding again."

She waved, then hurried out of the house. Gracie closed the door behind her and leaned against the frame. She felt as if she'd just had a close encounter with an alien from a different planet. Did Vivian really think she could seduce her fiancé back into marriage? Gracie had only met Tom a couple of times but from what she'd seen, he seemed like a rational, sensible sort of man. His points about her sister were all valid. She hoped he was strong enough to force Vivian to grow up a little, but who knew. Of course if he *was* weak enough to be done in by a naked woman in his hallway, then he deserved what he would get.

"Not my problem," she said as she turned back toward her bedroom. She caught sight of the clock in the hallway and shrieked. It was nearly six-thirty and fabulous took way more than thirty minutes.

Riley paused outside of Bill's Mexican Grill and squeezed Gracie's hand. "If you keep breathing that fast, you're going to hyperventilate. We don't have to do this. We can leave now and I'll call Mac from the car and tell him we're having take-out at my place."

Gracie shook her head. Her normally straight blond hair moved in a cascade of curls that had him itching to touch. Makeup emphasized her wide eyes and full mouth. She was gorgeous.

The clothes were just as good. A short skirt emphasized her long, tanned legs. A kind of sweater thing hugged breasts he knew to be soft, erotic and luscious. She was a poster girl for sexual desire and he wanted to subscribe to get the autographed set.

"I can do this," she said, her voice low and determined.

He'd been so busy thinking about how much he wanted her, it took him a second to catch up. "Dinner?"

"Uh-huh. I'll be fine. I'm completely okay with this. I have nerves of steel. I'm invincible." She glanced at him. "Do I look okay?"

He grinned, then lightly kissed her cheek. "You're beautiful. I've been impressed for a long time, but now I'm in awe."

"Wow. Awe works." She leaned close. "Whatever happens, promise you won't leave my side?"

"My word of honor. Ready?"

She nodded and pushed open the door to

the restaurant.

Inside the combination of voices and mariachi music from the bar assaulted them. He knew the restaurant would be quieter in the back, where Mac had booked their table. Riley gave his name to the hostess standing in front.

"The rest of your party is here," the teenager said with a smile. "If you'll follow me."

She wove her way through dozens of tables. Gracie gripped his hand hard enough to snap bone.

"People are staring," she whispered. "I can feel it. Oh, God, this was a really, really bad idea. It's because we're together. How could we do this?"

He pulled his hand free and wrapped an arm around her waist. "You're fine. If anyone is staring it's because you look like a goddess. Every guy in the place wants you."

That made her laugh. "Oh, please. On what planet?"

"I'm serious. If I'd known how great you were going to turn out, I might have paid attention to you all those years ago."

She snorted. "I was fourteen. I could have *been* a goddess and you still would have ignored me."

"The age difference seemed bigger back

then," he admitted. "Plus the whole go-to-prison thing. You were jailbait."

"I'm not anymore."

He squeezed her closer. "Is that an invitation?" he asked in a low whisper.

"You bet."

He was about to say that dinner no longer interested him when he saw Mac and Jill sitting at a table in the corner. The other couple rose and waved them over.

"Hi," Jill said brightly, as she settled back in her chair. "We saw this corner table was open and thought we should grab it while we could. It's much less conspicuous."

Gracie winced. "Because people are going to talk, right? That's what you're saying. I knew it. I think I'm going to be sick."

Mac looked wary. "For real, or is this drama?"

Gracie placed a hand on her stomach. "I don't know."

"It's drama," Riley said and pulled out a chair. "A few chips and salsa will make you feel better."

Gracie brightened. "I do like chips. They're not dangerous."

"Like bread?" he asked.

"Exactly." She beamed at him. "You remembered."

She sank into her seat. He and Mac

exchanged a look that said "women — what can we do?" then they sat down as well.

"How's it going?" Mac asked Riley.

"Okay. Poll numbers are down since the debate. Not a surprise. Zeke, my campaign manager, is coming up with some strategies."

"I never liked the mayor," Jill said with a sniff. "He's so smarmy." She shivered. "I want you to kick his butt. In the election," she added when Mac raised his eyebrows. "Not literally, although I wouldn't mind that either."

"And here I thought you were sworn to uphold the law," her husband said as he put his arm around her.

"No, honey. That's you."

They smiled at each other. Riley studied their easy exchange. When he'd first heard his old friend had taken the job as sheriff and remarried, he'd actually felt sorry for the guy. Who would want a life like that? But now, watching them together, he saw they had a connection. He wasn't sure he believed in love, but if it existed, then Mac and Jill shared it.

"There's something different," Gracie said, leaning toward her friend. "What is it?"

Jill shrugged. "I can't imagine."

"No, there's something. You're . . . different." Gracie tilted her head. "It's not your hair. No highlights. Show me your teeth. Did you get them whitened?"

Jill laughed. "No."

Riley narrowed his gaze. Gracie was right. Something had changed. Jill looked radiant.

Suddenly Gracie shrieked loud enough for nearby diners to turn in their direction.

"Are you?" she demanded as she clutched her friend's hand. "You are. I can tell."

Jill blushed, then nodded. "I just found out this morning. I never thought it would happen so fast. We just started trying, but yeah. I'm pregnant."

"That is so great!"

Gracie flew out of her seat and rounded the table. Jill stood and they hugged. Riley leaned over to Mac and offered his hand.

"Congratulations," he said.

"Thanks. We're both happy." Mac looked sheepish. "It's a little fast. I thought we'd have a couple of months, but I guess we got it right the first time."

Gracie and Jill returned to their seats. "Are you in shock?" Gracie asked.

"Oh, yeah," Jill said. "I haven't even bought any baby books."

Riley watched the women. Was Gracie pregnant as well? They still had a few days until they would know. What would he think if she was? From his perspective, he doubted he would consider the idea "getting it right the first time."

"Well, well, isn't this something."

Riley turned and saw two older women standing by their table. He started to rise, but the one with sausage curls put a surprisingly firm hand on his shoulder.

"Don't get up. Not that I don't appreciate the manners."

Mac shifted uncomfortably. "Riley, I don't think you've met Wilma. She runs the sheriff's office."

"Hi." The shorter of the two women stared at him. "This is my friend Eunice Baxter."

"My neighbor," Gracie whispered. "Hi, Ms. Baxter."

"Hello, Gracie. My, my, don't you young people look so nice out together?" Eunice squeezed his shoulder. "I'm glad to see you've come to your senses, Riley. Gracie always did know how to love a man. When I think about all she did to get your attention, it does my heart good to see you with her now."

He wasn't sure what to say. "Um, yes, ma'am."

Eunice giggled. "Such fine manners. I

341

liked your mama so much. I'm sorry she's not alive to see this. You've done her proud."

"We should go," Wilma said. "Have a nice dinner."

The old ladies left. Gracie rubbed her temples.

"I warned you," she said. "I said this was really, really bad, that people would see and talk about us."

Jill patted her arm. "You're legend, and you're going to have to accept that."

"Can I be something else, like a pillar? I'd be a great pillar."

Mac grinned. "Maybe being seen with you will get Riley elected."

"Oh, I doubt that," Gracie said. "If anything, I've probably cost him points."

"I'm fine," Riley told her. "I didn't come this far to lose the election. Don't worry."

"I can't help it. Worrying is like a sport with me."

"Then worry tomorrow. Tonight we're here to have fun. Can you do that?"

She nodded.

The waitress arrived and asked for their drink orders. He and Mac each wanted a beer, while Gracie and Jill selected iced tea.

The reality of the situation struck him. She wasn't drinking. In fact the night they'd made love and played with champagne at the same time, she'd barely had any of the alcohol. He'd noticed her nearly full glass the next morning. He knew that Gracie normally didn't mind drinking, so the change had to do with the fact that she might be pregnant.

He'd known in his head it might be possible, but until that moment, the news hadn't sunk down to his gut.

What if she was? What would he do? Marry her?

He waited for the panic and frustration he'd felt when he'd had to marry Pam to swamp him, but there wasn't any. He wasn't even angry. So what the hell did that mean?

CHAPTER SIXTEEN

Neda Jackson turned out to be a bright, attractive woman in her mid-twenties with fabulous braids hanging halfway down her back. Gracie eyed them and wondered if she could pull off a similar look.

"Good to meet you," Neda said as she walked into Gracie's rental house. "I've been doing my research and I have to tell you that all your brides are very happy with your cakes. One of them even invited me by after the wedding. Her mom had saved me a piece." Neda's dark brown eyes widened with pleasure. "Delicious. I love how the cake tasted, and I'm not a big cake eater. So what do you put in it?"

Gracie laughed. "Sorry. House secret. I played with various cake recipes for over a year until I perfected the one I use. It's a white cake recipe that I modify for chocolate or yellow cake."

"What are you working on now?" Neda asked.

"Staying sane. It's the busy season. I have at least three cakes to make every week for the next eleven weeks. Then it drops off to just two cakes a week. Some of the designs are simple and only take twenty or thirty hours. Some take double that."

"But you work alone, don't you? There aren't that many hours in a day."

Gracie nodded. "Tell me about it. I save a lot of time by making the decorations in batches. A lot of them can be made in advance."

"And you do it yourself. That's so great. I have to tell you, I've met some wedding cake makers who really cut corners. As much as these cakes cost, that makes me crazy."

Gracie led the way into the dining room where hundreds of leaves and individual flowers sat on stacked trays.

Neda moved close. "What are these? Plastic flowers you buy at a craft store."

"No. I made them. They're edible."

"You're kidding." Neda moved close and stared. "They're icing. Even the leaves. You made the leaves? You don't buy those?"

"I make each one by hand."

Gracie led her back into the kitchen where

she had a two-layer shower cake on the counter.

"How do you get the frosting so smooth?" Neda asked. "It's beautiful."

"The cake is frosted in buttercream icing. Over that I've placed rolled fondant. That's what makes it so smooth. The sides are decorated with little dots in two sizes." Gracie showed her how to apply them. "Roses circle the base of the two layers."

She picked up a premade rose and gently set it into place. "The process isn't that difficult, but it's time consuming."

Neda laughed. "Not to mention that you have to be able to design the cake in the first place and make all the decorations."

"It helps."

"I could never do that." She set her notepad on a kitchen chair then dug in her bag for her digital camera. "Okay, let me take some general pictures, then I want to shoot you decorating this cake."

"Sure."

Gracie worked on the shower cake while Neda circled her and took pictures. There was a partially assembled wedding cake on the other counter and Gracie worked on that as well. As Neda took photos, she asked questions.

"Why wedding cakes?"

"I like making them. I enjoy the challenge of coming up with a new design. I like being a part of a couple's special day."

"Any disasters?"

Gracie sighed. "Someone dropped the top layer once. The bride's brother had picked up the cake, which was in six boxes. I was going to assemble it later. I received a frantic phone call that the top layer, including the blown-glass antique ornament, had been destroyed."

Neda stared at her. "What did you do?"

Gracie slipped three more roses in place. "I was making another cake for the following day and they were about the same size. I put a new top layer in the oven for bride number two and quickly changed the frosting on the one I already had. We still didn't have an ornament, so I put a call in to the florist. By the time I arrived at the reception location, she had delivered five dozen miniature roses in the bride's colors."

Gracie shivered at the memory. "It was a three-layer cake with pillars in between, so everything was visible. I had less than an hour to make it all work. I pretty much pulled off most of my decorations, to make the bottom two layers more plain, then I cut the rose stems off and piled the buds on each layer. I used leftover petals to dress up the table and tacked a few decorations on the top layer. No one ever knew, except the immediate family."

"Talk about pressure," Neda said.

"It got my heart racing."

Neda took several more pictures, asked a couple more questions, then announced that the interview was finished.

"I'm so impressed," the reporter said. "I love your work and I'm going to say that in my article." Neda loaded up her bag. "I'm engaged. We're thinking of a Christmas wedding. Do you still have room in your schedule for my cake?"

Gracie smiled. "Absolutely. Let me give you a card. You can call me in the next month or so and we can talk about what you'd like. Holiday wedding cakes can be so beautiful. All those jewel tones."

"Good. Thanks. You've been terrific."

"My pleasure."

Gracie led her to the front door, then walked her out to her car. As they approached Neda's Mustang, Gracie noticed a couple of boxes lying on the driveway next to her own car.

"What are those?" she asked as she moved closer.

When she caught sight of the familiar *cake mix* logo, she froze in place.

"What is it?" Neda asked.

Gracie couldn't move, couldn't breathe. She could only stare at the two boxes that had obviously fallen out of her Subaru. No wonder, what with the back end of the vehicle being jam packed with what looked like hundreds of cake mix boxes.

"Are you kidding?" the reporter asked, sounding disgusted. "You use cake mix? That's your secret ingredient?"

"No! These aren't mine. You didn't see them when you drove up. I haven't used a cake mix since I was twelve. Someone did this."

Neda shook her head. "Oh, sure. Someone knew I was coming and just happened to figure out when so they could plant this on you. Forget what I said about you making my wedding cake."

Gracie picked up the boxes. They were full. "You have to believe me."

"I don't think so. You're not special after all. I should have known."

Neda opened her car door and tossed in her bag. When she turned around, Gracie saw the digital camera in her hand. Before Gracie could stop her, she'd already taken half a dozen pictures.

"Oh, and never mind about the article. We're a reputable magazine," Neda said as she climbed in her car. "I can't believe you did this. Don't you realize you're spoiling people's weddings? That's so low. You seemed so nice, too, but I guess that was as much a lie as your cakes. You probably didn't even make those decorations yourself. That's why they were all stacked like that. You bought them somewhere."

With that Neda slammed her door and sped away. Gracie stared after her. This couldn't be happening, she told herself. It just couldn't.

But it was, she thought as she stared at the cake box in her hand. Someone had set her up. And there was only one name she could think of:

Pam.

But even as she told herself no one else would bother, she honestly couldn't think of a single reason as to why Pam would do this to her. The woman had been nothing but friendly and pleasant since Gracie moved back. She'd even rented out her kitchen.

Gracie fought tears as she dropped the boxes in the trash. Then she walked in the house, grabbed her purse, made sure the oven was off, then hurried to her car.

Riley wrapped up the meeting and walked

back to his office. As he crossed in front of the elevators, they opened and Gracie stepped out. He took one look at her face and knew the worst — whatever that might be — had happened.

"What?" he asked as he put his arm around her and led her into his office. "Is someone hurt?"

She shook her head and gulped in a breath. "The cakes. I don't understand how it happened. I told a few people, but no one knew when exactly. I think it's Pam, but why? She's been nice. It can't be Jill, and I want to suspect my sisters but I never even told them. God forbid we talk about anything but them."

He ushered her inside and closed the door. When they were alone and in private, he pulled her close and wrapped his arms around her.

"Start at the beginning," he said gently. "Tell me what happened."

Instead, she began to cry. His first clue was the long silence. Then her body began to shake and finally he heard the soft sobs.

"I'm ruined," she managed after a few minutes. "Completely ruined."

"Not possible," he said and kissed the top of her head. "What happened?"

Her answer was to cry harder. Riley had

351

never been a fan of tears on a woman —
they'd always seemed like a manipulation.
But with Gracie, he felt differently. She
didn't want anything from him — except
possibly for him to ease her pain.

She sniffed. "I need a tissue."

He pulled out a handkerchief and handed
it to her.

She blotted her face, then turned from
him and blew her nose.

"I'm not attractive when I cry. You should
look away."

He pulled her close again. "Right. Because
I'm just in this because of how you look.
Tell me what happened."

"I had my interview with the bridal magazine person today."

"Okay and then what?" He led her over to
the sofa in the corner and tugged her down
next to him. After angling toward her, he
cupped her face. "I know you were charming and brilliant and you made a fan."

Tears filled her blue eyes. "You'd think,
wouldn't you? She even asked me to bake
her wedding cake. She's getting married in
December. But now. . . ."

Her voice wavered and her shoulders
slumped.

"Now, what?" he asked gently as he wiped
her cheeks with his thumbs.

"She was leaving and I walked her outside. One of the things she wanted to talk about was the secret ingredient. I don't tell anyone what I put in my cakes. I worked on the recipe forever and it's really good."

"I know. I've had your cake."

She sniffed again. "There were boxes everywhere. Someone planted cake mix boxes in my car. They were spilled out onto the ground. She got mad. She took pictures and called me a liar and now I'm ruined."

She covered her face and began to sob. He drew her close and settled her against his side.

The typical male side of him wanted to promise that everything would be all right, but he didn't actually know that and he wasn't about to pretend to Gracie. Her business survived on reputation and word-of-mouth. He knew what the mention in *People* had done for her career. If word got out that she was a fraud, clients could disappear overnight.

Frustration bubbled inside of him. He didn't have a clue as to how to fix the problem and the need to do so burned hot and bright inside.

"Who would do this?" he asked. "Who would want to set you up? Are other cake decorators mad because you're doing so well?"

She kept her head on his shoulder and wiped her face with the handkerchief. "I don't know. We're not exactly a close-knit group. No monthly meetings or any of that. I've met a few at wedding expos. They seemed nice enough. How would any of them know what I was doing or even where I was?"

"Who knew about the interview?"

"You, me, Jill. I'm sure she told Mac, but he would never do anything like this. And Pam."

"Pam, my ex-wife?"

"Uh-huh. She was there when I got the call. She was really excited for me."

"Yeah, right. Pam's never been happy for anyone but herself in her entire life. Okay, she's a prime suspect."

Gracie straightened and looked at him. "I agree that of all the people who knew, Pam is the only one I don't trust. But why would she do it? What does she care if I get a write-up in some bridal magazine? It's a big deal with me, but not to anyone else. It's not as if she has a rival bakery. My success, or lack of success, doesn't impact her at all."

"Good question. But there isn't anyone else."

"I know." Gracie sighed. "I just don't get it. Why? And what do I do now?"

"Do you want to confront Pam?"

"Not really. I want to crawl back home and have this never have happened. Can we do that?"

He stroked her hair. "Gracie, I know it's horrible, but what's the worst-case scenario? You don't get the nice spread in the bridal magazine. You were doing well before — is not getting the notice going to be all that bad?"

She sat up and looked at him. "No, that's not so bad. But I'm afraid that's not the worst of it. I've made cakes for famous people — that makes me loosely linked to them. And there's nothing anyone likes more than a scandal related to movie and television stars. If Neda just bad-mouths me at the magazine, I'll be okay. But if she sells the story and the photos to a tabloid, then I'm completely and totally screwed."

Pain darkened her eyes. Pain and a kind of hopelessness that made him want to lash out at someone — anyone, so long as it would make her feel better.

"What can I do?" he asked.

"Nothing. But I appreciate the thought." She stood.

"You've been great, but I have to get going. There are more cakes to finish before my career flushes down the toilet."

He rose. "You don't know that will happen."

She nodded. "Maybe I'll get lucky, but I don't think so."

As he watched her leave, he tightened his hands into fists. There had to be something he could do, some way he could fix the problem. Or if not this problem, then another one. Because he had to do something. He couldn't leave Gracie in that much pain.

Gracie lost herself in work. Home seemed the safest place to be and with the worry that she could be trashed in some tabloid at any second, she desperately needed to work while she still could.

She avoided everyone, even Riley. She talked to Jill by phone, but didn't mention the botched interview, and she stayed away from Pam and her bed-and-breakfast. Better to have to turn the pans every ten minutes than risk that encounter, she thought, still not sure why Pam would have done it.

Three days later, the world came calling in the form of someone knocking on her front door. She walked out to the small foyer and looked out the window.

"Just what I need," she murmured as she saw her mother standing there. "Another emotional beating."

But there was no way to hide, not with her car parked in the driveway, she so braced herself for the forthcoming lecture and opened the door.

"Hi, Mom," she said with a cheerfulness she didn't feel. "How's it going?"

"Okay." Her mother stepped into the house. "Not great."

Gracie drew in a deep breath. "I'm sorry to hear that. Honestly, I didn't come back here to make trouble, but that seems to be what's happening. Apparently, there are forces at work I can't control. In truth, while I appreciate your concern, I can't handle one more lecture. I don't want to talk about my relationship with Riley, my past, my issues or any of that."

"That's not why I'm here."

"Okay." Great. More wedding talk. Had Vivian's plan of nakedness worked?

Gracie led the way into the small living room and motioned to the sofa. "You want anything?"

"No. I'm fine."

Her mother settled on a sofa and waited

until Gracie took a club chair before speaking.

"I'm sorry," her mother said. "I'm more sorry than I can ever say. I've been a horrible mother and a worse person. I'm disgusted with myself." Tears filled her eyes.

Gracie figured that was four-for-four on the Landon women sobbing in the past couple of weeks. It had to be a record.

"Mom, I have no idea what you're talking about."

"I know." More prepared than Gracie had been during her meltdown, her mother withdrew a small package of tissues from her purse. "I've tried to ignore it all, but I can't. It's just like it was all those years ago. I know what I did and I refuse to do it again. Those bitches can just go to hell."

Gracie blinked. She wasn't sure she'd ever heard her mother swear before. "I'm all in favor of bitches in hell. Really. But who are we talking about and what did they do?"

"It's not them. It's me." Her mother drew in a deep breath. "Oh, Gracie, you were always such a bright, happy child. Then your father died and your world collapsed. You were his favorite." She gave a shaky smile. "Parents aren't supposed to have favorites, or if we do, we aren't supposed to say, but everyone knew your father loved you best.

358

And when he died, you were so lost."

Gracie swallowed. She remembered her father. How he'd always made time for her, how they'd done things together. "I missed him a lot."

"I know you did. I was worried, but I thought you'd be fine. Then that Riley boy moved in next door and you fixated on him. I knew it had to do with you losing your father and needing a man in your life. I thought it would blow over. But it didn't."

Gracie's warm fuzzy feelings faded. "We've been over this, Mom."

"I know. Here's my point. Things got out of hand so quickly and soon everyone knew you had a crush on him. People talked. There were those stories in the paper. You became legend. A lot of people thought it was sweet, but some women around town weren't so kind. You were so creative and they were cruel. They laughed at you and at me. I felt exposed and humiliated. As if I couldn't control my own daughter. Every week there was a new Gracie story."

Gracie felt her cheeks get hot. She'd never considered her actions from her mother's point of view. "I'm sorry," she whispered.

"Don't be. You were young and it was your first crush. I should have been able to handle it. I should have told them you were my daughter and I would stand by you. Instead I tried to make you stop, which didn't work. Then Pam turned up pregnant and there was the quickie wedding. I knew I had to get you out of town so nothing happened."

Gracie nodded as she remembered the pain of being sent away.

"But it didn't matter," her mother continued. "At Pam and Riley's wedding, you were all anyone talked about. They placed bets on whether or not you would show up. They recounted their favorite Gracie story and talked about how you loved that boy with your whole heart. Some people admired that, but others were less kind."

Gracie winced. "I didn't know that."

"I'm not telling you now to be cruel, just to explain. The fault is mine. I didn't think I could face the ridicule anymore. When my sister offered to take you, I let you go because I was selfish and weak. And I'm sorry."

Her mother started to cry again. "I missed you so much. Every day I reached for the phone to tell you to come home. But then someone would say something and it all came back to me. In time the talk died down and it was such a relief to me. But on the inside I felt so guilty for being a coward.

I let my so-called friends influence me and because of that, I lost a daughter."

Gracie didn't know what to think. She was numb. "You didn't lose me."

"Yes, I did. You and I aren't close. You're angry with me for what I did, and I deserve that. I have no excuse. I was spineless and foolish. I'm sorry, Gracie. I'm so sorry." She pressed a hand to her mouth. "And I'm a bad mother because of my three girls, you're the one who turned out the best. Vivian is spoiled and selfish and Alexis is a drama queen. I think I did that. I think it's my fault."

Gracie moved to the sofa and hugged her mother.

"It's okay," she said.

"No, it's not. I lost you and I only have myself to blame. I'm so sorry."

Gracie held on. "I'm sorry, too. I never meant to embarrass you."

"That was me, not you. You were a little girl in a lot of pain. I should have seen that."

Gracie supposed it was true, but she still felt self-conscious about it all. "Remind me to never have a crush on a guy again," she said.

Her mother gave a strangled laugh. "I think you're over all that now."

Gracie pulled back and eyed her suspiciously. "That's not what you were saying a couple of weeks ago."

"True, but I know better now. If Riley Whitefield makes you happy, then you go on seeing him." Gracie half expected the earth's crust to open and gnomes in pointy hats to appear. "Really?"

Her mother nodded. "I don't want to lose you again, Gracie. I know we can't recover what's lost, but I want us to try to be close again. I'm willing to be patient and earn your trust."

Gracie felt her heart opening and stretching. "Oh, Mom. It's okay."

"It's not now, but I want it to be." They hugged again.

"What changed your mind?" Gracie asked.

"Alexis and Vivian were over the other night and I realized that part of our family was missing. I felt so sad, I couldn't stop crying. I want us to be together again. I hope you can want that, too."

Gracie nodded. It might take her a little while to shift her thinking, but she was willing to make the effort.

Her mother squeezed her tight, then let go. "All right, now that I've dumped all over you with my problems, how are you? How's the cake business?"

"There are a few bumps in the road."

"Like what?"

She hesitated for a second, not sure if she wanted to say anything, then drew in a deep breath.

"I had an interview with a reporter from a bride magazine a few days ago."

"That's great."

"Not exactly."

Gracie told her what had happened.

When she'd finished, her mother looked stunned. "Who on earth would have planted those cake boxes?"

"I haven't a clue. No one really knew about the interview. Just me, Riley, Jill and Pam."

Her mother's lips curled. "Pam's a bitch. How did you get messed up with her?"

Gracie couldn't help laughing. "Talk about a snap judgment."

Her mother dismissed the comment with a flick of her wrist. "I never liked Pam. No one does. She's only out for herself. But why would she want to set you up?"

"That's the question of the hour."

"I'll ask around," her mother said. "Maybe someone has heard something. Too bad Vivian didn't plan the wedding at Pam's little B&B. I would enjoy constantly canceling and upsetting her plans."

Gracie winced. "About the wedding. . . ."

"Not your problem," her mother said. "And except for making the phone calls, it's not mine, either. I'm tired of running interference for Viv. She needs to grow up and accept the consequences of her actions."

"Really?"

"Cross my heart." Her mother hugged her again. "Any leftover cake?"

"Absolutely. Come on."

Riley read through the detective's report again. Nothing. No sign of a mystery reporter, no hint that the mayor was up to anything. Riley had even asked the man to keep tabs on Pam for a few days and so far she'd been a model citizen.

It was all frustrating, he thought as he drove through Los Lobos. He was no closer to figuring out what was going on than he had been before he'd hired the detective. Worse, he had no motive for anyone to set up Gracie.

As he couldn't fix that problem, he'd decided to deal with another one. Which was why he parked in front of Zeke's insurance office just before closing and strolled inside.

"Is he in?" Riley asked the woman at the front desk.

"Yes. May I say who's . . . Oh. Mr. White-field. I'll announce you."

Riley gave her a quick smile. "Not necessary. I'll find my way back."

He walked down the short hallway and opened Zeke's door without knocking.

Zeke looked up. "Hey, boss. What are you doing here?" He glanced at his calendar. "Did we have a meeting I missed?"

"Nope." Riley walked to Zeke's desk and perched on the corner. "Did you know that when I left Los Lobos I headed north?"

Zeke frowned. "No. Should I have?"

Riley shrugged. "Not really. I crewed on fishing boats in Alaska. It's hard work. Long hours. I was a kid from a small town. I didn't know shit about the world. But I learned fast. Got into a lot of fights with guys bigger and older. After getting the crap beat out of me, I learned to hold my own."

Zeke shifted in his chair. "Probably not good campaign material."

"But it's interesting. Oil rigs are even worse. Confined quarters, a lot of independent men. When fights start there, they can go on for hours."

"You want to beat up the mayor?"

"No. I was thinking more of taking you on."

Zeke's eyes widened. He scrambled to his

365

feet. "Me? What did I do?"

"You're keeping secrets and I gotta tell you, I don't like it. They upset your wife, which doesn't matter to me, but then she tells Gracie and Gracie gets upset. Gracie does matter. This whole mess with the pictures started because of you. I can't solve the other problems in Gracie's life, but I can solve this one. Where the hell are you going at night and what are you doing when you get there?"

CHAPTER SEVENTEEN

Gracie stood in front of her schedule and wondered how long it would be until it all hit the fan. While she wanted to believe that Neda Jackson would simply keep the news to herself, Gracie knew her luck wasn't that good. If Neda couldn't write her article for the bridal magazine, she would be out some serious money. Which meant the reporter would have to make up the money elsewhere. As tabloids had a reputation of paying big for a scandal, Gracie had a feeling that was where Neda would go.

But how long would it take? Gracie didn't know anything about the world of weekly publishing. Was it days? Weeks? When would it hit?

Not that it mattered. She still had cakes to bake and decorate. Since the debacle with the cake mixes, she hadn't been back at Pam's place. Somehow she couldn't shake the feeling that the other woman was

367

involved and until Gracie figured out how to prove it, she didn't want to confront her.

A car pulled up in her driveway. Since reconciling with her mother, Gracie felt less worried about visitors. With luck, she would really like this one.

She hurried to the front door and smiled when she saw a familiar Mercedes next to her car and a handsome man walking toward her.

"Don't you have a bank to run?" she asked, trying to ignore the fluttering she felt inside. Liking Riley was one thing, but *really* liking Riley could be a big mistake.

"I have a staff," he said as he approached, then bent down to lightly kiss her. "It's one of the perks of being the boss."

"A staff, huh? I might have to get me one." She stepped back to let him in, then led the way to the kitchen. "What's up?"

He moved close and put his hands on her shoulders. "I have good news about Zeke. He's not having an affair. Not even close."

She'd been expecting him to say about a thousand other things. "What? You talked to Zeke?"

"I can't solve your really big problems, but I knew I could take care of this one."

Which was really sweet, she thought happily. "Okay, what's he doing on his nights when he disappears?"

"Brace yourself."

Riley was touching her. The only thing she really wanted to do was get closer and purr like a well-fed cat.

"I'm braced."

"He's doing stand-up."

Gracie stared at him. "Excuse me?"

"That was my reaction. Apparently Zeke has always dreamed about being a stand-up comedian. Then he met Alexis and fell in love. He put the idea aside, but lately it's been bugging him. He doesn't want to live his whole life with regrets, so he's trying to make it now."

Stand-up? "I never thought of Zeke as that funny. Why didn't he tell Alexis?"

"Beats the hell out of me. Part of it is they're talking about starting a family and he didn't think quitting his job would make her feel secure. He's been going to clubs in Santa Barbara and L.A. working on his act. A couple of weeks ago, some guys from Leno saw him, so he's been waiting for a phone call."

Gracie couldn't believe it. Not only that her brother-in-law's secret life was something she never would have thought of but that he and Alexis were thinking of having a baby. There was a lot of pre-pregnancy going around these days.

"Is he going to tell Alexis?" she asked.

"I convinced him that was the best plan."

"Do I want to know how this convincing took place?"

Riley looked pleased with himself. "I threatened him."

"With physical violence?"

"Oh, yeah."

She chuckled. "Was it good for you?"

"The best. I haven't been in a fight in years, but I was willing to take him on. Zeke never was a real physical guy. He backed down right away."

"I'm so proud of both of you." She stepped closer to Riley and he wrapped his arms around her. "One problem down, fifty million to go."

"Is that how it feels?" he asked as he stroked her back.

"Every minute of every day."

"So we'll tackle the next one. Pam and the cake boxes."

She didn't want to think about that. "Why would Pam be involved?"

"Not a clue, but she makes sense as a suspect. We just have to figure out what's going on with her."

Gracie winced and thought longingly of an antacid. "Tell me we're not going to watch her house."

Riley stepped back and grinned. "I'll be here at eight. Dress in black. Oh, and bring your camera."

When Riley left, Gracie went to work on baking. As she had to turn the pans every ten minutes, the job was far more labor intensive than it should have been. She'd just pulled layer one from the oven when her cell phone rang. She grabbed it and pushed the talk button.

"This is Gracie."

"How could you?" Fury filled the unfamiliar female voice. "I can't tell you how horrible I think you are. Bitch doesn't even come close."

"What?" Gracie blinked. "Who is this? I think you have the wrong number."

"Oh, you wish. I hate you. I'll never forgive you. And dammit, I want my deposit back right now. How dare you pass yourself off as a professional? You're a hack. You're a liar. My father's a lawyer and I'm going to talk to him about suing you for . . . for I don't know what, but something. You're disgusting."

Gracie's stomach turned over as the room seemed to get very, very cold.

"Who am I speaking with?" she asked as

calmly as she could.

"Sheila Morgan. You're supposed to be making my wedding cake next month. You lied, Gracie. You *lied* about everything. Now I have to find someone else. I hope you rot in hell. Oh, I'm so mad, I can't think of bad enough things to say to you."

The phone call ended abruptly. Gracie pushed the end button and stared at her phone. Then she turned it off.

Twenty minutes later she stood beside the check-out line of the local grocery store. The weekly tabloids were still stacked together, tied in bundles. She scanned the headlines of the first two before seeing the teaser on the third.

Wedding Cake Planner To The Stars Stirs Things Up With Bad Baking.

Next to the headline was a crumpled box of cake mix.

She pulled the tabloid out and flipped through it until she found the article. It wasn't very big, maybe half a page, but there was a picture of her car filled with cake mix boxes and another shot of herself looking more than a little upset.

The text damned with innuendo. No one came out and said she used the cake mix, but the way it was written, no one had to.

By six, eighty percent of her cakes had

been canceled. She'd been on some of the bridal internet bulletin boards and had seen the angry posts there. Even the editor of the bridal magazine that had commissioned the story in the first place had called to yell at her.

Gracie lay curled up in bed, staring at her cell phone. Every time she turned it on, there were more messages from brides canceling their orders. They were all furious and she had no idea how to tell them she'd been the one betrayed, not them.

This couldn't be happening, she told herself. It was a really, really bad dream. She'd worked so hard for so long to build up her reputation and now it was gone. Just like that. No one cared about how many nights she'd stayed up making sure each cake was perfect. No one wanted to hear the truth.

The room got dark and she told herself she had to get up and do something, but she didn't have the energy. Instead she pulled the pillow over her head and willed the world to go away.

Sometime later she heard pounding on her front door. She ignored it, even as she remembered she and Riley were supposed to go watch Pam's house. What did it matter if Pam had done this to her? The dam-

373

age was irreparable. Gracie's career was ruined.

After a few minutes, the pounding went away. Gracie dropped the pillow onto the other side of the bed and stared at the ceiling. Shadows filled the room. In the distance, she heard a door open, then footsteps.

Under normal circumstances, she would have imagined the worst — robbers or aliens or something — but right now she didn't care.

"Gracie?"

Riley's voice. The man didn't give up.

"In here," she called, her voice low and thick with pain. Everything hurt.

A light clicked on in the hallway. Seconds later he appeared in her room.

"What happened? Are you sick?"

"I wish. At least I could get better. Or die. Either way the problem would be solved."

He sat on the edge of the mattress and brushed the hair out of her face. "Tell me what's going on."

She picked up the cell phone and pushed the buttons to replay the messages, then handed it to him.

He listened for a few minutes. When he turned off the phone, she found herself fighting tears.

"I didn't do anything wrong," she said. "If

I had, I could accept what they're doing. But I didn't, and no one will listen. My business is all about reputation. Now it's gone. I get to keep the two cakes for this weekend because it's too late for the brides to find someone else. Just about everyone else has canceled, except for the stupid sheet cake the historical society wants me to do and I'm sure the only reason they haven't canceled is that I'm doing it for free."

She saw anger tighten his expression. He bent down and kissed her.

"We'll fix this," he promised.

"Not to make trouble, but how?"

"We'll figure something out. We're a great team. Come on. We're going to go stalk Pam. I've already got my detective working on learning everything we can about her. There are secrets in her past and we're going to find them. In the meantime, let's go get some incriminating pictures."

Gracie shook her head. "You go."

"Not without you."

He grabbed her arms and pulled her into a sitting position, then he crouched in front of her.

"Come on, Gracie. Let's go ruin Pam. It will be fun."

The urge to simply curl back up in bed

nearly overwhelmed her. She would have given in except she had the thought that if she did, she might never get up again, and that couldn't be good.

"Okay. Give me a second to get changed."

She stood and walked to her closet. The clothing choices seemed overwhelming. Riley moved next to her then reached inside for a pair of black jeans and a dark purple T-shirt.

"Very fashion forward," he said, draping the clothes over her arm and pushing her toward the bathroom. "You have three minutes to get changed."

"Where did you ever hear an expression like 'fashion forward'?"

He grinned. "Are you kidding? The style network is really big on the oil rig. All those half-naked models draw us in, but the runway news keeps us riveted."

She smiled, which felt weird, but nice. "I'll be right out."

Ten minutes later they were in his car and heading across town in the rapidly dwindling twilight.

She stared out the windshield and tried to keep her sighing to a minimum.

"You don't have time for this," she told him. "The election is in a couple of weeks."

"I've got it covered. I'll start going door-to-door in a day or two."

"Are you behind in the polls?"

"I'm holding my own."

She looked at him. "Tell me the truth."

"I'm —"

"Riley, I'm not a baby. I can handle it. What are the numbers?"

"Still falling."

How much of that was her fault? If she hadn't come back to Los Lobos, none of this would have happened.

"I'm sorry," she said. "About all of it."

"I'm sorry about the cake disaster, but not the rest of it."

"What? Are you crazy? You could lose. Have you considered that? It's ninety-seven million dollars."

"I won't lose."

"But if you do. And what if I'm pregnant?"

That seemed to get his attention. "Are you?"

She slumped down in the seat. "I don't know. I don't think so. I can take the pregnancy test in three days. But what if I am?"

"We'll deal with it."

He spoke calmly, which wasn't what she expected. In his position, she had a feeling she would be both furious and screaming. But after the day she'd had, she appreciated the lack of dramatics.

"I'll try not to be pregnant," she said.

"I don't think it works that way."

He drove down a street she thought she recognized, then parked behind a minivan.

"Pam's house is over there," he said, pointing to a house on the corner. "We'll walk the rest of the way."

"Shouldn't one of us be humming the theme from *Mission: Impossible*?" she asked as she climbed out of his Mercedes.

"Only if it's important to you."

"I guess not."

She followed down the sidewalk. Streetlights illuminated much of the area, but there were still puddles of darkness to hide in.

When Riley ducked into a side yard, she followed. They made their way into the backyard and crouched by some bushes.

"She didn't close her blinds," he whispered.

"She probably didn't expect to be spied on. It's not something I think about either. Although given what's happening in my life, I guess I should."

"There," he said, pointing.

Gracie strained to see in the window. Pam stood in the kitchen, pouring something from a large bowl into a —

"That bitch has my baking pans!"

The loud words filled the silence of the night. Even as Riley grabbed her and pulled her down next to him, she slapped both hands over her mouth.

"Sorry," she mumbled. "I didn't mean to do that."

"I know." He spoke the words directly into her ear.

The soft sound was distracting enough, but when combined with the heat of his breath and the way his strong arms supported her, she started to go all gooey inside.

This was neither the time nor the place, she reminded herself as she dropped to her knees and shoved her hands into her pockets.

"She has my baking pans."

"I gathered that."

"Why would she take my baking pans?"

"Not a clue."

Gracie considered the possibilities. "To make her own cakes? But why?" She rose up slightly so she could see in the window again. Pam bent over the oven, positioning the cake.

"The rack's too high," she murmured. "The edges are going to burn. If she was planning to steal my business, she should

379

have asked more questions."

She turned to him. "Is that it? Is Pam going to steal my business?"

"Why would she want to? She seems to have enough money of her own."

"You're right. Someone is paying for very expensive clothing," Gracie said. "And there's the bed-and-breakfast. That wasn't cheap. Okay, now I'm completely confused. What is she doing?"

They stayed out in the bushes for nearly two hours in an attempt to find out. The only thing they discovered was that Pam was a really bad baker. Gracie felt some small measure of satisfaction when the cake turned out lopsided and burned on the edges. The pleasure peaked when Pam attempted to remove the cake from the pan and only about sixty percent of it fell onto the cooling rack.

"It was a complete disaster," Gracie said cheerfully as they headed back to the car. "My first cake was much better than that and I think I was all of ten when I made it. I guess I don't have to sweat her stealing my clients anytime. . . ."

Her voice trailed off as she realized she didn't have any clients *to* steal.

"We'll figure it out," Riley said as he put an arm around her and drew her close.

"We'll watch her for as many nights as it takes."

"Good thing sweeps month is over on television and there's nothing to watch."

He looked at her and raised his eyebrows. "You would rather watch television than spy on Pam with me?"

She smiled. "Never! Did I say that? Absolutely not. You sure know how to show a girl a good time."

The next two nights of spying produced similar results. Pam baked. Badly, Gracie thought with some measure of satisfaction. Pam also didn't take good care of the pans, which were getting dark and scratched, but that was the least of Gracie's problems.

But on the third night there wasn't a cooling rack in sight. Pam barely came into the kitchen and when she did it was to pop a cookie sheet of store-bought appetizers into the oven and pull a bottle of white wine out of the refrigerator.

"Company," Riley said with satisfaction. "Let's see who Pam hangs out with these days. Maybe we'll get some answers there."

"The only possibly interesting person could be the mayor," Gracie whispered. "And it can't be him. She thinks he's just as creepy as everyone else."

"Are you sure?"

Gracie realized she wasn't sure about anything except that she was getting a cramp in her leg.

"We'll go around to the side yard," Riley said. "We'll be able to see who's arriving."

Gracie followed him, making sure to stay low. When they were in position in the side yard, she fumbled with her camera. Might as well get a picture of Pam's visitor.

A car drove down the street. Gracie rose so she could brace herself against a small tree. She raised her camera to her face and squinted to see out the tiny viewer. The car got closer.

"Come on, big guy," she murmured.

Riley chuckled. "Big guy?"

"Just an expression."

"Okay. The car's pulling in."

She wasn't sure what happened next. Maybe it was wet grass or leaves. Maybe it was just being clumsy. Maybe it was fate. Whatever the cause, just as she prepared to snap the picture of Pam's visitor, Gracie's foot slipped. She found herself sliding and falling. As she instinctively reached out to grab something, she squeezed the button on the camera. The flash exploded in the darkness. The tired mechanism pushed out a picture and whoever was in the car backed up and sped away.

"Come on."

Riley grabbed her free hand and dragged her out of the yard and toward their car. Lights popped on in Pam's house. The front door opened.

"Who's out there?" Pam yelled. "What's going on?"

Gracie threw herself into Riley's car and ducked down below the dashboard.

"Drive. Drive!" she insisted.

"I'm driving."

He started the engine and made a U-turn. It was only when they were a couple of blocks away that he turned on the lights. Gracie slowly straightened.

"I'm sorry," she said, afraid to look at him and see how mad he was. "I didn't do that on purpose."

A strange sound made her stiffen. Was he . . . laughing?

She turned her head and stared at him. "What is so funny?"

"You," he said with a chuckle. "I know you didn't do that on purpose. I watched you start to slide, but I was too far away to prevent it. You were like a cartoon or something. Slow at first, then faster and faster." He glanced at her. "I'll give you this, Gracie. You're never boring."

"Great. You can put that on my tomb-stone. In the meantime, we *still* don't know what Pam's up to or who she's hanging out with. Did you see the car?"

"No. It was too dark to figure out make or model."

Gracie pulled the covering off the picture and stared at a section of Pam's roof and a bunch of darkness she figured had to be the sky.

"If I don't get my baking career back, I'll never make it as a photographer."

"You'll get your baking business back."

"How do you know?"

"Because we're going to solve this mystery, and then whoever did it will make it right. Even if I have to stand over him or her and physically force them."

She liked the sound of that. "You can be so sweet."

"Because I'm willing to beat people up for you?"

"Yeah. It's great."

He reached over and touched her cheek. "You need to rethink your standards."

"Not even a little." She turned her head so she could press her mouth to his palm. "Want to sleep over?"

"Absolutely."

She liked that he didn't even have to think

about it.

"You're a good man, Riley Whitefield."

"I'm a bastard. You can't see it."

"I don't think so."

Sure, he had his flaws, but who didn't? The important thing was he'd been there for her, almost from the beginning, and this despite their rather odd and scary past. He'd obviously gotten over her being stalker girl. He was protective, caring, funny, smart and, when they made love, she touched a whole new dimension because of him. He made her feel safe. He made her feel sparks.

She watched him as they drove back to her place. After he parked in the driveway next to her car, he leaned over and kissed her. As she wrapped her arms around him and held on tight, she wondered if it was the least bit possible that she might very well have picked the man of her dreams at the tender age of fourteen.

CHAPTER EIGHTEEN

Riley woke to a sunny room and an empty bed. He brushed his hands against the rumpled sheets and figured Gracie had to be somewhere in the house and that she'd show up here eventually. Then he would grab her and pull her down next to him and have his way with her. Again.

He closed his eyes and smiled at the thought. He liked having her in his bed. He liked how she looked and smelled and how she made him feel. She was good for him, and he couldn't say that about many people he knew.

"Whatcha smiling at?"

He opened his eyes and saw her approaching. She wore a long T-shirt and, from the way her breasts swayed with each step, very little else.

"You."

"Yeah?" She sat next to him and brushed the hair off his forehead. "Were you thinking about last night? You were an animal."

"You weren't bad yourself." He turned his head to glance at his left shoulder. "I think you bit me."

She grinned. "I *know* I bit you."

"You left marks."

"Complaining?"

"Only if you don't do it again."

She chuckled, then bent down and brushed her mouth across his.

"You're violating the three *F's* code and soon the three *F's* police will come and arrest you. The good news is you won't have to worry about being a daddy while you're locked up." She held out a white plastic stick. "I'm not pregnant."

He'd forgotten it was time for her to take the test.

He reached for the stick, but she held it out of reach. "I peed on that. I don't think you want to touch it."

"Good point." He studied her face. "You're sure?"

"Yup. Not just from this." She waved the test. "But I've been getting symptoms. I'll be getting my period in the next day or so. I'm guessing it's late because of all the stress in my life. That happens."

"Are you okay with this?"

Her eyes widened. "I'm completely fine.

Be happy. This is what we wanted. Isn't it?"

"Of course." An unexpected pregnancy wasn't a part of his five-year plan.

"We've kept using protection after that first time, so no worries." She stood and tossed the plastic stick into the trash. "I've made coffee. I have some eggs if you want. I'll even scramble them for you."

He sat up, then grabbed her hand and squeezed her fingers. "I only eat cake."

She laughed. "You're my kind of guy. Want to shower first?"

"Thanks."

Riley left about thirty minutes later and drove home to change clothes before going to the bank. He'd promised to call later so he and Gracie could figure out their "Pam" strategy. He also had a meeting with Zeke about the campaign and a host of other responsibilities.

But all he could think about was Gracie and the fact that she wasn't pregnant. A good thing, he told himself. So why wasn't he more happy? Had he wanted her to be?

No way, he told himself. Then what? He would have had to marry her and be a husband and father. Neither were part of his game plan. He wasn't the kind of man who settled well in one place and Gracie. . . .

Well, all right, maybe Gracie was the kind of woman that if he *had* to settle down she would make it okay. But he wasn't looking for a commitment. Not his thing. He didn't care.

Except he did care about her. He didn't want anything bad to happen to her and he was determined to make her life right. He liked being around her.

Interesting, but not important, he told himself. When the election was over, win or lose, he planned on walking away. Nothing about that had changed.

"We're doing girl bonding," Alexis said. "Please say you'll come."

Gracie wasn't sure she was in the mood for her family's definition of togetherness, but she did want to see her mother. They hadn't spent any time together since clearing the air on their past.

"All right," she said. "What time?"

"Vivian has a half day today, and Mom and I are taking a long lunch, so say noon? We're doing a potluck. Do you have any cake?"

"Of course. I'll bring some. I have tuna salad, too."

"No thanks."

Gracie chuckled, then sighed. "Is Vivian's

wedding back on?"

Alexis hesitated. "To be honest, I haven't a clue, and I'm not sure I want to even know. If we go back and forth one more time, I'm going to have to kill her."

Gracie could relate to that. "What about Tom? Has she talked to him?"

"I don't know that, either. I guess we'll find out. See you in a couple of hours."

"I'll be there."

Gracie hung up the phone, then wandered into the kitchen. Selfishly, she wouldn't mind if her sister's wedding was back on simply to have a cake to make. Right now the only thing on her calendar was the cake she was making for free for the historical society. While she planned to give them more than just the sheet cake they'd asked for, the event wasn't appropriate for something too fancy.

Not that she had her actual design. She'd left that at Pam's along with all her really good pans. At some point she was going to have to go back and get them, but not today. In the meantime, she would recreate the design and figure out her work schedule. At least now she didn't have to worry about fitting it in around other cakes.

At a little before twelve, Gracie drove over to her mother's house. In some ways, she actually felt better about everything. One by one her problems were being resolved. She wasn't pregnant and she wasn't fighting with her mother. Now if she could just get her career back on track, she would be pretty darned close to perfect.

She parked behind Alexis's car. Her sister waited while Gracie collected a pink bakery box from the passenger seat and stepped out.

"How's it going?" Alexis asked, looking especially happy and cheerful.

"Good. What about you?"

"I'm great. Zeke and I have spent the past few nights talking." She grinned. "And doing other things. Did Riley tell you about him wanting to do stand-up?"

Gracie nodded. "How do you feel about that?"

"Honestly, I was shocked at first and I pretty much went crazy. Then I thought about it and I realized that Zeke deserves the chance to follow his dreams. Plus I kind of like the idea of being married to someone famous."

Gracie nodded, as if that made perfect sense to her, even as she realized however much she might *want* to be emotionally close with her sisters, it was probably never going to happen. And the reason had nothing to do with being raised by her aunt and uncle. Instead it was because they were completely different people.

"After the election, he's going to quit his job," Alexis said as she knocked once, then opened the front door. "I'll be supporting the two of us."

"You're kidding." Gracie couldn't imagine Alexis taking that on.

"Doing my best to be the supportive wife. He can repay me later with really great jewelry."

"It's an interesting plan," Gracie said as she tried to keep an open mind. While she could appreciate that Alexis wanted to help Zeke out, she wasn't as comfortable with the payback mentality. But then she'd never been married. Obviously it worked for them.

"You guys made it," Vivian said as she walked out of the kitchen. "Gracie, is there lots of cake, because I'm doing a real sugar thing right now."

"A ten-inch triple-layer cake with chocolate filling."

Vivian sighed. "Perfect."

Gracie watched as her baby sister took the bakery box, then peeked inside. Somehow Vivian seemed older than when she'd last seen her, and thinner. There were circles under her eyes and a sad set to her mouth.

"What's up?" Gracie asked.

"The sex thing didn't work?" Alexis asked with a grin. "Coulda told you that."

Gracie winced. "Are you okay, Vivian?"

"No, but I will be. This gets better, right? Heartache."

"Tom will come around," Alexis said. "A couple of weeks without him getting any and he'll be yours to command."

Vivian shrugged. "I don't think so. He's been pretty clear about it. Come on. Mom's in here."

She led the way into the kitchen where their mother had set four places at the large round table.

"All my girls together," she said. "This is lovely."

She hugged them all in turn. When she gathered Gracie close, she whispered, "I'm so glad to see you."

"Me, too," Gracie murmured back and was pleased to know she actually meant it.

They sat down. Vivian passed on the sandwiches and salad and cut herself a piece of cake. But instead of eating, she chased crumbs around her plate.

"So what happened with Tom?" Alexis asked as she picked up a chicken salad sandwich and took a bite.

"Not much. We've talked a couple of

times. He's standing firm. I just. . . ." She swallowed and looked at Gracie. "I guess you were right. I should have been honest. It's just I never have been. Not with a guy. I thought being mysterious and unpredictable was the way to keep them interested. Plus Mom, remember how you'd never tell Dad stuff. You'd buy us all new shoes, then make us promise not to say anything for a few weeks."

Her mother looked at Vivian. "I didn't want him angry because I'd spent too much money, but that has nothing to do with being honest. Is that what you remember?"

"I was only nine. I don't remember very much at all." Vivian turned to Alexis. "Do you tell Zeke everything?"

"Of course not, but that's different. We're married."

Gracie did her best not to react to Alexis. "I wonder if your threatening to call off the wedding time after time made Tom feel that you didn't love him enough."

Vivian straightened. "Yes. That's what he said. He wasn't sure of my feelings. He was afraid I'd run off every time there was a problem. I wouldn't. Once we were married, I'd be committed."

"Maybe he needed proof of that *before* the wedding," Gracie said softly.

"I guess."

"Things will get better," their mother said. "If you two are meant to be together, you'll find your way back to each other."

"I hope so." Tears filled Vivian's eyes. "It's just I miss him so much. Plus, I feel really horrible about everything that's already paid for. I'm supposed to pick up the wedding dress on Friday. What on earth should I do with it?"

"Keep it," Alexis said cheerfully. "I told you — he'll come around."

"I don't think so. And even if he does, I don't think we'd have the same wedding." Vivian stared at her cake. "He was really angry about how much everything was costing. He said he was going to call you and talk about repaying you for the deposits."

"He already did," her mother said.

"You're kidding. What did you say?"

"That I would handle it, but I appreciated the offer."

Gracie found herself regretting that the wedding was off. Tom sounded like a great guy and someone who would treat her sister well.

"Keep the dress," Gracie said. "If you don't get back together, you can sell it on e-Bay."

Vivian nodded. "I can. You're right. I just

have to. . . ." She squared her shoulders. "Mom, have you canceled everything already? I mean, I can make some phone calls and stuff."

"It's all done, but thanks for asking."

Vivian shook her head. "No. I need to do something. It's not right that you had all the work and all the expense. I know I said I'd work to help pay for my wedding dress, but I wasn't very responsible about it. I really want to commit to working in the store. We'll come up with a schedule, okay? I'll promise at least fifteen hours a week until I've paid you back."

"Honey, you don't have to do that."

Vivian gave a shaky smile. "I think you'd better let me. It might be the only way I'll ever grow up."

"Good point," her mother said.

Alexis rolled her eyes, but Gracie felt a tugging sensation around her heart. Maybe there was hope for Vivian after all. If she matured, she would certainly have a shot at winning back Tom.

Vivian turned to Gracie. "Maybe you could give me some pointers on getting over the only guy I've ever loved. How did you recover from Riley?"

Gracie opened her mouth, then closed it. A month ago, she would have said time and distance. Today, she wasn't sure she was over Riley, and she wasn't sure she wanted to be. He was everything she'd ever dreamed of finding in a man with a few bonuses thrown in for good measure.

She blinked. "I'm the wrong person to ask," she said slowly. "I'm not over him. In fact, I'm in love with him." She looked at her mother. "Sorry, Mom. I know this isn't what you wanted."

"Ha. I'm done caring about those vultures I've called friends. If you love him, then I want you two to be happy. Are you?"

"I don't know. Right now I'm in shock."

"It's all because of me," Alexis said smugly. "I'm the reason they got back together."

"Is it a good thing?" Vivian asked. "Do you *want* to be in love with him again? Does he love you?"

"I don't know," Gracie said, feeling both shocked and more than a little bubbly. "I think he cares some, but . . . I don't know."

"You're going to tell him, aren't you?" her mother asked.

"Sure. Of course. After the election."

"What?"

The other three Landon women spoke at once.

"I have to wait," Gracie said. "He's behind

in the polls. I can't distract him from the election."

Although if she did and he lost, he couldn't close the bank and the loans wouldn't be called.

No! She refused to work like that, dealing behind his back. It was wrong.

"I'm so confused," she admitted. "I will tell him, but not just yet."

Vivian eyed her. "What size are you? Want to buy a beautiful but never worn wedding gown?"

Gracie gave a strangled laugh. "Let me get back to you on that one."

"Come," Riley called without looking up from his computer screen. Diane's distinctive knock meant he always knew when it was her.

"We have been approached by the historical society ticket committee," she said after she'd stepped into his office.

"They have a whole committee to sell tickets?"

"It's really only two people, but they like to sound bigger than that."

He pushed the save button and turned to face his secretary. "Fair enough. How many do they want me to buy?"

Diane pressed her lips together. "Obviously as many as you would like, but I informed them you were not interested in supporting local civic charities and that it was unlikely —"

"I'll take fifty."

He had the pleasure of watching Diane's mouth drop open.

"Excuse me?"

"Fifty tickets," he said, speaking slowly, as if not sure of her cognitive abilities. "Buy them and pass them out to the staff. I want one, as well. Leave the extras on a table for those interested to take them for family members."

Her mouth closed and her eyes narrowed. "Why do you care about the historical society?"

"I don't."

"But you're buying tickets. They're ten dollars each." He leaned back in his chair and grinned. Ruffling Diane's prickly tweed-covered feathers was turning out to be a lot of fun. "Maybe your attempts to guilt me into doing things I don't want to do have worked," he said.

"I doubt that."

"Then maybe I want to preserve our historical past."

"Not even for money."

He chuckled. If he were sticking around,

he would want to give her a raise. "Gracie is baking the cake. Everyone who attends will try it and word will get out that she's amazing."

"I see."

The words were obviously loaded but he couldn't say with what. "Care to expand on that?" he asked.

She shook her head. "I'll go call the committee?"

"Which half?" One corner of her mouth turned up in an almost smile. Then she excused herself and left his office.

Riley stared at the closed door. He liked Diane. At first she'd simply been efficient, but now she was someone he respected and enjoyed working with. He would miss her when he left. Not that it mattered.

He returned his attention to his computer, but after a few minutes, he shut it down and grabbed his suit jacket. Suddenly the bank president's office had gotten too small.

He told Diane he was leaving and headed toward the parking lot in the rear. As he approached the double glass door, he saw a woman hurrying toward it. She had a small child by each hand and something about her was familiar.

He held open the door and smiled. "Afternoon."

400

"Oh, Mr. Whitefield. How nice to see you." She nodded. "I'm Becca Jackson. I have the loan for the daycare center in my home."

"Oh, right. How are you?"

"Great. Busy and tired, but business is wonderful and I love what I do. Thank you again for approving my loan. You're a life-saver."

"My pleasure."

She stepped into the bank and he moved toward his car. As he walked, he wondered how difficult it would be for her to obtain other financing after the bank closed. She shouldn't have much of a problem. Of course the new bank would want to go over her profit and loss statements, and as a starting business, she wouldn't have much in the way of profit.

Not his problem, he told himself and got in his car.

As he drove through town, he found himself noticing different businesses that had loans with the bank. Some would be just fine, but others would never be able to find other funding. Then there were the houses. How many had their loans with him? Ten thousand? Twenty?

He reminded himself he didn't care. These people were nothing to him. He had a plan, and it wasn't about staying in Los Lobos. He wanted to destroy everything his uncle had ever cared about. Maybe then he would be able to sleep at night.

He turned into a residential neighborhood and pulled up to the sidewalk. Small, one-story homes lined the street. The lawns were well kept, the trees nearly touched over the center of the street. Families lived here. Babies were born and grew up. Fathers mowed the lawns on Saturday morning.

He'd wanted that once. Years ago, after his dad had walked out, Riley had dreamed about a simple life filled with everyday activities. He'd wanted a house instead of a single wide. Two parents instead of just one. He'd wanted his mom happy, not crying when she thought he was asleep because she couldn't stretch the money far enough to buy him school supplies or get them cable. Sometimes she'd only made dinner for him, while she went hungry.

He'd hated that more than anything. And his uncle, who could have fixed it all, had simply turned his back on his only sister. The old bastard had even let her die.

Riley wouldn't forget that — not ever.

He parked the car and turned off the engine. After slipping into his jacket, he walked up to the closest house and knocked on the front door. A woman in her early forties answered.

"Good afternoon," he said cheerfully. "My name is Riley Whitefield and I'm running for mayor."

The woman glared at him. "I guess you are. I recognize your picture. If you're here about the election, you can forget it. I would have voted for you before. I don't like that weasel Yardley, but compared to you, he's a saint."

"Excuse me?" Riley had no idea how he could have offended someone he'd never met. "What changed your mind?"

"Gracie Landon. I don't actually know her, but I've heard all the stories. She was crazy about you. Loved you with her whole heart and you never appreciated it. You still don't."

No. This was not happening.

"I can assure you Gracie and I never . . ." Never what? Slept together? "She's not pregnant and if she were, I would marry her right away."

"Oh, sure. That's romantic. You'll take her on if your careless behavior screws up her life. Wow. Talk about noble." She shook her head. "You don't get it, do you? Gracie is a legend. She loved with a fearlessness we all admire. But you never understood what a gift she offered. You only saw her as a pain in the ass. Well, you're wrong. Her love is a precious gift and if you're too stupid to see that, you're too stupid to be mayor."

CHAPTER NINETEEN

"How did it go?" Zeke asked later that evening when they met at Riley's house to finalize their campaign plans.

"Interesting."

Riley was already on his second Scotch. He figured he might as well go for a third later. The situation would be a hell of a lot easier to deal with drunk. Not that three drinks would even get him close, but it was a start.

"Define interesting," Zeke said. "Interesting good?"

Riley closed his eyes as he relived the afternoon he'd spent going door-to-door in Los Lobos.

"I visited about thirty houses where someone was home. I'd say about eight-five percent of them basically told me they wouldn't vote for me until hell froze over."

Zeke swore. "It's the Gracie thing, isn't it?"

Riley nodded. Who knew that something from his past would jump up and bite him so firmly in the ass? "It was those damn newspaper articles," he said grimly. "People who had never heard of Gracie or me feel as if they lived a part of our lives with us. They feel involved. Right now they're taking her side and assuming I'm the bastard in all this."

To think he'd come so far only to lose it over something like this.

"You must want to kill her, huh?" Zeke said.

"Not really."

Riley knew it was probably the logical reaction, but he couldn't bring himself to blame Gracie. She hadn't done anything wrong. Oh, sure, he was past angry. It was ninety-seven *million* dollars and more importantly, a chance to screw his uncle. But the disaster wasn't Gracie's fault.

Which brought him to an interesting question. Why *wasn't* he blaming her? If she hadn't come back to Los Lobos, none of this would have happened.

And that was the kicker, he thought as he stared at the bookshelf across from his chair and finished his drink. He didn't want to take back what had happened. Not the part that included her.

"So what are they saying?" Zeke asked. "That you should treat her better?"

"That I should marry her."

"So why don't you?"

Riley turned to his office manager and glared. "Marry her?"

"For the election. Listen, it's not a crazy idea. You could work something out with her. A temporary marriage to win the election. You wouldn't even have to marry her. You could just get engaged. Gracie's a sweetie. She'll say yes."

She probably would, he thought. Knowing Gracie. She would feel horrible about what had happened and do everything in her power to make it right.

"No."

Zeke stared at him. "What? No? Just like that? You're not even going to ask her?"

"No."

"Why not? It's the perfect solution. What's the problem?"

Interesting question, and one Riley couldn't answer. He would have married Gracie if she'd been pregnant, but he wouldn't do it this way. Not even a fake engagement. Besides, with his luck, an engagement wouldn't be enough. He'd have to go through with it.

"I won't screw with her life like that," Riley said. "Leave it alone. We'll come up with another solution."

"I don't have another solution."

"Then you're going to have to find one. That's why I pay you the big bucks."

Zeke looked cornered. "Riley, the election is in less than a week. I can't fix this in a week without using Gracie. You have to know that."

"Find another way."

"But . . ." Zeke closed his mouth and nodded. "I'll see what I can come up with."

It had been forty-eight hours and Gracie still had trouble grasping the truth of the situation.

She loved Riley. Loved him. Crazy or not, he made her heart beat faster, her body tingle and when they kissed, she saw sparks. Even better, he was a great guy. She could imagine being with him always, growing old with him, having kids with him. The only thing she couldn't picture was how she was going to tell him the truth.

"After the election," she reminded herself as she stretched the rolled fondant onto the last of the cakes. "He'll be able to deal with me then."

Until that time, she would simply bask in her newfound feelings and work on the cake for the historical society.

Her plans, and her good pans, were still at Pam's, but Gracie remembered the basic design. She'd planned on a square three-layer cake in the center with smaller layer cakes spread out around. Almost like houses in a town. She'd gone with a white fondant and a basket weave pattern on the sides. Simple flowers would decorate the top.

She'd made a duplicate sketch from memory and consulted it now as she began decorating the cakes. Her head felt a little fuzzy, as if she hadn't been getting enough sleep. Which was partially true, but not enough to make her feel so weird.

Maybe it was Riley withdrawal, she thought with a smile. They'd been talking several times a day on the phone, but he'd been so caught up in election stuff that he hadn't been able to stop by. Too bad — she was going to need another fix soon.

The strips of basket weaving went on easily. Gracie had created cakes like this dozens of times before. The roses were all prepared. When she finished the basket weave, she would anchor them in place.

Over the next few hours, the cake came together, even as her body seemed to be falling apart. Her head ached, her body felt heavy. Putting on the final roses seemed to take every bit of her concentration.

Finally she had the separate cakes in pink boxes and ready for delivery. She carefully put the boxes in the refrigerator so that she could take them over in the morning. She closed the door and felt the room tilt. Not a good sign.

Gracie checked to make sure the oven was off, then made her way to the bedroom where she collapsed onto the bed. A voice in her head said she should at least kick off her shoes or get under the covers, but then she got very, very sleepy and very, very weak and the whole world just faded away.

Gracie wasn't sure what time it was when she woke up. The room wouldn't stop spinning and she couldn't believe that she was both burning up and shivering. Her mouth was dry, her body ached and she really wanted someone to shoot her and put her out of her misery.

Instead she did her best to stare at the clock and try to figure out if it was the next day or not. There was sunshine. Had it been sunny when she'd taken a header on the bed?

When the swirling numbers refused to focus, she forced herself to her feet where she staggered through the house until she found her cell phone and called a number she'd only recently put in her directory.

"Hello?"

"Riley?" It hurt to talk. Her throat felt as if she'd been snacking on fire.

"Gracie? Is that you? What's wrong?"

"I just . . ." She shuffled to a chair and sank onto the seat. "I don't feel very good. I have a bug, or something. I can't. . . ." Rational thought faded. What was her point? Oh, yeah. "The cake. Is it Saturday?"

"Most of the day."

"Okay. Good. I haven't missed it."

I haven't missed it. Why did that line sound familiar? It was from a movie, she thought hazily. Yeah. A movie she liked. She closed her eyes and concentrated.

"A Christmas Carol," she said triumphantly. "I haven't missed it. The spirits have done it all in one night."

There was a long pause on the other end of the phone.

"How sick are you?" Riley asked.

"Not a clue. But the cake has to go to the historical society. I can't take it. Can you take it? Can you take it and set it up? Can you take it and set it up and make sure it's okay?"

"Yes. Stop trying to talk. Do you have any food? Are you eating?"

411

"My tuna salad, but I had a bunch yesterday and I don't want any more."

"Are you drinking?"

"Not sure liquor's the answer."

"Obviously not. I'll stop and bring by supplies. Give me an hour."

"I'll just be here." She closed her eyes. "Maybe I'll go back to bed." She touched her hot face. "I don't think I look very good. I might have to throw up."

"I can handle it. Just try to rest."

"Sure. No problem."

The phone slipped from her fingers. Gracie thought about trying to pick it up but the ground was so far away. When had it gotten so far away?

"Last week," she said as she pushed to her feet. She swayed for a second, then made her way back to her bedroom where she did her best to get out of her clothes. The shirt was easy, as was the bra. But her pants proved insurmountable, so she left them on, along with her socks. She'd already lost her shoes somewhere.

She dug a nightgown out of a drawer, although the act of bending over nearly had her passing out. She managed to pull the nightgown over her head, then she had to fall onto the bed and sleep.

She came awake to the sound of someone

412

pounding on the door. The loudness of the banging, along with the semifrantic speed told her that whoever it was had been at it for a while.

"I'm okay," she said, though her voice sounded faint and scratchy. She pushed into a sitting position, then forced herself to her feet. Once there it wasn't too hard to sort of walk and bump her way along the hallway wall.

"It's like pinball," she said with a giggle as she reached for the front door. "I want extra points."

That statement was made as Riley pushed inside. "Points for what?" he asked as he looked her over, then touched her face. "You have a fever."

"Huh." She pointed at the bag in his arms. "Whatcha got? Something for me?"

She took a step forward, intending to look inside the bag. But somehow her feet got caught or didn't move or something because she was falling and falling and there didn't seem to be a way to stop herself.

Then big strong arms scooped her up and she was flying down the hall and into her bedroom.

"Tylenol for fever," Riley said as he set her on the mattress. "I called Diane and asked. Then I bought some. And soup. But

I don't think I should leave you alone."

She sank back on the bed and sighed. "Then you should stay. It's fine with me." Her eyes slowly closed for a second, before she forced them open again. "The cake. You have to take the cake. It's Saturday, right?"

"Still. Yes." He sat down next to her and brushed the hair off her forehead. "I'm going to call your sister. Give me her number."

"Which one?"

"She has more than one phone number?"

"What? No. Which sister. Alexis. Call Alexis. But don't bother her. I'm fine."

She read off the number. Riley punched it into his cell phone and started speaking. Gracie did her best to listen. She wanted to tell him not to bother, that she would survive on her own. Had he brought soup? Was there soup?

"She'll be here in a couple of hours," he said. "I'll wait."

That sounded good to her, except . . . "The cake. Just take it over now, please. They've got to be worried. It's in boxes."

"More than one?"

She nodded, then wished she hadn't when her head began to ache. "Five. I was going to connect them like a street thing. You know. A map or whatever, but just set them out so they look nice. There are five boxes.

414

Did I say that?"

"Yes. Why are you wearing your jeans under your nightgown?"

"They were too hard to get off."

"I can help with that."

He bent over her and quickly removed her jeans, then pulled down her nightgown.

"Slide under the covers," he said. "I'll tuck you in."

She liked the sound of that. She liked having him around. In the back of her mind, a thought nagged, but she couldn't put her finger on it. Was she supposed to tell him something? Or was she keeping a secret?

"How's the campaign going?" she asked.

"Good."

He didn't look at her as he spoke, which made her wonder if he was telling the truth. Was there —

Oh! She loved him! That was it. The secret. She found herself wanting to blurt it out right now. To say the words and see how he reacted. If he cared about her, maybe it would be a good thing. Maybe —

"Gracie?"

She heard him speak her name, but the sounds came from far, far away. Her eyes were far too heavy to open. Everything was heavy. And hot. And just too . . .

■ ■ ■ ■

Gracie rolled over and found herself drenched. Her body was cold and chilled, her nightgown soaked. Her eyes popped open and she looked around, half expecting to see the ocean in her bedroom.

Instead Alexis sat on a chair in the corner. She looked up and smiled. "Are you sane again?"

Gracie blinked at her. "When wasn't I?"

"You've been out of it ever since I got here. Riley said he got a couple of Tylenol down you and I guess they kicked in. Or you beat the fever. You were burning up for a while. How do you feel now?"

"Like I just fell into a pool."

Alexis stood and walked to the bed. "That means the fever's broken. Good for you." She touched her sister's forehead. "Yup. Cool to the touch. Are you hungry?"

Gracie considered the question. "Starving. I don't remember falling asleep. I don't remember much of anything. Oh. The cake for the historical society."

"Riley's taking care of it. You called him. Remember?"

"Not really." She had a few hazy images that were more dreamlike than anything

416

else. "Whatever bug I picked up was strong, but short-lived. I think I'm okay now."

"Why don't you take it easy? I'll go fix some soup and toast for you." Alexis fingered the damp sheets. "Can you move to the sofa? You can lay down there and I'll change these later."

"You don't have to do all that for me. It's the weekend. What about Zeke? Shouldn't you be with him?"

"Don't worry about it. He's working all day on Riley's campaign then picking me up about six so I can go with him to see him do stand-up at a club in Ventura tonight."

"Sounds like fun."

Gracie sat up and tested her equilibrium. The walls and floor stayed exactly where they were supposed to. She felt tired and a little weak, but otherwise, fine.

Alexis helped her to her feet, then led her to the sofa in the living room. As she went to work in the kitchen, Gracie had the thought that she wouldn't have expected her sister to come through for her like this. Which just went to show that she'd pretty much been wrong about every member of her family. Maybe in the future she should simply let them be and not try to predict or assign value judgments.

"What does Zeke have to do today for Riley?" she asked as Alexis puttered in the kitchen. "Are they still going door-to-door?"

"Not exactly."

"Why not? The election is in a few days."

There was a long silence, as if Alexis was considering what to say. The longer her sister was quiet, the more Gracie began to wonder what she didn't know.

"Alexis," she said. "What's going on?"

"Nothing."

"I don't believe you."

"Everything is great. Really."

Uh-huh. As if Gracie would believe that high, tight voice. "You're not a good liar. Tell me."

Alexis appeared in the doorway. "Zeke wasn't supposed to say anything to me. If Riley knew I knew, he would never have asked me to come over."

Gracie's stomach tightened and it had nothing to do with acid or lack of food. "What do you know?"

Her sister shifted her weight from foot to foot. "Just that Riley's poll numbers are really down. They went up when everyone thought the two of you were together, but since the debate, they've been falling. The people in town are taking your side in this, which is really nice for you. But they hate

Riley because, well, you know."

Gracie didn't know but she could guess. Because of those stupid newspaper stories, half the town felt as if they knew her. Now, all these years later, Riley was the bad guy for not falling in love with her and giving her what they thought was her happy ending.

Of course the irony of the situation was that she really *was* in love with Riley and she wanted to be with him, but that was her business, not theirs.

"Is he going to lose?" Gracie asked quietly.

Alexis nodded.

Ninety-seven million dollars gone because of her.

"I have to fix this," she said.

"How?"

"I don't know. I'll go talk to him when he's done delivering the cake and we'll come up with something."

"It's going to take a miracle," Alexis told her.

Gracie wished she had one of those in the corner of her suitcase. As she was fresh out, she would have to think of something else.

There were several security guards on duty at the large house on the hill. Riley had never paid much attention to the historic value of some of the older homes in Los Lobos, but now as he walked up the wide front steps, he felt as if he were stepping back in history.

The Victorian mansion had been restored to its original fussiness. Rockers and tables were scattered across the long front porch. Flowers decorated the pillars.

"Can I help you?" a rent-a-cop said from his position by the front door.

"I'm delivering the cake for the fund-raiser tonight," Riley said, motioning to the large box in his arms. "There are four more of these in my car."

"Sure thing. Go on up. Then drive around back and use the rear entrance. It'll be closer for you."

"Thanks." Riley jerked his head to the three guards by the driveway and the two security vans set up by the fence. "Why all the firepower?"

"A lot of items are on loan," the guard told him. "Apparently they're worth so much, the insurance company insisted." He grinned. "So don't try anything."

"Not me. I'm just the guy with the cake."

Riley followed his directions to the main reception area in the ballroom on the second floor. As he walked into the huge open room, he saw the tables set up for the buffet, two bars and a lace covered table complete with several pink bakery boxes.

"What the hell?" he muttered as he walked closer.

He set down his box and looked at the others. It was a cake. One that looked amazingly similar to the one Gracie had baked. Nearly identical. The same basket weave on the side, the same flowers. Except, now that he looked more closely, he saw the weave was crooked and the individual pieces of it were poorly done and broken. The flowers looked as if they'd spent one too many nights out on the town.

Questions crowded his brain. Who had done this and why?

Riley moved his box to the edge of the table and crossed to the window overlooking the rear of his property. Just then a familiar Lexus sped down the driveway.

Pam! He swore long and loud, then reached for his cell. Gracie picked up on the first ring. "How you feeling?" he asked.

"Better. The fever's gone. Alexis has fed me and I just had a shower. I think I'll live."

"Good to know. I have a situation here. I'm delivering the cake, but there's already one here. I also just spotted Pam heading away from the scene of the crime."

Gracie gasped. "Is *that* what she was doing with my cake pans? Making a cake for the benefit? But why? And how does it look?"

"Like crap. I don't get it. What's the point? This can't be to get her business. No one will know she baked it."

"No, but they'll think I did. Taste it."

"What?"

"Taste it. I have to know if it's horrible."

"Hold on."

Riley eyed the pink boxes, then grabbed a fork from the pile by napkins and stuck it into the small layer cake close to him. He sucked in a breath, then took a bite.

"Jesus," he said as he spat it out. "What's wrong?"

"Salt instead of sugar. At least I think that's it." He grabbed a paper napkin and wiped off his tongue. The horrible flavor lingered.

"Riley, you have to get her cake out of there. She's trying to make sure I can never recover from the scandal about my cakes. Get hers out and put mine in its place."

"Will do."

"Can you call me when you're done? I have something I'd like to talk to you about."

Normally those were words to make him head out to sea, but not this time. "What's wrong?"

"Nothing. I just want to talk about the election."

Damn. "What do you know?"

"That you're in trouble."

"I'll be fine."

"How?"

He eyed the table. "Look, I need to get the cakes changed. I'll call you when I'm done, then come by. Fair enough?"

"That's great. Thanks."

He clicked off his cell phone and dropped it into his pocket. Then he collected two of the small boxes from Pam's cake and carried them back to his car.

It took him three more trips to get Gracie's cake inside. He set it up as best he could and was leaving with the largest layer of Pam's cake when a guard met him at the top of the stairs.

"Not so fast," the burly man said. "What have you got there?"

"A cake. Two were delivered by mistake."

The other man didn't look convinced. "We just got a call that someone would try to trade out the cakes as a joke. Something about the election and one of the candidates wanting to make a fuss." His eyes narrowed. "Funny how you just happen to look like that guy running for mayor."

Riley couldn't believe it. Pam had sure as hell covered her bases on this one.

"This isn't what you think," Riley said as he tried to inch his way around the guard. "The new cake is in place and it's delicious. Take a bite of it if you don't believe me. This is the bad cake." He held out the box in his hands. "Big mistake to eat this one."

"You just hold it right there. I'm going to have to call this in." The guard reached for his walkie-talkie and pushed a button.

Riley tried to judge the distance to the front door and wondered if he could make a run for it. When he heard the guy on the other end of the conversation say "Hold him," he knew he didn't have a choice.

He started down the stairs, noticing too late that someone was coming up the stairs — a big guy carrying a case of wine. Riley went left, the guy went right. They ended up on the same step and tried to avoid the crash.

It happened anyway. The impact knocked Riley off his feet. He grabbed for the railing, slipped and reached for it again. The cake went flying. The other guy lost control of the box of wine. Riley and the other man fell at the same time, bouncing down the stairs in a tangle of arms and legs.

When they hit the ground, they landed

onto wine-soaked cake and a floor full of glass.

Every part of him hurt. Riley knew this couldn't be good, an opinion that was confirmed when he heard sirens in the distance and getting closer.

CHAPTER TWENTY

The cell phone woke Gracie early the next morning. Her first thought was that whatever bug had gripped her had been firmly squashed. The second was that Riley had never called or come by. Was this him?

"Hello?"

"Gracie, it's Mom. Have you seen the paper?"

"Huh? No." She rolled over in bed. At least she knew this time whatever scandal it was couldn't be about her. She hadn't left the house in two days.

"It's Riley," her mother said. "He was arrested."

"What? Are you kidding?"

She scrambled out of the bed and hurried to the front door. After flinging it open, she raced to the edge of the porch where the morning paper waited. A quick glance at the headline had her cringing.

"Mayoral Candidate Arrested for Drunk

426

and Disorderly Conduct."

The picture showed Riley covered with cake and surrounded by broken wine bottles in the foyer of the historic mansion.

"I'm going to throw up," she whispered as she walked back inside and closed the door. "This is all my fault."

"You were sick in bed. Alexis told me."

"Exactly. I got sick so Riley took the cake over for me. Only Pam had already been there to put a nasty-tasting cake in its place. He was helping me out and somehow things went wrong."

"Then I guess you're going to have to fix them. How can I help?"

The support made her eyes burn. "I don't know, but as soon as I figure something out, I'll be in touch."

"I'll be waiting. We're here for you, Gracie. I want you to know that."

"I appreciate it, Mom. I'll let you know."

She hung up and quickly punched in Riley's number. Several seconds passed before he answered.

"Are you okay?" she asked frantically. "I just saw the paper. What happened?"

"I just got home and I need to take a shower," he said. "Come on over and I'll tell you everything."

She had a thousand questions, the first

one being why he was just getting home.

"They kept you in jail?" she asked, outraged.

"It's a long story."

"Okay. Go take your shower. I'll be right there."

"I'll leave the front door open."

Gracie dressed in record time and made her way to Riley's house. She felt a little weak, but a big breakfast should take care of that, she thought. After parking in the driveway — at this point what did it matter if anyone saw her car there — she walked inside and headed upstairs.

She found Riley in his bedroom. He'd already showered and shaved and was just pulling on jeans as she walked in.

After a brief thought that she was sorry to have missed the good part of watching him dress, she moved close and hugged him.

"This is all my fault, and I'm really, really sorry."

He pulled her against him. "It wasn't you. It was Pam and circumstances. Don't blame yourself." He cupped her face in his hands and kissed her.

The melty sensation began instantly, but Gracie told herself this wasn't the time to get distracted. There were too many other things to worry about.

"What happened?" she asked when he drew back. "How did you end up covered in cake? And who arrested you? And why didn't you get home until this morning?"

He released her and picked up a shirt on the bed. After shrugging into it, he started on the buttons.

"One of the guards figured out I was taking out a cake as well as bringing one in. Someone had called to warn security I might try to pull something."

"You? That's crazy."

"I saw Pam driving away, which means she saw my car. I'm guessing she made the call to get me in trouble and it worked perfectly. The guards tried to detain me, I didn't want to stay. What I didn't see was the liquor guy coming up the stairs. We collided and both went down. The wine broke and we fell in it and the cake."

Her breath caught. "What about all that glass? Are you hurt?"

"A few cuts. Nothing serious. Then the deputies arrived to take me away. There was enough blood that we had to stop by the hospital first."

"Blood? Where?"

He pulled up his shirt and turned so she could see the bandages on his back. There were five and none were very big.

"Did they have to pick any glass out?" She asked, feeling more horrible by the second.

"Some. I have a couple of stitches."

She winced. "I'm so sorry."

He dropped the shirt and set his hands on her shoulders. "Not your fault. Remember that. This is Pam's doing and by God, she's going to pay."

Gracie wanted to ask how, but she had other, more pressing questions.

"Why didn't Mac release you right away?"

Riley tucked in his shirt. "He wasn't on duty and the damned deputies wouldn't call him. They didn't want me to call anyone either. They finally did let me and I got in touch with Zeke who drove out to Mac's house, but he wasn't there. Apparently Mac and Jill went out of town for the night. Zeke called around to hotels in Santa Barbara until he found them. Mac drove back and let me out."

"And I slept through the whole thing," Gracie said mournfully.

"You were sick. Alexis left when you fell asleep. Don't sweat it," he told her. "I'm fine now."

"So how are we going to get Pam?" she asked.

"Too bad she's a woman. If she was a guy I'd just go beat the shit out of her."

"We could confront her and threaten her. That would be good."

"Sounds like a plan," he said. "You have your camera in your car, just in case we find something interesting?"

She grinned. "You bet."

They drove to Pam's house and parked right in front.

"I don't care who knows we're here," Riley said as he climbed out.

Gracie agreed and followed him to the front door, which was standing ajar.

They both stared at the slight crack of space just begging to be entered.

"Is it a setup?" Gracie asked in a whisper. "Is she going to have us arrested for breaking and entering?"

"Prove that it wasn't," he said, nodding to her camera.

"Oh. Great idea."

She snapped a picture of the half-open door, then winced at the loud *click* and *whirr* of the picture being shot out. She grabbed it and handed the picture to Riley to shove it in his jeans back pocket. Then he pushed the door open wider and they stepped inside.

Gracie's first impression was of elegant furnishings and plenty of light. "Nice house," she murmured.

431

Riley shot her a glance that said this wasn't the time to be discussing Pam's decorating ability, then motioned to her to follow him. He pointed to the hall.

Gracie wondered why until she heard a faint sound. A faint rhythmic sound that was familiar. And intimate.

"She's doing it!" she whispered. "We've got to see who the guy is. Whoever he is, he's helping her!"

Riley pressed a finger to his lips and led the way. The noises got louder. There was heavy breathing, a cry of "Oh, yes, I'm close," from Pam, then a low groan.

"Get ready," Riley mouthed, pointing to the camera.

They paused outside the half-closed bedroom door for a second, then Riley pushed it open and rushed inside.

Several things happened at once. As Gracie followed, the couple on the bed noticed the intrusion. Pam screamed, which made Gracie jump and maybe scream a little, too. But she was careful to keep her camera positioned.

Through the tiny lens she got an eyeful of Pam's breasts, some guy's back and then the guy turned and she found herself staring directly at the still-erect private parts of Franklin Yardley.

432

"Oh, yuck," she yelled, even as she started clicking pictures.

"Get out!" the mayor demanded.

He grabbed for the blanket, jerking it off the bed, but not before Gracie got several pictures of him and Pam in what could only be described as compromising circumstances. The ever-lovely Mrs. Yardley was not going to like this.

Riley was careful to catch the pictures as they popped out of the camera.

"Interesting," he said with a grin. "It's about time someone else starred in the local paper. I'm getting tired of all the notoriety."

Yardley grabbed for the pictures, but Riley kept them out of reach.

"You'll pay for this," Yardley said.

"How?" Riley asked. "A picture's worth a thousand words." He looked at Pam, who had pulled the sheet up over her breasts. "When did your taste get so lousy?"

She glared at him. "Don't talk to me about lousy taste, you bastard. You're the one sleeping with Gracie." Her face tightened and her voice rose. "How could you want that bitch?"

Gracie jumped. "I'm not a bitch."

"You're disgusting and horrible," Pam yelled. "I *hate* you. Do you hear me? I hate you. I hate everything about you. I wish you

433

were dead. You ruined my life. All those damn articles back when we were in high school. Everyone thought you were so sweet and I was just the whore who wanted to marry Riley for the money. You ruined my wedding. It was supposed to be *my* day, do you hear me? My day. And it was all about you. All everyone could talk about was Gracie Landon. 'Do you think she'll show up?' " Pam said in a mock high voice. " 'What will precious Gracie do'?"

Pam narrowed her eyes. "I wanted you punished back then, but I couldn't find you. So I waited and planned and I've got you now."

"Pam!" Yardley move away from the bed. "You're unbalanced. What have you done?"

Pam turned on him. "What?" she shrieked. "Oh, don't you dare pretend you weren't in on this from the beginning."

Yardley's eyes widened. "I swear, I have no idea what she's talking about. Pam, have you broken the law?"

Pam screamed. "Don't you play innocent with me, you old goat. You're in this up to your eyeballs."

Yardley turned to Gracie. "I swear, I have no idea what she's talking about."

Pam swore. "Fine. If that's the way you want to play it." She turned on Riley. "Oh, this is good. I might have to go down, but I'm taking your precious Gracie with me." She swung her attention to Gracie.

"I ruined you," she said with glee. "I ruined your precious business and now you have nothing." She turned back to Riley. "I've ruined you, too and I'm glad. You know why? Because when you left me, you said Gracie was right. I've never forgiven you for that."

Gracie turned to Riley. "You said that?"

He shrugged. "You were."

"Wow."

Pam screamed, "I never got a penny out of that divorce and I want my money now. Do you hear me?"

"Pam," the mayor said. "Be quiet. You're obviously not feeling well. I had no idea you were harboring all of this anger."

"Anger?" Pam started screaming and crying and laughing. Gracie wondered if she *had* gone over the edge.

"I hate you both," she said as she sank back on the bed. "Dammit, I worked so hard. I hate you all."

"Pam!" Yardley sounded shocked. "I don't know you anymore."

"Oh, like you ever did," Pam said, sounding defiant. "I only ever slept with you because you're getting most of the estate when Riley fails. I was planning to take half of it and run as soon as we were married." She looked at Riley. "He keeps a separate set of books in his office. He has a secret drawer in his desk. He's been skimming money for years."

"Pam, no!" Yardley protested.

She stood and jerked the sheet free, then wrapped it around herself. "I nearly got everything." She glared at Gracie. "I suppose you're feeling fine."

"Sure. Why would you . . ." Gracie stared at her, remembering her sudden illness. "What did you do to me?"

"Mixed some very old mayonnaise in your stupid tuna salad. My God, how can you eat that? It smells like cat food. I wanted to get you out of the way and I did. I planned everything." She kicked Yardley. "Until you messed it all up. I'll never forgive you."

Riley took Gracie's arm. "This is our cue to leave."

Yardley stared at Pam as if he'd never seen her. "But I loved you."

"Oh, sure. That's why you screwed all your assistants. You're old and you can barely get it up and you're lousy in bed." She turned her attention to Riley. "You're crap in the sack, too."

With that she stomped into the bathroom,

closed the door and clicked the lock.

Riley led Gracie out of the bedroom. She couldn't believe all that she'd heard.

"It was them all the time," she said, feeling as if she'd just watched a very intense live show. "The photographer, the cake mixes. Everything."

"Looks that way."

"She tried to poison me and it worked. I can't believe that."

"I'm sure the sheriff will want to talk to her about that."

She glanced at him as he walked them out of the house. "You're not really lousy in bed."

He grinned. "Thanks."

Back at his house, Riley fixed a pot of coffee and then spread the pictures out on the long kitchen counter. There was plenty of evidence — unfortunately it wasn't the kind he could use.

"You're going to call Mac, right?" Gracie asked as she took the mug he offered and sipped. "He can arrest Yardley today. And Pam, although I care less about her. We'll ignore the sexual stuff, because sleeping with his assistants is gross but not illegal, but he's been stealing money for years. Isn't that great?"

"Uh-huh."

He turned his back on the pictures and stared out the window at the large backyard.

Funny how he'd hated this house when he'd first arrived in Los Lobos. The big space had represented everything he'd hated about his uncle. But in the past few months, he'd grown to like the house. The room, the quiet. Just as he liked the bank. He enjoyed working with numbers, making things right for people. He enjoyed the challenges of playing the funding market, getting the best deal for his customers. He would miss it.

Gracie shook his arm. "Are you listening to me?"

"No."

"I didn't think so."

He looked at her face, at the dark blue of her eyes, the easy smile, the way she lit up when they were together. He couldn't think of a single thing he didn't like about her. She was . . . perfect. Or at least perfect for him.

"I was saying that as soon as the mayor is charged, you have to go on the radio and talk to the town. You can tell everyone it will be a smooth transition and they'll really like having you as mayor."

"It won't work," he said.

"What?"

438

"Yardley's accused me of some things. Now I'm going to accuse him of worse things. Who are the voters going to believe? Someone they've known for sixteen years, or me?"

"But the charges."

"It'll take a couple of days to get him formally charged by the D.A. It's Sunday. Nothing's going to happen until well into next week and the election's Tuesday. Yardley can stall long enough to tell everyone the truth about my uncle's will. Once they know why I'm running, do you think they'll care about what he's been doing? It's all true, Gracie. I was only doing it for the money."

"But . . . but . . . No! We have to come up with a way." She set down her coffee and grabbed his arm. "You've worked so hard. I won't let this happen to you. Can't you want to stay and be mayor? You could say you've had a change of heart."

He smiled at her. "I have, but who's going to believe me?"

"I will. I'll —" She opened her mouth, then closed it. Color flooded her face. "Marry me. That's what the town wants. Their happy ending. So marry me. We'll have Jill draw up some papers right now. I don't want any of your money and I'll say that in writing. We'll get married today. We can fly to Vegas and be back tonight. Then we make a big announcement tomorrow. You'll win for sure. Then we can split up later. It could work."

She was so damned earnest, he thought. Bright and willing to do anything to help.

"It's ninety-seven million dollars," she said.

"I know the amount."

"Then?"

He'd been feeling something for a long time. A vague feeling he couldn't identify until just that second.

He tucked her hair behind her ears and kissed her.

"I love you, Gracie Landon," he said quietly.

She stared at him. "W-what?"

He grinned. "I love you. You're the most amazing woman I've ever met. You lead with your heart and I admire that. I want to marry you, have babies with you and grow old with you."

She opened her mouth to speak and he pressed his fingers against her lips.

"But I won't agree to anything until after the election."

"What?" The word came out as a yelp. "Are you crazy? Why are you waiting?"

"Because I don't want you to ever wonder if I just did it for the money."

She covered her face with her hands. "This is *not* happening," she said, then dropped her hands. "Riley, listen to me. We can announce our engagement." She grabbed him by the shoulders. "I love you, too. I have for a long time. Maybe fourteen years, I don't know. I love you so much, I will not let you throw this away. It's ninety-seven million dollars. It's this house and the bank and I know you've started to care about the town. You want to stay here and settle down. We can do that."

"I have money."

"It's not about the money." She grabbed him by his shoulders and tried to shake him. "It's about your heritage and belonging and having roots."

"I have money from the oil rigs."

He loved her intensity and how much she wanted to convince him. Funny how she hadn't figured out she was all he needed.

"It's not about the money," she repeated. "I have a good business. At least I had one. I can rebuild it. I'll make Pam issue a statement or something. I know I can do it. Anyway, that's not the point. It's about having choices. Don't walk away from this without trying."

"It's not about trying," he said. "I meant what I said. I love you and I don't want you to ever have to question that."

She couldn't believe it. She had water on her brain or something. "It's ninety-seven million dollars. No one is worth that."

He pulled her close and kissed her. "You are. I'll come find you Tuesday night, after the polls close. I'll get down on one knee and propose and you'd better be prepared to say yes."

Gracie didn't remember driving home. Luckily there weren't many other cars on the road and she arrived unscathed. She felt battered and numb and in total and complete shock.

Riley loved her. He'd said so about fifteen times and had promised to propose. She felt all warm and happy inside. They were going to be together.

But at the same time, she battled outrage and indignation. How could he be willing to walk away from everything just to prove he wasn't marrying her for the money? She knew that. She would always know that.

It was completely stupid and pigheaded and male for him to turn his back on his inheritance.

She walked into the house and pulled her

cell phone out of her purse, then she pushed in a number. Dealing with Pam's poisoning attempt and the sheriff's office would come later. First, she had important business to deal with.

"Hi, Mom, it's me. I need your help. Vivian's and Alexis's, too, and we don't have much time. Can you get them to come over in half an hour? I need to call Jill and a few other people. Uh-huh. I'll explain it when I get there. Oh, do you know anyone at the newspaper office?"

CHAPTER TWENTY-ONE

Riley spent the rest of Sunday by himself. Gracie had called to say she wasn't feeling well and wanted to rest. Although he'd wanted to go over and see her, he wanted her better more so he'd stayed away.

In the afternoon he'd driven down to Santa Barbara and looked at engagement rings. He'd wanted to find just the right one for Gracie. Something beautiful and special.

He'd found it in the fourth store he'd gone to and now it sat on his dresser until after the election when he could propose for real.

Funny how he'd never thought he would get married. He'd assumed he would live his life alone. Two months ago if someone had told him he would fall in love with Gracie Landon, he would have punched the guy. But she'd swept into his world and had changed everything — most of all, him.

Monday morning he woke up early and

collected the paper. The mayor's arrest was front-page news. Riley grinned as he read the start of the article. He might have lost the election but at least Yardley would be doing some serious time in jail. He had a feeling things wouldn't go so well for the mayor once he was there.

There was a separate article on Pam where she confessed to messing with Gracie and planting the cake boxes in her car. If Riley knew the good citizens of Los Lobos, they would make sure Pam wasn't ever able to live here again.

So they would all be leaving, he thought as he drank his coffee. He would miss the town. It had finally begun to feel like home to him. But without the bank, he didn't have anything to keep him here. It wasn't as if he could set up an oil rig in the center square.

He studied the picture of the mayor being led into the sheriff's office. No doubt the news would lose the older man a few votes, but not enough. If Riley had taken Gracie up on her offer and married her, he would have had the election nailed. Not that he would have. Yeah, it was a lot of money, but she was more important. He'd never been in love before and by God, he was going to do it right.

He turned to the second page and nearly

spit the coffee he'd just sipped. Instead of a recap of local, state and national news, there was a two page ad with Gracie's face smack in the middle. Across the top, huge print proclaimed: I Need Your Help To Get My Man!

Riley swore. What had she done now? He scanned the text, which was a letter addressed to the town.

Dear Los Lobos,

It's me. Gracie. I know most of you remember me from those articles in the paper, both fourteen years ago and recently. The ones about my crush on Riley Whitefield. You followed the tragic story of my unrequited love and felt my pain when it ended with Riley marrying another woman.

So here's the thing. I'm still in love with Riley and I want to marry him. And you know the best part? He loves me, too. But he has this crazy idea he can't propose until after the election.

Riley is a great guy. He'll be terrific for this town and honestly, I want to be with him here . . . in Los Lobos. But for that to happen, I need your help. I need you to vote for Riley on Tuesday.

You've always been proud of the fact

that I loved with my whole heart. That hasn't changed. The only thing different this time is I'd like you to be part of that. I'm pulling off the biggest stunt of my life and I can't do it without you. If you've ever rooted for me and Riley, please vote for him on Tuesday.

Thanks, Gracie.

He read it twice, then set his coffee on the counter and picked up the phone. Of course Gracie didn't answer.

Five minutes later he was dressed and out of the house. As he drove toward her place, he saw hundreds of Gracie Says Vote For Riley posters and flyers plastered everywhere.

He made it to her house in record time, but she wasn't there. He tried her mom's house, then headed to the bank. Could she have done this and then left town?

But as he drove up to the bank, he saw a huge banner hanging from the side of the old building. Gracie Says Vote For Riley flapped in the morning breeze. Waiting in front were all his employees, Zeke, Gracie's mom and sisters and Gracie herself.

She walked to his car, then stood on the sidewalk while he shut off the engine and stepped out.

"What do you think?" she asked, sounding more than a little nervous.

God, she looked great. "That you're crazy."

"Good crazy or bad crazy?"

"There's a difference?"

"Oh, sure. I was bad crazy before, when I stalked you. I like to think I've changed."

He reached for her hands. "Don't change for me. I love everything about you." He nodded at the banner. "Why did you do this?"

"Because you want to be mayor. It's not all about the money. I know you can do a good job and I think we could be happy here. I believe you love me, Riley. You don't have anything to prove. You've always been a better man than you believed."

He drew her close and hugged her. Feelings flooded him — feelings he'd never had before. "I love you. I want you to know that."

"I do."

He looked at her and grinned. "Practicing?"

"Should I be?"

"Absolutely. I bought you a ring."

He kissed her and in the background he heard cheering. "I think I just lost my authority with the staff," he said.

448

"No, they'll work harder because they care about you."

He kissed her again and breathed in the scent of her. "Marry me, Gracie. Marry me and let me take care of you. Let me love you and prove it each and every day."

She looked into his eyes and smiled. "Only if you let me love you back."

"Always."

She sighed. "You've officially violated the three *F's*, big guy. They're going to throw you out of the club."

He cupped her cheeks and let himself get lost in her. "There's only one *F*. Falling. Falling for Gracie."

EPILOGUE

They held the rehearsal dinner at Bill's Mexican Grill because it was Los Lobos and where else would they hold it?

"We only have a few minutes," Riley said as he glanced at his watch, then at the big television Bill had wheeled into their private banquet room.

Gracie leaned against him. "I can't believe Zeke is going to be on Jay Leno. Isn't that the best?"

"It's pretty great," he said, although not his idea of the best. The best was being with Gracie. He would marry her in the morning, and then they would fly to Hawaii for a romantic, albeit short, honeymoon. They had to be back in five days for the swearing-in ceremony.

"If you're going to be called His Honor, the mayor, do I get to be Mrs. His Honor, or am I Her Honor?"

He chuckled. "I haven't a clue."

"It's time," Vivian said from the far side of the table. "I wonder if we'll be able to see Alexis in the audience. She must be so nervous."

"But proud," Tom said.

Riley glanced at the younger couple. They weren't engaged yet, but they were dating and Gracie had high hopes.

"Turn up the TV," someone called.

Gracie hit the volume button on the remote, then she tucked her arm around Riley's and sighed.

"You know I love you, right?" she whispered.

"Oh, yeah."

She looked at him. "About that family we wanted to start right away. . . ."

His heart stopped. He felt the absence of thudding and everything else went still. "Gracie?"

She leaned close and lowered her voice. "I have a stick I peed on earlier. Want to see?"

He started to laugh. As Zeke had just told his first joke, everyone else joined in. Riley pulled Gracie onto his lap and started to kiss her. They would tell their friends and family later. Right now it was enough to know and have her close and in love with him.

"You're sure?" he asked, more delighted

451

than he could say.

"Absolutely." She grinned. "This is going to make the town love you more."

"But you're the one I care about."

"Sure, but I'll have competition. All the old ladies in town will start knitting. It's going to be great."

"The best," he said. "You always make it the best."

ABOUT THE AUTHOR

New York Times bestselling author **Susan Mallery** has entertained millions of readers with her witty and emotional stories about women. *Publishers Weekly* calls Susan's prose "luscious and provocative," and *Booklist* says "Novels don't get much better than Mallery's expert blend of emotional nuance, humor and superb storytelling." Susan lives in Seattle with her husband and her tiny but intrepid toy poodle. Visit her at www.SusanMallery.com.

The employees of Thorndike Press hope you have enjoyed this Large Print book. All our Thorndike, Wheeler, and Kennebec Large Print titles are designed for easy reading, and all our books are made to last. Other Thorndike Press Large Print books are available at your library, through selected bookstores, or directly from us.

For information about titles, please call:
  (800) 223-1244

or visit our website at:
  gale.com/thorndike

To share your comments, please write:
  Publisher
  Thorndike Press
  10 Water St., Suite 310
  Waterville, ME 04901